TRANSFERENCE

A NOVEL

By Ellen Metter

Denver - Colorado

Dedicated

To those who enjoy the Twilight Zone television series,

To loved ones, who allow me abundant project time,

And to Mark, an exceptionally fine fellow.

Cover photo: Cat Eye in Bright Sunlight by Xil. CC BY-SA 3.0
https://commons.wikimedia.org/wiki/File:Cat_eye_in_bright_sunlight.JPG

Front Cover design: Rita Toews

Cat Paw Print: J_Alves

Cataloging-in-Publication Data
Metter, Ellen.
Transference : A Novel / Ellen Metter.
ISBN 978-1537758558
1. Title.
PS3613.E746T172 .2017

First printing 2017

CHAPTER 1

The flutter of eyelids. The quick inhalation of breath. The slow exhalation through parted lips. It added up to a visual of pleasure, accompanied by a soundtrack of sighs.

Hiri peered at the webbed form a few yards away, then grunted before returning to his screen tapping. No problem at the moment. Maryl's trip was going well. More than well from the sound of it.

"Unnh." The sound was an almost comical groan of pleasure. Buried in her thoughts and sensations, Maryl didn't hear her own sighs. What she did hear was Lena's voice, high and sing-songy.

"Mooshie, you're such a *freaking* pretty girl," Lena cooed, as she switched mode from deep back rub, to intense ear massage. "I tend to go for guys, but in your case, I've gotta' say, you're one helluva sexy gal." Maryl watched as Lena bent down, face looming, planting a ticklish kiss on the bridge of Mooshie's nose. A rush of contentment enveloped Maryl's mind as Mooshie's purr swelled.

The cat rose and stretched full-length, each movement elongating, then calming, her muscles. Maryl, her own distant body snug in the tendrils that hugged her, gasped in pleasure. That luscious sensuality could still, after all this time, be a delicious shock.

Passing through the lab Cavnee saw Maryl's head, nestled in the shining mesh, move slowly side to side, a gentle smile on her face, deep into the DT process. He stopped, dropping his face within inches of hers. He called softly to the others in the lab.

"Teesh, Hiri, look at this, would you? She's actually working to bring herself back, even though it's obvious she's getting a mind-exploding massage."

Cavne's head moved to mirror the lazy sway of Maryl's. He straightened. "I stand in awe of her amazing capacity for denying pleasure. When that kind of stroking happens to me, I stay until I'm drooling."

Hiri offered a half grunt response, not looking up from his slumped position in the control panel back-up seat. Teesh, standing by the monitor, grimaced as he pushed light-colored hair from his forehead and walked to Cavnee's side, his slim form rocking to the rhythm of his seesaw walking style. Teesh edged Cavnee away from Maryl, suspended and vulnerable in the web's fine threads, his signature exasperated eye roll in full roll.

He spoke in low tones. "The image of you …dribbling… is lovely, Cavnee. I thank you so much for lodging it in my mind."

Cavnee flashed Teesh a "you're very welcome" smile as the lab lead continued, intoning as if delivering a lecture.

"Maryl knows Lena can pet a cat rather endlessly on autopilot when absorbed in something. If it's obvious Lena's not going to launch into one of her monologues, or do something else of interest to us, it's a waste of time. Hers, mine, Hiri's, VRC's.

Cavnee shook his head as he continued to an adjoining lab space and Teesh returned to the control panel to bring Maryl back.

The fibers around Maryl began to loosen and retract into nearly invisible slots, responding to Teesh's machinations at the control board.

Maryl shook her head groggily, the smile still intact.

Teesh called to her. "You need any help, Marylsune?"

As Maryl became aware of her newly changed surroundings she pulled her arms and legs from their disintegrating cocoon, readying to stand on her own with help from a single remaining strand extending from the ceiling. At the public Travel Centers, an aide would have been nearby to support her as the web retracted. But Maryl was no novice, and the trip had been uneventful. Hiri, charged with assisting if needed, barely lifted his eyes from his screen.

"I'm ok. Maybe a sensuality after-shock." She grinned. "I can't complain."

Cavnee called from across the room. "What "after-shock"? You hardly let yourself have any fun. I saw you. You were thinking about work, probably thinking about tomorrow, even in the middle of that beautiful stroking you were no doubt getting from Lena-with-the-magical-fingers. Lovely Maryl. There are times you need to com-pletely unwind."

Maryl stretched in the now empty space.

"Cavnee. Please tell me this. If you were doing tomorrow what I'm doing, wouldn't you be a tad on edge? Maybe thinking ahead? I probably shouldn't even be transferring at this point, but I wanted a distraction."

Cavnee shrugged.

Maryl shook her head as she walked to the RT area adjacent to the lab. She was used to the good-natured teasing of her friend.

"All right," she said. "I wish you all a good night and thank you for your kind ministrations." She paused and turned with a smile. "No, I thank Lena for her kind ministrations. I'm going to do a quick RT follow-up and then head home."

Teesh replied. "Everything's set for tomorrow. Don't you lose a minute's sleep thinking about it." He nodded toward Cavnee. "If he's here, which I'm sure he will be, I'll keep him quiet. Good night, Marylsune."

CHAPTER 2

Rob inclined his head graciously, holding fiddle and bow to chest as party-goers clapped and whistled their appreciation. He glanced over his shoulder as he always did after a set, checking Matilda's cage on the mantle. He was happy to see his cat sitting Sphinx-like within her enclosure, gazing out with half-closed eyes.

For Matilda, it was a comfortable and quiet evening in her padded carrier. To observers, the metal cage looked humble, adorned as it was with two loosely tied pink bows, and filled with washed-out pieces of cloth odds and ends. To the cat, the discarded t-shirts and nearly disintegrating boxer shorts felt like pillows designed for a princess, and no annoying pea in sight.

As Rob leaned over to place fiddle and bow on their stand, Matilda stretched her paws forward, and arched her back into a waterslide stretch. Rubbing against the carrier door, she turned on her astounding purr. Rob's band members, within a few feet of the lawn-mower-like sound, turned to smile and shake their heads.

"That is the loudest damn cat on God's green earth," said Matt, shaking his head while disengaging his banjo strap and depositing the instrument on its stand. Entwining his fingers, he stretched his arms palms out.

"Yeaah, that's good. All right, then. Time for another keg trip." He nodded to Rob. "I 'spect I'll see you there soon?"

People gathered around the band, some intent on handing out compliments on the group's hip-shaking bluegrass, others inching toward Matilda, curious about the presence of the tiny black cat nestled above the fireplace.

Rob stood in front of the shoulder-high carrier, Matilda pressing her nose through the wire-wall door. He waggled his finger in front of the cat, urging her to shift to playtime mode.

Eying the fiddler's long, slim physique, the party's hostess pressed in beside Rob. Her voice echoed her New England upbringing.

"Andrew told me we'd have a feline visitor tonight. It certainly adds an unusual touch to your band. That's part of the reason we chose you, when we read about you and your cat on your promo site. Although your music certainly stands on its own merits."

Rob smiled. "Well, thank you, Mrs. Stewart. And Matilda thanks you, too."

The hostess inclined her head to one side, enjoying Rob's smile and manner nearly as much as his figure. She found the whole package appealing, including Rob's hazel eyes, a sexy match to his shaggy light brown hair, mustache, and goatee. Making her usual error, when assessing young men as potential lovers, the hostess, herself well into the over-40 category, guessed Rob at a decade older than his 24 years.

"So what's the story? How in the world do you get a cat to nap with all this excitement?"

Rob tapped his ear. "She's hard of hearing. She has been since she was a kitten, and some idiot kids lit a firecracker near her."

Rob had told the story endless times before, but he didn't mind telling it again. Matilda's near deafness explained her imperturbability in the face of bluegrass or any other kind of music. It also explained the monstrously loud meow and purr from such a small creature. It seemed to Rob that her minuscule body was home to maybe a few internal organs, and the rest filled with voice box.

"MEOWWW."

Matilda's enormous meow validated Rob's thoughts, and Mrs. Stewart reacted with widened eyes and a laugh. "I see! She is a noisy one!"

"So your husband told me you a have a bunch of dogs around here, right?"

The woman rolled her eyes and gave a wry smile. "Mmm. A bunch is right. Five of all shapes and barks. But of course we prepared for the cat, and they're nicely tucked into their backyard kennel."

"I was going to see if you'd mind if Matilda roamed around, but with five dogs, maybe not."

"Ha. I guarantee you it wouldn't be a problem. She could wander to their gate, and taunt them with her stare. From the looks of her, she might enjoy it. And those slobbering monstrosities couldn't get out if they grew battering rams from their foreheads. Our kennel is quite secure. In fact, I tried to get in on my own once, and it defeated me. Thank God. Now I have an excuse for never taking care of them."

Rob gave a half smile. Though not much of a canine fan himself, he wasn't sure how to react to a dog owner who shared his opinion.

"Well, it would be great if she could stretch her legs. She's dying to get out."

"I have no objection." Mrs. Stewart saw the drained beer cup near Matilda's cage. "I'll bet you're ready for a freshen up?"

"Can't say I'd say no."

"Well, how about I get you one while you get Martha started on socializing, or roaming, or whatever."

Mrs. Stewart gave Rob a slow smile as he handed her his beer mug. She turned away, showing a tanned back and a halter top held on with a bow that looked ready to undo itself.

Rob wondered if the woman was flirting with him. He never knew. It seemed like when he was most certain, was when he most embarrassed himself. Well, Lena was coming to pick him up later, anyway. Not that he was married. But Lena had his full attention at the moment, and at this point he knew he wouldn't bite if Mrs. Stewart offered a taste.

As he turned back to the cage, he saw that a clutch of cat-people had gathered, the type who melted at the sight of whiskers and a pair of pointy ears. Rob knew the feeling.

"Hey." He reached over to the carrier through the cat lovers. "Let me take her out and you can get to know her. Her name is Matilda, named after my maternal great-grandmother who loved cats as much as she loved her husband. Some say even more, though that's a family secret."

As Rob opened the cage door, Matilda released a magnificent meow and sat blinking at her audience. The group burst into laughter as a 50-something bleached blonde woman reached toward Matilda.

"Honey, little as you are, I think you need a big woman to handle you."

Matilda seemed to think the offer a good one, and leapt into the woman's arms.

"Oh, you fickle cat," said Rob. "Feel free to hand her around. At some point she'll squirm away, but don't worry about it. She'll be back when it's time to go home."

Rob moved off in search of Mrs. Stewart and his beer, leaving Matilda's admirers exclaiming over the kitty.

Through the patio sliding glass doors, Rob saw the hostess and Matt in what looked like intimate conversation, the woman with head tilted to one side. Looked like he had two chances for getting a beer through waiting: slim and none.

Rob slipped through the open glass door and eyed the kegs. He leaned over the tap labelled "Guinness" and prepared to take the time needed to fill a plastic cup with the frothy brew, a process that took at least two draws.

As he looked back toward Matt, he saw that his band mate was now solo, and trying to catch his eye. Matt sauntered up. "Smoke?" He inclined his head toward the back yard.

Rob shook his head. "Nah, but I'll join you for a sit down. Just finishing the pour." Matt stood, hands folded, waiting respectfully for the final Guinness draw.

Beers in hand, the musicians headed into the immense back area to a ring of trees. Rob saw no sign of the kennel. Good. Dogs might not appreciate the sweet aroma of their visit. Matt had switched on a key chain flashlight, which now illuminated lawn chairs tucked into the suburban grove.

"Well, now ain't that comfy," said Matt. "Come take a load off."

Matt and Rob knocked leaves off the chairs and sat down, Matt putting his beer on the ground, his hat on his lap, and a cowboy-booted foot on a conveniently located stump, as he pulled a joint and lighter from his pocket. He lit up and inhaled.

Rob leaned back in his chair. "Nice to take a break. Especially since this bunch looks like they'll be waving bills for an encore. So. I noticed you and our hostess were enjoying some conversation?"

Matt shook his head as he held on to his hit, letting out the smoke slowly as he smiled.

"Just conversation, that's all. She's married. I don't go there."

"Since when?"

Matt coughed out a puff of smoke as he laughed.

"Hey, don't make me waste this nice stuff I'm smokin'. And what do you mean, "Since when?" I've never gone there, dated a married woman." He offered the joint to Rob who replied with a little head shake.

"Anyway. I've got studying to do tonight. I knew cats had a ton of bones – 245 if you care to know - but I never thought I'd need to know quite so much about some of 'em." Matt stubbed out his joint on the log. "Well, I keep hearing that being a vet is better than studying to be one, so I'm going to hang in there."

Grasping his hat by the top, Matt eased it from his lap and back on to his head.

"So you know our not-so-young, but still-pretty-hot hostess has her eye on you. First thing she asked me was about your general availability."

Rob raised his eyebrows and sipped his beer. "Really."

"Really. I told her that a gal has been seen in your close vicinity for, what, more than a few months now? So, how is Lena doin'? Haven't seen her lately."

"Oh, she's good, good. No complaints."

"That Lena's a wild girl."

Matt reflected on the last time he'd seen Rob's girlfriend Lena. She could be fun. But she also seemed bitchy. Maybe it was partly her being five years younger than Rob. Well, for whatever reason his friend seemed to dote on the girl. He'd long ago learned not stick his nose into other people's relationships. Or at least to avoid sharing the whole truth unless absolutely necessary. And maybe Lena wasn't so bad. She could definitely be a hoot.

"So? Anything on the horizon? Like living together?"

Rob's mind flashed to the intimate times with Lena, legs intertwined, him whispering how nice it would be to wake up with her each morning; her giving a half smile, pulling away, and saying it was about time for some coffee. She had the air of being happy to stay around as long as no string of the attached kind was in sight.

"Mmm, not quite yet. But it's crossed my mind...oh crap."

Rob's last words were a reaction to sounds usually inspired by a blowing siren; dogs barking and wailing in unison and, in this case, noises that Rob guessed were the result of massive canine bodies flung against a chain link fence.

Jumping from his chair, Rob first began striding, then running, in the direction of the racket. Other party-goers appeared from the direction of the house, Mrs. Stewart pushing through the crowd and assuring them that the "monsters" constantly had "major freak outs."

"Believe me it's nothing," she said. "Those idiot dogs will use any excuse to bark like hyenas. A mosquito probably passed by their yard and shook its ass at them."

The small group fell silent as they heard a man's yell.

"Holy Mother of God. You scared the hell out of me, you little beast!"

Rob emerged from the woods with Matilda, puffed to twice her usual size, claws seemingly imbedded in Rob's chest, struggling and meowing with a vengeance.

"Ouch, watch the damn claws Tilda, would you? You're ok now, girl. Calm down." He looked from the cat to the group, now aware of the eyes on him.

"Sorry, I didn't mean to scare you all. Matilda gave me quite a start, shall we say, when she jumped from out of nowhere onto my shoulder. Luckily she grabbed a little more t-shirt than skin. But still – ow." He shook his head. "I got a glimpse of those dogs, Mrs. Stewart. They really do foam at the mouth, don't they?"

Matilda, still meowing loudly, wasn't responding to Rob's attempts to calm her with pets.

"Can someone grab her cage? Thanks."

Matilda's bleached blonde friend disengaged herself from the crowd and started back toward the house.

"Got it. Be right back."

"Yes," said Mrs. Stewart. "Perhaps that's enough pet interaction for the night." She turned and smiled at her guests. "Shall we all go back to the house? Maybe hear a little music? I must say I'm glad I'm not that cat right now. To be her size and encounter those behemoths up close? Terrifying. Come."

In his webbing Danyin muttered "Baata preserve me. What *were* those hideous things?"

CHAPTER 3

It was finally tomorrow.

Maryl's hands tidied a wandering piece of her smooth auburn hair, her mind considering the dark outcomes predicted by colleagues of today's communication. They said expect panic. Violence against...who? Against any number of imagined enemies.

Maryl knew it was true. Fear could lead to illogical action. Through the blur of thoughts, and the murmurings of those milling around the staging area, she heard Cavnee's whisper to Teesh.

"She should roll down the collar of that shirt. She looks so...stern, don't you think?"

Maryl's eyes focused as the off-stage comment found its way to her brain.

"No, Cav." she said. Don't worry. More will be revealed later, so to speak. Although you shouldn't care. I'm way too old for you."

Cavnee admired Maryl's oval face, brown eyes, hair styled attractively to flow with the lines of her jaw.

"Well, just hardly."

"No, plenty. And I'm taken."

Teesh called from across the room.

"All right kislings, enough flirting. And yes, she's gorgeous but yes, she's too old for you, Cavnee. And taken. And so are you. So." He looked around the space at the technicians ready to record Maryl, and the scientists ready to stand witness.

"Do we have all questions accounted for? I promised Maryl I'd keep the environment as quiet as possible, so…" Teesh pressed fingers of one hand against his own lips and pointed with the other at Cavnee. "…Ok?"

Teesh turned back to Maryl where she sat positioned on a chair in front of RT transmission equipment.

"Ready to make history, Mar? Good." He called again for quiet and turned back to Maryl.

"You can start whenever."

RT || Maryl Tymin

"This is, as we believe you know, our second transmission. You'll be glad to know this one answers more questions. The first communication was meant to just let you know about us, to help you get over the simple shock of our existence. Believe me. We were pretty shocked when we found out *you* exist."

Maryl paused before the next scripted statement.

"We've told you that we've been able, in a very limited way, to observe you."

Maryl didn't know that her head dipped slightly as she told the official lie. Deception wasn't an ideal path toward their aim of fostering a trusting relationship with those on Earth, but it was the agreed upon course.

"We had suggested that you share our contact with only a few others right now, for reasons we explained. We made the interpretation of that first transmission as complex as possible, to at least try to steer it into the hands of responsible parties. Like we said last time, we just don't want to cause a panic.

Ultimately, of course, the choice is yours regarding how to share what we send you."

She paused, creating a natural stopping point for those who would go back and analyze the message to that point, as they would no doubt do thousands of times.

"The Virrius Research Center, the VRC, for short, chose me for this message. I'm told my appearance is pleasant, unthreatening. I hope so. Also, I've been deeply involved in the research I'm going to tell you about. So, I talk to you as a scientist. The final reason I was chosen?" She leaned in and grinned. "I wouldn't quit bothering my boss until he said I could do it! And yes, that was a joke, which is something you seem to enjoy as much as we do."

Maryl saw the slight shake of Teesh's head. He'd thought the joke reference was distracting. But the comment had been approved.

"To begin. My name is Maryl Tymin. If you're one of the first to access this transmission then you're listening to me, but not seeing me. We know you can use your existing technology to hear me, and then later, you can use the explanation at the end of this recording to build what's needed to see me."

"First, I'll say I hope my English is acceptable. I've been studying, practicing, for about six of your years. I'm quite sure you'll catch mistakes, but hopefully it's not too bad. Others here have learned other Earth languages, but it seems to us that English is widely used. At the end of this broadcast, everything I'm saying will be repeated in the language most used on our planet, and some basic words and phrases will be taught."

Maryl leaned forward. "We know these transmissions must be overwhelming, exciting, incredible. But it is real. And

I'll say right now that we only hope we can get a similar communication from you. Soon."

Maryl glanced at Teesh to gauge how he felt things were going. Teesh nodded and swirled his hand for her to continue.

"First, a few words on the RT's, which, as I've said, we've given you instructions for building. RT stands for Rate-current Transition Link. We use the RT for general communication, and also to store information. An RT can both record and project images of living beings, like me, for example, which seem perfectly real, though the image can be disrupted by solid objects in its path. Sounds are also transmitted from the projected area. We keep RT activation pads everywhere in our everyday lives -- built into furniture, walls, transports -- and we've also got portable ones."

"RT's only project images of living creatures and items that retain some warmth, like a fragment of the seat I'm on now. If the RT is projecting in a way that covers the warm part of the seat, it will look like I'm floating, since you can't see the cooler part of the seat. But," she smiled, "I'm not floating."

Maryl leaned over to pick up a glass.

"In a moment, you'll see a portion of the object I just picked up. I'll hold it in such a way that as my hand warms it, you'll see some of it appear."

Maryl waited, and Teesh signaled her when he could see the suggestion of part of the cup Maryl lifted on his RT monitor.

"One day we'll work out how to have objects appear in RT's without the need to warm them up."

Maryl continued as she returned the container to the surface next to her, the surface invisible to the RT viewer, and the outline of the cup segment that could be seen a moment before, quickly dissipating.

"We also store and access digital data on devices we call hovi's. We'll go into detail on those another time, since those are more like technology you have. Possibly identical."

"As I said, I'm the one who will get you oriented to who "we" are, where we come from, and why we're contacting you now. Let me start with why, since that's easy. The answer to why is that we're excited about the existence of other intelligent beings, and we're curious about you."

"Who are we? We're called kisans. Where are we? Kisa, a world with many similarities to where you live, Earth. At the end of this RT, I'll supply information to help you pinpoint Kisa in relation to Earth, though it's possible you won't be able to locate us. The distance between us is vast."

Teesh, Cavnee, and the others in the room watching Maryl were silent, some nodding in agreement with Maryl's words.

"What if you could come to my home? How would our planet appear as you approached? Well, it's a question we can't answer. You see, the ironic situation is that we kisans can clearly see details of planets well beyond our own, but we can't see our own. At least not from the perspective of an outsider approaching our world. So far, our atmosphere has proved impenetrable."

At this confession of her planet's isolation, Maryl paused a beat before continuing.

"The inner view of Kisa I can easily describe, and that's lovely. First, I'll tell you what you see when you lift your head to the sky."

Maryl tilted her head, eyes, and hands upward.

"The blue you'd see might make you think you were on Earth, until you noticed the threads of lavender clouds, some lighter, some darker, all in constant motion. The cloud stream sometimes thins, and sometimes expands, blanketing the blue sky and muting the light from our two suns." She looked down and ahead again. "And yes, we have twice as many suns as you do."

"The purple clouds, and blue sky they're nestled in, are not only beautiful, but they also protect us from the source of our entrapment. It's called virrius gas. It circles the planet, invisible to the eye. Not only does the virrius devour artificially-created objects, it also carries a lethal contagion."

"We are not trapped on our planet due to lack of creative effort. The variety of contraptions we've developed to try to pierce our atmosphere and just move from place to place on and under our planet's surface, verges on the excessive. We have vehicles and attachments that let us fly, roll, glide, float, and leap at any pace you'd like, for long trips and short. But they're all compensations for the bleak reality of our planetary cage. None can safely penetrate the virrius."

Maryl lifted what appeared to be strings with small packets attached.

"One of our favorite travel devices is called the sarpac. These let us fly with only the merest of attachments on our bodies. And you better believe it's an exhilarating ride!"

A quiet "mmm-hmmm" of agreement from the sidelines was stifled quickly by Teesh's disapproving look. Teesh shook his head, sharing his displeasure with Cavnee, his eyes rolling upward. Cavnee shrugged in mock deep sympathy, as they both returned their attention to Maryl.

"Imagining the sarpacs in action will help you understand the virrius and just how impassable it is. We love to literally tumble around the sky in sarpacs. Sometimes we get careless and fly too near the virrius. And that can be a quick death. If the sarpac brushes against even a wisp of that destructive vapor, the device dissolves and we plummet. And we break."

"This gas has so far eaten through all materials we use for travel. So. We exist in a lovely purple-blue fish bowl. Some don't care. They fly their sarpacs, roam the planet's hollows, travel by surface transport, walk through forests, or just stay put."

"Quite a few of us do care, though, which is why you're hearing me now. Some of us have always wanted to slice through the virrius. I grew up with only broadcast glimpses of stars and worlds beyond the clouds, seen through breathtakingly expensive equipment, which disintegrated after capturing only a few seconds of these impossible sights."

Maryl paused and smiled.

"Then came the breakthrough. The portal."

CHAPTER 4

It was a typical morning for Lena. She was pinned to the bed, unable to rise. She managed to lift her head.

"Guys. *Come on guys.* Time to up and at 'em."

In her mind, she edited her proclamation. *Up and at 'em.* A cliché. Please. "Poor writing loves cliché." She laughed at the editors' textbook etched into her freelance writer's brain.

The two cats, Mooshie and Einstein, one spread the length of her legs, the other her torso, and perhaps offended by the worn-out phrase chosen to admonish them, were slow to respond.

"You guys are lucky I'm more patient with kitties than I am with people."

Lena decided to give up for the moment, settling back onto the pillow. She was still sleepy. As she should be. 4:30 AM! She couldn't believe she needed to be out by 5:00 to be at her destination in time for sunrise. She marveled at the insane things she'd do for a story. Like this morning. At the moment she felt vastly older than her 19 years. But then two extra-large cats on your body could you make you feel that way. She lifted only her head and stared at the two pairs of eyes leveled on her.

"OK!" Her loud pronouncement startled the cats, as intended, and they jumped to the ground, emitting discontented meows.

"OK!" This one she meant for herself, and it also had the desired effect. Pulling her body up and her legs over the side of the bed, she stood. "OK. Percussion."

The summer solstice ritual at the Red Rocks Amphitheater would already have begun, dark shapes on seats nestled in an earthen bowl silhouetted against dramatic Colorado red boulders. The drums would already be awakening.

In the winter, the thrumming of the Red Rocks solstice drums urged the lengthening of the days; in the summer they were said to welcome the warm months of growing, and the harvest to come. Or at least great eats at the local farmer's market, thought Lena.

Lifting a lumpy cloth bag from the floor and putting it on the bed, she pulled the drawstrings back to examine the contents. Tambourine. Maracas. Sleigh bells. Cow bell. Claves. And that wonderful three-headed, multi-colored straw shaker, a gift from a generous, sexy, enthusiastic and shit-faced drunk participant at a Seattle music festival a few weeks ago; particulars on the origin of both gift giver and instrument unknown. She smiled at the memory of the indulgent weekend.

Bring her own drum? No. There'd be plenty. Last year she'd walked in the darkness, up and down the stone seats set into the hillside, weaving her way through drums of all types, the tapping, shushing, tinging, and ringing sounds she made with her percussion instruments accentuating the rhythmic and arrhythmic beats from each clutch of players.

She dressed quickly and leaned her backside on the bed as she more neatly packed her instrument sack, shaking her head at herself as she worked. Lena didn't think of herself as a spiritual person. She didn't believe the seasons would stay forever fixed if she didn't help coax them to change. But last year, when she'd attended the rite, her heart had soared with the sun as she saw the shapes around her emerge into what they were: people creating magic and making it real by believing in it. And this time she'd pay special attention since she'd write about the experience.

Too bad she couldn't convince Rob to join her this morning. He contended that a gig ending at 2am, as his would, and early morning solstice celebrations, weren't the best combination. His loss. Maybe hers, too. Lena sighed as she thought of Rob.

Rob. A mixed-emotion subject. On one hand, Rob was the guy who followed Sierra Club rules and stayed on hiking paths instead of gathering bouquets of mountain flowers. He was the guy that had the manufacturers label stuck to his mattress, because the tag declared it unlawful to remove it. Rob crossed at the green and not in between.

It drove her nuts.

Lena's own personal motto was "Follow rules when convenient. But don't break rules if that will screw up someone else." It wasn't a tidy motto, but there it was.

Of course, the guy wasn't strictly a straight arrow. Rob was also the last guy at the Irish music session in a downtown Denver pub, dawn not far away, still sawing his fiddle bow and laughing after the other musicians fell away, one by one. She'd rarely seen a proffered whiskey waved away by Rob's hand, and she couldn't forget one of the things she liked best about that fiddling Boy Scout: he loved cats. Why the hell were all those sexy rebellious guys' cat haters? Not that Rob wasn't sexy, she thought with a half-smile nudged by recent memories.

As if reading her mind, Mooshie jumped onto the bed next to the instrument sack and nuzzled Lena's arm, as if to prove cats were indeed loveable, yes? Lena pulled the bag's drawstring and laid her hand on Mooshie's head, working her fingers through the fur of the cat's head.

Rob. She shook her head as she thought of him and imagined his smile. She knew their relationship could be cut short, and that she'd be the one to drop the ax. The ache she felt at the thought told her she didn't necessarily want that ending. But it was an outcome she practically took for granted after junior high and high school years of falling in and out of love, time and again. She knew Rob was ready to pledge his love. He said he'd wait through pre-college adventuring – which was now - as well as college years.

Crap. She knew such declarations should just make her exit. Serial monogamy seemed more her style for now. And there was that guy she'd interviewed last week for the article on 14'ers mountain hiking. He'd called. And he was in good shape. He had to be to climb those 14,000 feet-above-sea-level behemoths. And he was funny.

Lena sighed. Falling in and out of love. Yes, that was the lyric from the ancient Pure Prairie League song. She should just change her name to Amie, the heroine the song lamented, so at least the guys she dated had a heads up on her whole "no-commitment-thanks-anyway" situation. If she was being honest with herself, she knew "that hiker guy" was almost beside the point. It could be anyone that caught her eye and imagination. As long as it wasn't who she was with.

Ah, well. She had time to make mistakes. She was young, though at this wretchedly early hour she didn't feel it.

Mooshie, leaning her 13-lb thick-furred bulk against Lena's side, brought Lena back to the moment. Lena gasped as she glanced at the clock and saw the time. Mooshie issued a meow of complaint as her human support rose quickly, grabbed a brush from the dresser, and pulled it through her blonde mane, not bothering to see the effect in the mirror.

"Mooshie, Einstein, no time for breakfast. It's early! Go back to bed. Enjoy it for me!"

CHAPTER 5

RT || Maryl Tymin

"Imagine you're sitting in a park on a summer day, alone, enjoying the sunshine, lost in your thoughts. Suddenly, you realize you must have been drowsing since you look around and see people everywhere. Children playing and laughing, couples strolling and snuggling. It's energizing and wonderful to watch. But it's also overwhelming since a moment ago you were sure you were the only one around. That's the feeling all of us on Kisa had after we learned about the portals, and saw what they revealed. Without warning, we all understood we were not, and had never been, alone."

"The dream of VRC researchers was to design visual gateways we could use to peer through our planet's cloud-roof. And that dream came true. The portals revealed beings on two other planets."

"On the first world we monitored, there seemed to be no life. Just brown soil, stretching from horizon to horizon. But portal adjustments over time showed that yes, there were tiny residents, only just visible to the eye, leaping, crawling, skittering and flying. Bugs. Many here at the VRC are still learning from this planet, periodically announcing a new total number of species, which is in the hundreds now."

"The second world the portals uncovered, which we call Kelmin, is a frigid place for four of its five seasons. The animals are, of course, equipped to stay warm. The biggest are the lumbering, fur-covered beasts we call bondins."

Here, Maryl couldn't help but pause and smile, thinking of the soft-looking, roly poly monsters.

"I was assigned to a team that studied the behavior of those blubbery giants. For creatures who could crush me or you with a careless step, they're actually quite endearing. With their gray and white coloring, and stubby snouts, they seem like giant cuddle toys ...until you've seen one use its square, digitless paw to deal a hammer blow to a tiny Kelmin animal. Which it then eats whole. With, what appears to be, great satisfaction. My team members often commented they were glad we were watching the bondins through the portals, and not within chewing distance."

"Still, I was engrossed in our bondin study. That is, I was, until I saw the images beamed from the next inhabited planet we discovered."

"At first we called that third planet Mesto, named after the researcher who first gained up-close visual contact. It was later we began referring to it by the name its native dwellers gave it. The planet with creatures on it much like us. That was Earth. And those creatures would be you."

The first stunning images of Mesto had slipped, unplanned, from VRC confines, and made their way to public hovies. Maryl learned of the discovery at home, along with the rest of the world. Still staring at the hovi images, she'd fumbled for the RT pad, embedded in her kitchen counter, choosing the quick-reach function whose settings she knew by touch.

She spoke as an image gathered in her kitchen.

"That you, Brae?"

The dark eyes, dark skin, dark hair, and even darker fur of Braelind Carsinsen filled the screen. The predominant tisani line in his ancestry was especially evident in his lightly furred neck, and the ears sporting the slight, quintessential, tisani curve. His broad face also revealed a smattering of kyan, the other type of kisan, in his background.

Braelind looked like he'd been startled by the sharp sound of the quick-reach transmission, though his expression relaxed as he saw the caller. As head of the research division at the Virrius Research Center, Braelind Carsinsen didn't always receive calls as pleasant as this one would likely be.

"Brae! Have you selected the new researchers yet? For the new planet? The one with kyan-type kisans on it? And mynies. Baata, it's amazing isn't it?

"Well, hello there, Dr. Tymin."

Braelind answered in his usual measured, deliberate manner. Maryl thought, as she often did when chatting with Brae, that perhaps only a charging rundy, its claws extended and jaw open, heading straight for a delicate part of Braelind's anatomy, would make this kisan move quickly. Brae continued.

"As usual, you cut through the niceties and get on with communicating. If we could bottle your enthusiasm, we could probably use it to pierce the virrius in no time."

Braelind smiled as Maryl shook her head at her boss's imperturbable nature. His RT receiver made it appear that Maryl was floating above the chair across from his desk. To Maryl, Braelind seemed to be relaxing in the center of her kitchen, suspended in a sitting position, with only splinters of a chair arm branching under one elbow.

"Well, I hate to be slacking off on my duties, Maryl, but we have only known about this planet for about, let's see, six hours. So, no. I must admit that the research teams are not yet in place. To be frank, we didn't want the information transmitted so widely, so quickly. There was a leak." His frown turned into a look of resignation. "I know. It's all over the hovi's, and that's the situation we've got. It will be fine."

He shook his head. "Rush, rush, rush these days. Well. It is, indeed, amazing and most exciting." He paused. "And. I was about to contact you and some others to discuss this. Can you come to VRC now? I know it's late, but…"

"Of course I'll be there! I'll see you in person before you melt."

"All right. See you soon."

Maryl spoke as Braelind leaned in to break the RT connection.

"Brae. One thing before I go. I want to let you know…"

"Yes?"

"Put me on the new team. I'm ready to be reassigned."

"Reassigned, huh?" Braelind leaned back on the unsubstantial air of Maryl's kitchen, the place where she knew the comfortable back of Braelind's chair existed in his office. He eyed her mildly. "And here I thought you loved watching those big jolly killers."

"The bondins. Yes, you know I do. It's been the opportunity of a lifetime. But Brae. This new thing. This is perfect for me. You know my past work in mynie research."

"I know. And I know you have two meowing housemates you love as much as I love my kislings."

"Actually, I have three now. I think the latest heard I was a softie, and found its way to my door a few weeks ago. Anyway, Brae. I'm probably more passionate about the inner and outer workings of mynie's than most anyone at the VRC.

I don't think I need to remind you of the massive amount of mynie Transference research I was involved in before and during the bondin work. Nearly a hundred trips. And really, that bondin thing is completely under control. The rest of the team wouldn't miss me."

"That "bondin thing?" That you were so passionate about last week?" He nodded and sighed. "Maryl, since you have the energy of three hyperactive kisans,. I doubt your team won't miss you. But, it's true I'm going to have to yank some of you from current assignments to work on this "Mesto thing.""

"So --? You'll think about it?"

Braelind sighed again, his nod turning into an unbelieving shake of his head. "Maryl, are you really a Reader and you just never bothered to tell anyone? Before you called I forwarded your name for the Mesto team. I'm not anticipating any disagreement, but we'll see. Meanwhile, get off the RT and over here."

Maryl shouted "Yes!" and "I will be right there!" Braelind watched her image dissolve in streaks of motion as the RT connection broke and the afterimage melted.

When Teesh called for a break in the transmission, Maryl's thoughts had wandered.

She'd always remember her RT talk with Braelind that remarkable night. Earth's discovery was a massive leap in the kisans' evolution of struggles to reach beyond themselves. In less than a lifetime they'd moved from experiencing the inner life of animals, to observing far off life nothing like their own, to this. Discovering lives comparable to their own. What would be next? What could be?

CHAPTER 6

Lena. Why did she spring to Rob's mind just then, in the middle of a long bow stroke across the center of his upright bass? Perhaps the resonant sound was evocative of the stirrings of his heart. A heart that both glowed and ached at the thought of Lena.

Lena. Wearing that shirt that had no secrets. The cinched waist skirt. The first thing he'd noticed when she'd approached him at the dance, that first time, was her shapely figure.

"Hi there," she said. "Are you interested in dancing after the break?"

Rob had been standing on the side of the dancehall, water in hand, wishing for a beer, knowing he'd have to wait a few more hours for that pleasure. He heard the question; someone asking if he'd join in the long lines of dancers doing the square-dance-like moves of the oddly-named "contra" dance. He heard the question, turned his head, and saw the tight sleeveless top and the dark blond hair, almost golden, voluminous, and long.

Rob smiled. "I would love to dance, but I can't. I'm in the band."

Lena had shaken her head and rolled her eyes.

"Oh god, I'm an idiot. I always listen to bands and always notice who the musicians are. I'm that one girl dancing in the corner at a concert when everyone else is standing around, you know?"

Rob smiled. "I do. Are you that girl?"

"That's me. Except tonight. This is my first contra so I've been absorbed in just learning the steps without maiming anyone. Without much success, I might add. Sorry, I didn't realize you were in the band. What do you play?"

"Bass."

She'd brightened. "Really? I love the bass. Such a rich sound."

"I love it too. Though honestly, for this gig, it's pretty boring. In old-time music, like we're playing tonight, I basically keep a beat. Tonight it would be more fun to be playing fiddle."

Lena nodded but didn't conceal a slight frown. "Huh. You know, I probably need to spend more time listening to violin." She gave a self-conscious laugh. "Actually, I'll just admit it. I don't always…appreciate violin."

"Well, actually, I don't play violin. Violin's fine. But I love the fiddle."

And so had begun a conversation on the driving sound of a fiddle, and the trilling sweeps of a violin, and the reality that the instruments were identical, though the playing methods and songs they appeared in different. Depending on who you talked to. Rob explained the topic was, had been, and always would be, a hot one among the fiddle/violin factions.

After the break, Lena found a dance partner, and Rob returned to the stage. As he thumped the bass and the dancers twirled, he watched his new acquaintance spin inexpertly with a man whose head rose well above her stooped one, and whose face contorted as she occasionally made firm foot to foot contact.

After the dance, while edging his bass into the back of his hatchback in the parking lot, Rob noticed Lena. He wanted to do more than nod a goodbye.

"Hey," he called. "Headed out?"

"Yes. Though after dancing I'm still totally awake. Maybe it was all those shrieks of pain from my partners? And they were close to my ear when they did it! Quite rude, really."

The two exchanged smiles.

Lena continued. "I don't feel like going home." She raised an eyebrow. "Any interest in stopping somewhere? A nightcap?"

Rob was interested. Lena wasn't bashful and he liked that.

They'd wandered the Denver streets, finding a late night place conducive to the tentative interchange of first date conversation; lights not bright, and all the tables for two. They asked each other the questions people ask when deciding if the spark they sense will last more than a night.

"Wruble. Is that Jewish?"

"Yes," Lena had replied. "I come from a proud Jewish heritage, which I'm completely demolishing when it comes to actual adherence. And if you heard a whooshing sound, that was my great-grandmother sighing from the great beyond. But, I still love matzoh ball soup, and you'll learn a lot of Yiddish words if you hang with me."

"Well, I know "gefilte fish.""

"Huh. A decent beginning. But I wouldn't recommend eating the stuff. *Totally* gross. So, your name. Rob MacIntosh. Is that Irish?

"Scottish, me lass. Though Rob is actually my middle name. And no one has ever guessed my given name no matter how hard they tried, so I'll just tell you. I only ask you not to laugh. Or at least not to laugh too much."

"I think I can at least promise not to laugh too much. At least I think I can! Good god, what is it?"

"Ok. Here it is. Ready? It's Gandalf."

Lena banged the table with her hand. "No. Come on. You can't be serious. I mean, sorry. But... come on."

"I'm serious. My legal name is Gandalf Robert MacIntosh. Luckily, my dad's more practical than my mom, and persuaded the family to call me Robert.

"Smart fella', that dad."

"Tell me about it. Though my mom still calls me Gandy when she's feeling particularly maternal."

"Well, I guess it was a creative impulse. Could have been worse. You could have been named, I don't know, Dracula, maybe? Or Dumbledore? Uh, Peter Pan?"

"All right now, I didn't name myself remember."

"Ok. Enough teasing. For now." Since the waitress hadn't asked for ID – thank god for dark eateries, and she was only shy of legal by two years, anyway - Lena sipped a glass of red wine, then returned the glass to the table, rolling her thumb and forefinger around the stem, her gaze moving from the glass to Rob's eyes. "Ok. Any particular reason for your parents choosing Gandalf other than being Tolkien fans?"

"Well, my mom and dad are very, shall we say, colorful people. You know, SCA-types."

Seeing her questioning look, Rob continued. "Have you heard of the SCA, the Society for Creative Anachronism?"

"Ohhh, yeah. Strange people who dress up in medieval clothing?"

Rob laughed. "They're not all strange! I mean, ok, well, strangeness could be a factor. But yes, the dressing up is a part of it. Have you ever been to the Ren Faire down in Larkspur? The Renaissance festival?"

Lena shook her head, a quirk of a grin on her face.

"The Ren Faire gives you an idea of what SCA people are into. Really anything from Europe, before, say, the 1600's or so. Culture, politics, clothes. So, at the Ren Faire you'll see plenty of wenches with lots of bosom on display. And men in tunics. "Garb," as they say."

"And good music, right?"

"Oh, great music. And comedy shows, phony battles, beautiful medieval-y things to buy, fantasy stuff. And there's more food than an army could eat in a century." He leaned forward, as if he had something to confide. "The SCA folks like to eat well."

Lena laughed. "Ok, that explains the buxom bosoms. Well, I definitely want to go." She looked down at her chest. "I could be persuaded to wear something bosomy."

It was Rob's turn to smile. "Yes. I'll bet you could."

Lena's hands had made their way to the middle of the table, the fingers of each restive, intertwining. Rob moved his hands closer. He looked at her, and then put his hands over hers. The spark glowed.

Rob kept talking as he looked at the small hands he'd begun stroking.

"So how could a woman as beautiful as you be at a dance without a partner?"

He saw Lena start to speak then stop, looking down at the hands atop her own.

"What?" asked Rob. "Were you supposed to be there with someone?"

"Let's say I could have been there with someone, but I chose not to be."

"O.K." He paused. "Next topic?"

"Yes, I think so." Lena pulled her hands from under Rob's to lift her wine glass and take a sip. She looked away for a moment and then made eye contact with Rob. "By the way, I'm really enjoying myself. I hope we'll do this again."

Rob nodded. "Me, too." They held the eye contact.

She broke the gaze. "So, are you a "real" musician? Or is it a passionate hobby?"

"Playing music is how I earn my living so yeah, I'd say I'm "real." How about you? You dance for a living?"

Lena laughed. "Not yet. No, I'm trying my hand at writing. Web articles and features, and a lot of stories that are really ads."

"Hmm. You can earn a living from that?"

"Not really. Well, not for me at this point, anyway. Only one thing makes it possible."

"Second job?"

"Parents. Since I was the whiz kid writer in high school, winner of lots of "watch out for her" writing awards, I got the ok to try my hand as a professional for a while before college. Without subsidized rent, and other minor assistance…ok a lot of assistance, I'd either be living in my parent's basement, or a dorm room."

"Dorm room's not bad."

"I know. And that'll probably happen soon enough. Meanwhile," she raised her glass, "welcome to my adventure." Rob raised his glass to hers.

The date lasted until a waitress stood by the table, her blinking eyes and pasted-on smile making them aware they were the last people in the restaurant, chairs being placed on tables around them.

They made plans for their next meeting. The spark was flaring.

The sound of a note from a string plucked by this own unthinking fingers brought Rob back to the present, back to his practice room, back to noticing a fast-asleep Matilda on a table not a foot away from him.

He sighed, leaning the tall instrument against the wall. Enough of that damn memory-prodding bass.

CHAPTER 7

RT || Maryl Tymin

"It was on Mesto - Earth - that we found the beings that surprised us the most. That's because about half of the kisan population looks just like you. What you call humans, we call kyans. So, we weren't surprised by your alien appearance. We were surprised by the resemblance."

"The next obvious question is: What does the other half of the kisan population look like? The ones that don't look completely human, that we call tisani? Would you believe me if I said they have no arms, two heads, and tongues that flick in and out almost more rapidly than the eye can see? But, no. As I mentioned before, we like joking probably as much as you do."

Maryl smiled and caught both Cavnee's grin and Teesh's scowl from the side of the room. She'd lobbied to add that bit of silliness and had been surprised to get her wish.

"We'll be broadcasting images of typical kisans and, as I've said, we hope that sooner rather than later, you'll be able to construct your own RT's, and see what we look like. When you're finally able to see me, you'll see I'm a melding of both types of kisan, though my physical difference from kyans and humans isn't immediately obvious when I'm wearing clothing, as I am now."

Cavnee smiled from the sidelines. "Take it off, gorgeous. Show that fur," he said in an undertone. Teesh turned with raised eyebrows, his own excessively tisani features showing annoyance with a flash of pointy teeth. Cavnee put up his hands to show he got the message to stay quiet, as they both turned back to Maryl.

"I'm a kisan, just like the kyans are, but tisanies have characteristics that will remind you of an animal you know well. We call them mynies. You call them cats."

Cavnee couldn't help a glance at Teesh as Maryl described tisani characteristics. Teesh was the prototypical tisani kisan with his oval face, rounded eyes, faintly angled ears, short wisps of forehead whiskers stylishly unremoved, and sparse fur covering areas of his neck that Cavnee knew extended beneath Teesh's shirt, where it lightly covered the mid-section of his chest and torso.

"We have gradations of kyan and tisani. Some kyans, as I said, look precisely like you. That's the "full" kyan. At the other end of the spectrum, the full tisani, are those that almost look ready to crouch down on all fours. Not quite, though. You'll never see whiskers around the nose on any tisani; no fur on a face; ear placement is identical to kyan and human placement, and, although I'm sure they'd be handy, no one has retractable claws, or any claws at all. But the tisani skeletal and muscular structures do have slight differences that offer more flexibility and strength than the kyan structure."

Maryl opened the collar of her shirt which had, until then, been covering her throat.

"Ok, when you have visuals, you'll see what I'm doing right now. Just showing you a part of my physique that's slightly different than yours."

Revealed in the small swatch exposed by the opened collar was a light sprinkling of soft-looking fur, the mottled brown pattern a match to the brown of Maryl's hair.

"How did the two varieties of kisans occur? How are we related to the mynies, what you call cats, since we certainly appear to be? There's no evidence of a gradual evolutionary process. We think, with your help, we'll find answers to these questions. We think, as fantastic as it may seem, that the answers are with you. On Earth. You see, after we discovered you through the visual portals, we realized there was a possibility we'd already seen you."

Maryl remembered the gradual realization, learned through countless Transferences into dreaming mynies, that all the mynies had dreams featuring nothing but kyan-type kisans, the type that looked human, in what were then unfamiliar surroundings.

"We may have seen you and your surroundings through experiences we'd been having before the visual portals were created. I'll give you details soon. For now, I'll say we believe we may have seen your species and your planet through the minds of the mynies. In the dreams of what you would call our "cats." And it's not nearly as unlikely as you may first think. The process that allows it is a scientific one."

At home, the night of the first Mesto broadcast, what now seemed to be a lifetime ago, Maryl had told her little tribe of three the good news.

"Willo! Claudi! Valin!"

Two of the mynies came prancing in the room, tails and pointy ears erect. The one with gloriously-long fur and a face that could be featured on any hovi glam mag leapt to the top edge of a chair to be closer to eye-height with Maryl. Claudi. Around Maryl's ankles, chubby, gray, and vibrating with delight, Willo rubbed her face along Maryl's shins.

Maryl, still standing, bent forward and stretched one arm down to pet the mynie on the ground, the other up high to scratch the head of the mynie on the chair. "Typical," she thought. She looked around. "Valin?"

Valin, the newest addition to the household, likely didn't know his new name yet, having only recently stumbled, filthy and starving, into his new home.

Maryl smiled as she saw just half a mynie's head, at the far end of the room, peering around the corner. He was still shy.

Maryl scooped up the purring Claudi, whose brown and white coloring was similar to her own, and settled in a chair. Claudi's purr increased in intensity as she settled into Maryl's arms and chest. Maryl unconsciously reacted with her own tisani purr, the delicate sound only heard well when leaning an ear on the chest of a pleased tisani, making it an intimate act between loved ones, including beloved pets.

Maryl poured out her news in the voice that seemed to always emerge when she talked to her four-legged kislings, a voice higher pitched, more emphatic, and musical then the one she used with kisans.

"Guess what mynies? I get to study far-away kisans and also mynies that look just like you! And you don't need to be jealous since they're quite far away." She kissed Claudi on the head. "Quite."

Willo jumped up beside Claudi on Maryl's lap, causing a two-second squabble that settled when Claudi realized she still had prime real estate in Maryl's arms.

"Well, aren't you at all impressed, guys?" She scratched Willo's right ear. "Will, as usual, you have amazing timing. You always seem to sense when I'm just about to get up. And that's when you thump on my lap and settle in."

Willo looked at her, all innocence, moving her head under Maryl's hand to get the pets she craved at that moment. Maryl looked into the clear gold eyes of her sweet Willo. They seemed so intelligent. Against all logic, she imagined her girl was thinking deep thoughts, and she longed to be privy to them. She planted a kiss on the furry grey head.

"Yes, it may well be true that you're cuter than a double sunrise. But, I'm still getting up and you're still getting dumped."

Willo and Claudi were momentarily shaken by the sudden impact of floor under paws as Maryl stood up, but quickly regained their composure and good humor as they saw Maryl was heading toward the kitchen.

The whir of the quick thaw was all that was needed to help Valin, at least momentarily, forget his timidity. Three pairs of eyes, some wide, some slitted, watched while she prepared their food. She scraped dinner into three small bowls. Three. Such a tiny number. At one point she'd had nine, after she'd inherited seven from her childhood and adopted two more later.

All her old, sweet mynies had died, one by one, of advanced age and disease. There was a time when she thought the pain of each loss was too deep, that she'd never again adopt a mynie after yet another had died. But she did.

Maryl set down the food for the mynies, each pet with its own bowl. Willo settled down to eat, with, as usual, one foot in her food dish. Maryl petted the tip of Willo's slate-colored tail while the mynie chomped with dazzling rapidity through her dinner. As happened often, Claudi sniffed the contents of her dish and made burying motions as if asking "What is this? Not food, surely?" And, as happened more often than not, Maryl emptied the bowl and replaced its contents with one of

40

the only foods the mynie would actually eat. A healthy varied diet was not on Claudi's agenda.

From the other room, Maryl heard the strains of a popular song from a decade earlier. "Bounce me up! Bounce me down! Bounce me round the streets of town!..." It was music from the RT signaling a call had come in. Maryl went to answer it and made a mental note that she really should change the song she'd selected for incoming calls so long ago. Her choice of "Bounce Me Up! Bounce Me Down!" had been a tribute of sorts to the playful bondins she'd been studying. Time for a change. Maybe "My Traveling Mind," or that song about wanderlust, "Above and Beyond." Yes.

It was Sumee calling. Maryl hit the RT button, and there was her friend, floating in Maryl's kitchen, just a portion of Sumee's mane of white hair visible above the torso of the shocking bright green and gold color of her dress. Her gray tisani eyes were as beautiful as ever under the merest suggestion of whiskers on her forehead. She appeared to be striding quickly though never coming closer, the wind caressing her sumptuously large frame. Though far more than a decade separated the two in age, they'd grown more intimate than twin kislings over the years.

"Sumee! You look gorgeous! Going to a session?"

"Hey, Marylsune. Just coming back, walking home. It's windy out here, but nice." She pointed at herself with a grin. "Thus the swishy fabric." Maryl knew Sumee delighted in creating dramatic RT images. "It should make a great melt."

Maryl imagined the green-gold coloring of Sumee's RT image scattering, "melting," when Sumee signed off later. Yes, it should be quite nice.

Sumee moved a stray flap of hair from her face as she strode. "So. I'm sure you've heard about Mesto?"

"Sumeesune, I was just spreading my great news to my kislings." Maryl gave her friend the details of her appointment to the Mesto research group.

"I figured as much. If you'd told me they hadn't picked you, now that would have been a surprise. Baatani be praised. Of course, as you may imagine, every corasan, including your little Sumee, is busy composing new songs about Mesto since we heard the news. I'll rely on you to pass on the juicier tidbits you come across about Mesto, yes?"

The musically-gifted kisans, the corasans, crafted songs that were sometimes based on history or legend, sometimes whimsy, sometimes the emotional extremes of life. The contact with Mesto seemed to be a tantalizing combination of history and myth, a once in a lifetime historic occasion, ripe to write music about.

Maryl foresaw corasans like Sumee refusing invitations for music visits, whether for home or public consumption, everything, in their frenzy to create lyrics and music that would appropriately herald Mesto's discovery.

It was common, on Kisa, to engage the musical kisans to bring the feeling to homes and psyches that only live music could impart. It was sometimes for the sheer joy of it, though a corasan visit could also be therapeutic, since some corasans, like Sumee, specialized in healing, listening visits. For these type of visits, intervals of music, intermingled with conversation, put the client at ease.

Sumee's striding ceased as she reached up for what was probably her home's door latch, took a few more steps, and gracefully reclined on what appeared to Maryl to be the air of her kitchen, but what was really one of Sumee's overstuffed, brightly-colored, chairs. A hint of yellow appeared behind one of Sumee's shoulders to confirm the existence of a chair.

One day they'll figure out how to broadcast surrounding scenery via the RT, thought Maryl, for probably the thousandth time. Some combination of the RT and hovi.

"Sorry, without the motion the melt won't be quite as spectacular. But I'm ready to faint for a while. Still, for my Marylsune, I will get up and spin around a bit when we click out."

Maryl laughed her thanks as Sumee smoothed her generous tresses. Her skirt-covered legs floated even farther from Maryl's floor as she folded them under her, settling in for a chat.

"So. To business. Tell me. Are there any cute kisans on your new team?"

Sumee had one other major passion beyond her corasan work: male kisans.

RT || Maryl Tymin

Maryl's thoughts often flitted to that night long ago when Mesto had been revealed to the kisans. So it was no surprise she thought of it now, even as she acted as her planet's ambassador on this communication.

"Our questions were obvious. Why did mynies, the creatures on our planet that look and act like animals you call cats, see what appeared to be humans in their dreams? Were they literally seeing images from Earth? Do the mynies have abilities that allow them to hear you and see you across the light years? This doesn't seem likely since the mynies dream of one place only. A rocky, desert-like area."

Maryl recalled the dry landscape of the often-repeated dream.

"One theory is that they're somehow intercepting the visual memories your cats harbor. Of course, we're not positive these dreams involve Earth at all. But we hope we can, with your help, discover the answer."

Maryl paused as some in the room shifted in their places, their body language revealing the unease they felt at Maryl sharing Kisa's secrets with others. Their concerns had been overruled.

"Regardless of this mystery, there are any number of other reasons for us, as a species, to reach out to you, with pure curiosity being the major one. A reason we think you can identify with. So, before I tell you more about our observation techniques, and our mynies' peculiar dreams, you do need to know more details about us."

"There's a type of kisan, the corasan, who is always tisani. The corasans are, on one level, music makers. They use voice alone, or accompany themselves using musical instruments and devices."

"Corasans sing and play during invited visits to our homes, our work, our schools, and in public places. Each corasan specializes in things like therapy, pure entertainment, or arousal. To imagine the possible range of corasan performances, just think of the many ways music and song might comfort, teach, or stimulate us."

"All corasans also share another commonality. You might say they're our historians."

"Corasans retell the events kisans, as a society, are most proud of; ones we most regret; and ones we recall sentimentally. All corasans perform segments of those happenings, their repertoire constantly growing. Of course, we also record our history in other ways. But hearing these essential elements of our past, these moments that reflect who we were, and who we are, hearing them sung and played, is an important ritual for us, as well as a way to learn. There's something about hearing events sung that helps you remember them."

"There's one more special thing about the corasans. It's a mystical aspect, and it's what identifies them as what they are soon after they start speaking. They alone share, from birth, the memory of what we call Baata, a heavenly arena where it's said the kisan life begins before it's released into our world; where kisans exist before we're born; where black angels nurture our pre-birth selves; where we are before we enter our mother's womb. At least that's the tale."

"Like most of us at the VRC, I'm a skeptic about mystical assumptions. But. The fact that a small segment of the population is born with the same, identical memory of Baata is not something that's easily dismissed."

Maryl heard the sound of clapping hands. It was Teesh.

"Ok, hold up." Teesh walked toward Maryl. "We're changing the acoustics. If you want to walk off a few minutes, go ahead."

Maryl blinked, feeling like a hand had stilled her body mid-leap. "Sure, I'll take a break."

There was much more to tell.

CHAPTER 8

While waiting for the recording to resume, Maryl's mind wandered to that first conversation with Sumee, after the Mesto discovery, back when the potential of portals could barely be grasped.

Maryl tolerated Sumee's chatter about romance. Even during that long ago RT conversation, when her thoughts flew with the possibilities presented by her new, upcoming research, she'd indulged her friend's favorite pastime.

Sumee's talk of love allowed fallow parts of Maryl's brain to creakily rise and peer about, if only briefly. Though moving rapidly into her middle years, her thoughts and life were relatively romance-free, despite Sumee's best efforts. Maryl's life had been so abundantly filled with scientific strides, that any energy remaining to pursue a love life was less substantial than an RT afterimage. Oh, there were encounters here and there with kisans who were interesting. But ultimately, they were not anywhere as intriguing as the discoveries she was part of that were affecting, to its core, her planet and her society.

Maryl tried to focus on the seemingly frivolous question Sumee asked her, knowing it was dead serious to her friend.

"So. Any cute kisans on your new team?"

"Well, let me think." Maryl closed her eyes to imagine the faces of the team members, most known to her from other VRC work, a few new.

"There was a kisan..."

"Tisani or kyan?" asked Sumee.

"Definite kyan."

"Oh." Sumee's "oh" was disappointed, reflecting her own preference for tisani-dominant kisans.

"Yes, definite kyan. I was busy thinking of more important things, of course…"

"More important than romance? Maryl. *What* am I going to do with you? Just tell me, please, since you're the genius."

Maryl laughed. "I don't know what you're going to with me, Sumee. How could I think that discovering a species on a distant world, that resembles a species on our world, and that we should soon be able to observe light years away -- how could I possibly think that could be more important than romance? Obviously, my brain has ceased functioning."

Sumee waved her hand, shooing away the sarcasm and talk of breakthroughs and revelations like so much dust on her gown. "Don't get distracted with all that. Go on. You were saying, about the kyan…?"

"Yes, the kyan. Danyin is his name, and he did strike me as charming, if not exceptionally handsome. He was sort of handsome, but, actually more charismatic, I'd say. You think he's attractive, because he acts like he's attractive, you know what I mean?"

Sumee nodded her head approvingly. "Yes, I do Marylsune, yes I do."

"Listen, no promises on me getting to know this kisan in anything but a professional way, all right? I'm going to be busy for a long time. We're talking eight-hour work days. Sometimes more."

Sumee used two hands to flip back her hair to accentuate her "Hmm."

"What's new about that, Maryl? You always overwork, you always have, you always will. All right. I won't ask you any more romance-related questions until, oh, our next conversation. What? Too soon? Ok. The conversation after our next conversation."

Maryl had smiled at the floating RT image of her friend. It was a battle she was sure to lose, so she wouldn't even try to engage.

Sumee's image stood up and her look grew thoughtful. "You know, I know someone named Danyin. Well, I don't actually know him. He's a Listener. And sometimes he sends me clients. We've exchanged written hovi messages. Mostly we know each other through reputation, and so far our referrals have worked out well. I've heard he's got that fantastic accent kisans from Robee have, though I haven't heard it myself. Danyin.... Mesterdide. Yes, that's his name."

Maryl grinned. "That's him, same kisan. Oh, that brogue. I must admit I find it charming. He could point out a blotch of food on my nose and it would sound appealing."

Sumee shrugged. "I'll admit that accent is all out sexy." She sighed. "But you say he's all kyan, hmm?"

Maryl put on a reproving frown, though a lingering smile was still evident. "Excuse me, but you do remember I'm a good part kyan myself?"

Sumee dismissed the idea with a flick of her upheld wrist. "Well, lucky you that your tisani part shines through and makes you fabulous."

"Sumee, do you reveal your prejudice to your kyan clients? I know you sing for kyans."

"Marylsune! I love my kyan clients! Some are the dearest kisans in the world, and closer to me than the color on my hair. It's not necessary that I feel the desire to partner with any of them. I'm being perfectly honest with you, my friend, in this private conversation." Sumee widened her eyes. "Would you prefer I be less than truthful?"

"Oh, Sumeesune. Quit it. Anyway. Now you know who I have a quarter of an eye on, while my mind is busy with other more important things, all right?"

"All right." Sumee sighed. "I'll click off for now, my busy friend." As she smiled and started spinning she said "You could devote *half* an eye to Danyin, instead of a quarter, Marylsune." Maryl paused to watch as her friend broke the RT connection. The swirling greenish-gold melt, one she remembered clearly to this day, had been marvelous.

Teesh clapped for attention. Cavnee put his hand on Teesh's arm and leaned in to speak.

"I'm out of here for now. You don't need me, right? I haven't seen Linny in, oh, I don't even know. But her last RT message said my afterlife will come more quickly than I wish if I don't see her today."

Teesh nodded distractedly. "Sure. No big deal here. Just making a little history. But you go, really."

Cavnee opened his mouth to speak and Teesh spoke first.

"Kidding, Cavnee. Go. Love to Linny from me."

Teesh resumed his clapping for attention, not realizing all had fallen silent.

"All right. Let's keep going. Maryl?"

Maryl pulled herself out of her reverie of memories of the two greatest changes in her world at large, and her personal world -- the discovery of Earth and her first inkling that Danyin would be an important part of her life.

"Ready?" asked Teesh? "All right." He clapped. "Go."

RT | | Maryl Tymin

"There's more to tell about the corasans, the musical kisans. But first, some background on how we arrived at this point."

"The portals were a remarkable technological advance. But second, perhaps, to another, earlier achievement on Kisa. Get ready to be amazed. The process is called Transference. And we soon learned we could meld Transference and portals together for remarkable results."

Maryl noticed that Endee had entered the room. As assistant to the rarely seen Head of VRC, she was an unfamiliar visitor. The diminutive kisan walked up to Teesh, and Maryl saw her gesturing with her hands as she spoke in a low voice to Teesh, the tall tisani angling his head to hear, occasionally nodding.

Teesh gave a final nod, straightened, and clapped. "Hold up. Good job, Maryl. Good job everyone. Something's come up and we're breaking for the day. I'll be in touch to let you know when we'll resume."

Endee leaned in again and lifted her head to speak a few more quiet words to Teesh. Teesh turned back to the group and added "Probably not tomorrow."

CHAPTER 9

The Earth RT's were on hold. They'd been told that a more accessible type of audio feed was being added.

Maryl, clearing her table after dinner, considered her mixed feelings of disappointment and relief at the delay.

The RT sang out the song that had now been programmed for years, "Above and Beyond." She glanced at the I.D. for the incoming call and clicked on the RT.

"Sumee! One of the few calls I never regret receiving." She admired her friend's appearance, the white hair swept to one side, nearly matching the white of Sumee's dress, which was crisscrossed, from the ample bosom down, with thin alternating lines of blue and silver. "Looks like you still hold the unofficial record for most fashionable corasan. So, what's news with you?"

Sumee nodded her acknowledgement of Maryl's compliment. "Mar, there's big news, actually. You ready? I'm taking a trip, if you can believe it."

Maryl paused with her mouth open before replying. "You? The last time you left the vicinity for a week you swore, in very colorful language, I recall, that you'd never do it again."

Maryl knew Sumee's sentiment was common among tisani kisans who adhered to the aphorism "Home is Far Enough," with "home" defined as an area about as far as a tisani could stride within an hour or two.

"So true. I'd rather dye my neck hair bright orange than travel. Which of course would clash miserably with *all* of my outfits. You know how I feel about orange." She mock shivered. "But it's because of my mother, Harit. She needs an operation."

"An operation? What's going on?"

"As far as major operations go, it's not. But it's "got" to be done. Harit's been croaking instead of singing, screeching instead of warbling. So this surgery is supposed to take care of the problem. She's quite beside herself as you can imagine."

"Well, yes. Sounds like a big deal to me."

Most corasans were descended from other corasans. In Sumee's case, her mother was among the most famous of her time. She still, decades after choosing Sumee's father, received sumptuous treats and aromatic bouquets from the kisans she'd both sung to and made love with in the time gone by when she had devoted her talents to sensual music and activities. Though now retired, Harit still derived deep pleasure from singing.

"I'm calm about the operation." Sumee pressed a hand to forehead, then alternate cheeks as she sighed. "Practically an unbroken success rate is what they say. And it's all over in less than a day. Nip, seal, go. But here's what's putting a crease in this delicate skin." Sumee pointed miserably to her smooth white forehead. "The operation is *only* done at a hospital in Gilbrit. Can you imagine? How primitive are we on this side of the globe?"

"Ah, Gilbrit. That's far, I can't deny it."

Though there were many ways to travel to Gilbrit, the least jarring way, for someone as travel-phobic as Sumee, would be by rolling tracktrain. Maryl and Sumee had watched the tracktrains spin by when she and Sumee were growing up together. Maryl had been engaged to watch out for the younger Sumee while Harit fulfilled corasan obligations. The two would picnic by the local tracks. Maryl vowed she'd one day ride far and wide. Sumee, though intrigued by the image created by the swirling giants, said she'd "rather wear bright orange" than travel anywhere, except for in dire emergencies. Both had honored their pledges.

"So, like it or not, I'm making reservations."

Maryl frowned in sympathy as Sumee sighed.

"Sumeesune, do you want me to go with you and Harit?"

Sumee's words tumbled out with her relief. "Yes, yes, yes! Did I say yes? Yes. Please."

Sumee sighed happily. "You are without question the friend of a lifetime. Should it turn out we have several lifetimes, you're the friend of all of them. It will all be so much easier to bear with you along." She paused. "Would you like me to wear orange, Mar? I know you love that color."

"Go ahead. Make the reservations. I'll tell Danyin and work out the time away from work. And I won't even hold you to wearing orange. I seem to remember that you in orange is not an appealing sight because of the frown it creates on your pretty face."

Sumee smiled at the compliment. "All right, my friend, my love, my Baatasune. I'll sign off now. Ok, I'm going to enhance the melt so enjoy." Sumee swirled her arms in front of her, making the blue and silver of her crisscrossed bosom an especially lovely tangle as the RT image faded in a shimmer of white.

CHAPTER 10

Maryl flexed the fingers of her cramped left hand. Was it possible that Sumee had gripped her hand for nearly the entire trip?

They'd boarded soon after one sun's rays brought a still-dim morning to life, the other sun still only a glow. The circular body of the train, suspended in its frame of upper and lower tracking, towered above them as they climbed into the cylinder's center, the space that would vibrate nearly imperceptibly as the exterior rolled forward around them.

Maryl had offered to drive the women to Gilbritz in her transport, but Sumee had refused, saying the train felt less like traveling.

Glancing around the variety of seating, some designed for full reclining, all made for legs-up comfort, Sumee pointed to a curved couch which faced the interior of the space.

"That's ours," she said. "I reserved the seating that looks *as much* away from the windows as possible."

Maryl had reluctantly headed for the center seating, envious of kisans curled or stretched in the sunny loungers by the windows. The three had barely settled onto the curved couch, Sumee in the center, when a lively melody broke out, one Maryl recognized as a tune Harit had written years before.

Harit laughed. "Oh Sumeesune. Do you keep that old thing on your RT? Or just for this trip to please me?"

"Mammasune!" Sumee feigned offense as she fumbled for the RT settings on her wrist, peering down to see the identifier text. "I've had that programmed for years. I love that tune! Listen, I'm going to take this, if you don't mind. It's my friend Bly. Well…he's someone from therapy who's becoming a good friend." She raised and lowered her eyebrows. "Very good." She smiled. "This shouldn't take long. I'll minimize and mute."

The realistic, though miniaturized, form of a handsome dark-haired kisan snapped into view in front of Sumee as she clicked on the RT.

"Bly! A third sun above wouldn't be a lovelier surprise. Hold on, I'm on a train so let me mute." She ejected the earpiece from its compartment on the wrist RT and put it in her ear. As she adjusted the insert she noted the worry on Bly's face, a look few would interpret as worry. The world saw someone who seemed never fazed, always unruffled, but Bly had allowed Sumee entrée beyond the façade.

"Ok. I'm plugged in. What do you have to say, my sune?"

"Well, what's going on with you? You're on a train. Are you going to move to the tropics? Then you'll send your poor clients a hovi scan after the fact?"

"Me? Move? Bly, I know we've still got a lot to learn about each other so here's something about me you should know." She leaned toward Bly's image. "The word "moving" is barely in my vocabulary. The phrase "let's frequently travel" is entirely banned."

She gave an exaggerated shiver. "Makes me feel furry just thinking about it. No. Me, I love exploring the world's nuances, creatures, ideas. And if I can do all that virtually, with zero actual travel, that's perfection. I'm on this rolling monstrosity because my mother needs an operation."

Bly watched Sumee's RT image as she turned her head side to side, obviously looking at others. Sumee looked back at Bly.

She spoke with stalwart conviction. "And I'm happy to do whatever I need to do to help out my mamasune. She's the greatest. Here. Meet her."

She turned her head, her pale hair falling over her cheek.

"Harit, my love, lean in over here."

Bly watched as the face of a lovely older woman appeared in the screen, the woman wisp-like in her thinness, in contrast to the curvy abundance of her daughter. Still, the resemblance to Sumee was obvious and brought a smile to Bly, the worried expression Sumee detected disappearing.

"Hello," said Harit. "I won't bother to put in the earpiece but I'll look forward to meeting you in person sometime. You two get on with your talking. Oh, wait, Sumee wants you to see her friend, too."

Harit moved out of the RT space and another kisan, brown-haired, with blended kyan and tisani facial features, stuck her head in from the opposite side of Sumee, mouthing "Hello" and giving Bly a quick wave before pulling her head back again.

Sumee's face reappeared. "That's my friend Maryl. I've told you about her. And also about her partner, Danyin Mesterdide. He's the Listener I've been recommending to you."

"Oh, yes. I think I have a few questions for Maryl since she's known you so long. I'd love to get some insight into your - unexpected and charming ways."

Sumee shook her head and smiled. "Save it for another time. She's already got her hands full. I'm here to help Harit, and Maryl's along to help me. She's the only one of the three of us that actually enjoys traveling."

She looked knowingly from her mother to her best friend.

"Strong legs. And did you see those green eyes? Dark green, to be exact. And his skin tone, not too pale you know, like me, for example, someone who is too pale."

Sumee waited for the expected protests from the others, assuring her that her skin was, indeed, perfect. She got them.

"And just so you know it's not only my eyes that are impressed, here's the amazing thing. He's got a personality as attractive as his looks."

"Give or take a few problems that you're helping him through?" asked Maryl.

"Yes, that is true. He needs some tweaking."

"I heard you recommend Danyin to your friend. That means he needs more than the usual tweaking, yes?"

Sumee shook her head. "I'm not going to tell you both too much yet. I don't want you to start forming opinions that just aren't right. So, for now, I'll ask you to trust me, and believe that Bly has a heart big enough for me, and everyone I love, with lots of room to spare."

Harit's expression turned skeptical. "Sumeesune. Are you taking on a partner with problems you can't handle? That maybe no one can handle?"

Sumee fanned her hands to deflect further comment. "Look. This tisani makes me swirl. Do you know what he does? He designs ornamental pieces for homes, things like delicate scrollwork for the center of a wall, beautiful knobs to open things, or open nothing, to just tempt and delight you. He creates beauty. His work is really something."

Sumee nodded as she continued to see Bly in her mind's eye, to feel the pleasure her imagination brought her.

"I think all those kisans I've seen in the past …"

"Lots…," said Maryl.

"…and lots," finished Harit.

"Yes, thank you my thoughtful and observant loved ones. There have been many males in my life. Look, Bly knows he has things to work through, and I'm impressed he acknowledges that. And I can almost guarantee that my remaining professional sessions with Bly will be morphing into strictly personal meetings in the near future. Maybe long, long, long term personal."

"Well, you must be exceptionally fond of Bli," said Harit. "He's made you forget entirely that we're traveling in an enclosed vehicle, rolling far away from home."

"Ow!" said Harit and Maryl simultaneously, as Sumee grabbed their hands. Sumee's moment of panic subsided as she held onto those she loved.

Later, looking down at her hand, Maryl had still been glad she'd been on the trip to support Harit and Sumee. Despite the aching hand.

CHAPTER 11

RT | | Danyin Mesterdide

Danyin mopped his brow as the RT began. He pulled at his shirt collar, and seemed to have difficulty comfortably arranging his barrel-chested body on whatever seating he was perched on, unseen in the RT recording. His brogue was even thicker than usual.

"That was, hands down, the most unnerving trip, ever."

He widened his eyes then sighed, composing himself. His accented, melodic voice, higher pitched than usual in his anxiety, was returning to normal.

"All right. I think I've pulled myself together."

He laughed.

"I feel foolish. Let's just say I know if I'd been in my usual body, instead of a feline body, you'd be working on reviving me right now! All right. To begin where it began."

"The beginning was interesting and sometimes fun. I was in my host, the mynie, uh, cat, we visit frequently, Matilda. It wasn't unusual, of course, to find myself in Matilda's carrier, traveling somewhere, since many of us have seen and experienced this scenario plenty of times now."

"So, I was relaxed, just wondering what sort of situation I'd end up in. Outside? In? Of course, I wasn't happy to see the fiddle case in the car, but then I remembered that the horrible screech that's so unbearable to other cats, is tolerable to our Matilda, on account of her poor hearing. She's lucky, that girl, I tell you."

"We ended up inside. At first the house was pretty empty, people obviously getting ready for a gathering. Rob, Matilda's owner, set me and Matilda on some sort of shelf. So far it's boring for me, and not valuable to VRC. Just the usual. Band sets up, band plays, people cheer, people talk to band when band stops playing, and people play with Matilda. Fine."

"As usual, some of the interesting data starts pouring in when Matilda is allowed to explore the environment she's been brought to. First thing of interest I'll mention, were three metallic looking vessels, flat on top and round around, less than a meter high, and a bit less than that side to side."

He mimed the container dimensions as he spoke.

"Each vessel had a hose coming out of it. Just at the top, I think. The vessels, which were set up right outside the house, were filled with a liquid that had a soapy-look to it."

"I'm thinking the liquid was like our mendo, since the humans went to fill their cups many times and seemed to be, shall we say, happier each time they returned."

"Well, our Matilda hung around the vessels for a while, taking a few sniffs. The metallic tang, mixed with a sharp but inoffensive smell, caused no particular reaction in Matilda, since it didn't translate into anything to be eaten or anything to fear. The scent images just revealed a warehouse-type place the vessels were stored before the party."

"So. Our favorite deaf kitty then headed out farther into the surrounding area, skittering away from partygoers who wanted to pet her along the way. I could sense she was in explorer mode, her eyes not interested in focusing on something familiar when there was new territory to be discovered."

"The yard was large and Matilda spent time nosing around foliage. No information for us. Trees, bushes, flowers; no varieties we haven't seen, described, and drawn before."

"As we wandered, we suddenly perceived a strong, unpleasant odor. The urge was to run from the stink, but, strangely enough, that reaction was matched by a feeling that compelled Matilda to stay and investigate. Oh, how I wish she'd ignored that feeling."

Danyin shook his head, the slight smile on his face belying the serious delivery of his wish.

"So, Matilda goes heading off toward this horrible smell, getting worse by the moment as she gets closer to the source. Soon we're outside a big fenced-in enclosure. You can probably guess what was in there. The animals we've come to know as dogs. They weren't like other dogs we've seen...but there were enough similarities for my guess."

"These animals were huge and, Baata bless her, tiny Matilda just had to have an up-close-and-personal look at the beasts. Before we approached, the dogs, let's call them, were curled up quietly along the inner edge of the fence. Not for long. Apparently Matilda's smell was as rancid to them as theirs was to us. As we approached and Matilda took full survey of the situation – five reeking monsters – I felt her back arch, and her fur rise. Their scents brought memories of bared teeth, and the memory quickly became the reality.

The dogs scrambled to their feet and started barking at a volume I could feel, I tell you. It could even be heard through Matilda's poor damaged ears. Matilda growled her heart out, but it was a pathetic murmur compared to those creatures. They were screaming for blood."

Later viewers of Danyin's RT would laugh, watching Danyin imitate Matilda's actions, curling his fingers into the semblance of paws with claws extended, as he told his tale.

"At this point Matilda seems to be rooted to the spot, on the verge of a cat heart attack – and me along with her - as these giants flung themselves against the fence, desperate to get a mouthful of the paralyzed creature."

Danyin shook his head in sympathy.

"Poor cat. We know all our attempts to communicate with our host have been useless, and this time was no different. I'm sure I was quite the sight in my web in the lab as I muttered things like "Move you crazy mynie! Let's go! What are you doing?" But, of course, she couldn't "hear" me."

"Luckily, Matilda is a well-loved cat, and her owner guessed quickly that the chaos involved his girl. Rob ran up to us, scooped us up, and sped back to the house. Matilda, unfortunately, was more in a fighting mood than a grateful one. The appearance of her owner did not calm her, though I sensed she was relieved to be whisked from the scene. Still, poor Rob will have a few painful memories, literally, in relation to this evening."

Danyin let out a breath that seemed relieved to be free.

"That's pretty much it. Of course, I was pulled back because my vitals were zinging, and Teesh does not take kindly to zinging vitals, which I much appreciate. All right. I'll make the graphics next, and then home to my nice, calm mynies."

The RT melt was the color of the dull gray of the recording room, Danyin's wearily shaking head creating wavy lines in the image.

CHAPTER 12

RT | | Maryl Tymin

Maryl waited for Teesh's "go" signal. Though glad the week-long recording delay was over, she was surprised to find more than adjustments to equipment had been made. Her script had fresh exclusions.

Teesh pointed to her and she began speaking.

"Some years before the invention of portals, we developed the remarkable process I've already mentioned. Transference."

Maryl saw Teesh and the others in the room, gazes fixed on her, all feeling the thrill of what she said on their behalf. They were sharing their most advanced knowledge.

"Transference is the ability to move, to transfer, all of one's senses, one's mind, if you will, temporarily into another living creature. Hard to fathom, I know. But true. I've done it hundreds of times now in my research, and almost everyone on our planet has done it as well. This miracle is now almost commonplace. You're part of a civilization with your own rapid advancements, so I'm sure you're not surprised to learn how such things can quickly be taken in stride."

"Once the Transference process was created, we experimented with discovering what types of transfers were possible. Our first attempts were same species transfers, and those experiments nearly led us to believe the process was a failure. When one kisan transferred into another kisan, he hit a hellish kaleidoscope of sensory input; an immediate, painful rush of colors, sounds, lights, shrieks, laughing, chatter. We think we were sensing "everything" at once: memories, thoughts, anger, feelings. But we couldn't separate them, keep them in check."

"We do continue to try kisan to kisan Transference, though, after an early attempt resulted in brain death of a scientist, we do it within very restrictive parameters. There have also been tragedies with non-scientists fooling around in ways they just shouldn't with a technology like this."

"In the case of the scientist, Gwinde, she decided she wanted to transfer into a kisan who was unaware of exactly when the Transference would occur. She had gotten the kisan's permission, but wanted the Transference time to be unknown, so that the host could accurately report any unusual sensation."

"Gwinde set up a meeting with a colleague, knowing the colleague would find her during the Transference process, and bring her back, if she hadn't already returned on her own."

"The colleague did find her. We don't know how long she was in for, but she came out unable to function. Breathing. But that's about all. And there was a smell. As if something had caught fire in Gwinde's lab. But no one could find evidence of anything burned."

Maryl had to pause and shake her head, recalling the combination of bright smile and sharp mind she associated with Gwinde before the incident. Afterward, her colleague's eyes were open, but seeing what? Gwinde's family had approved an experiment: Transference was attempted into the motionless kisan. Instead of being shocked by mind noise, the visitor was chilled by silence.

The charred smell made sense a few days later, after Gwinde died. The autopsied brain showed a scattering of burns, as if a shower of sparks had landed and slowly extinguished themselves in the surrounding brain tissue.

"Through our brief inter-species visits, we've at least come to understand how the host body responds to the visitor, since we can question the hosts, who are fellow researchers and volunteers."

"When entered, the host detects a muted flash of light. Saying the perception of the flash is brief is overstating it. If our volunteers weren't anticipating an effect, it's likely they wouldn't notice it. After the flash, there's nothing. No awareness of the visitor."

"We aren't certain that other species have the same reaction to a host transfer, but that's our theory. We think, and we hope, that our visits are largely non-intrusive. Some ethicists don't agree. They say we really don't know, so the practice of Transference cannot truly be seen as morally without question until somehow, we do know. I disagree. We frequently transfer into mynies. And no one loves mynies more than I do. I'm convinced no harm is done during mynie Transference. The best testing we can do, short of asking the mynies to testify themselves, supports that assertion."

A glance at Teesh showed Maryl that he looked satisfied with the RT's progress. He stood in an arms-crossed-over-slim-chest posture, absorbed. She continued.

"After our relative failure with same-species Transference, we looked at Transference into other species. The result? We found that quite a few conditions were not ideal."

"For example, transferring to aquatic creatures resulted in the traveler feeling claustrophobic and unconnected. We still do these visits, but they are nobody's favorites. Trying to inhabit avian animals has its own set of problems. We get the sensation of entering a vacuum, and an anxious feeling, as if things are happening too quickly in our bodies, and we can't catch our breath. Again, visits are possible but not popular."

"But, finally, we began having successes. When we finally found well-matched hosts, the sensation of being utterly attuned during Transference was immediate. We felt we were sharing the hosts' body, actually inhabiting it to a certain extent. For the most part we seemed to be feeling what they were feeling, and seeing what they were seeing."

"A number of animals are good hosts. We saw our surroundings rise and fall as we leapt with small creatures on Kisa who hop rather than walk. We felt the power of the fear inspired in other animals as we shambled through our dense forests within an animal similar to the Earth's bear. But no host has matched the experience we've had when transferring into the mynie, the being that seems identical to what you call a cat."

"Reete, the kisan who did our first mynie transfer, returned with the awe he felt evident on his face. In that well-recorded moment, still sung about by corasans, Reete smiled and opened his mouth once, then again, obviously looking for the right words to begin the description of his experience. The first thing that old scientist said -- and he was not known for poetic proclamations -- was "It's a perfect fit. As if we're meant to be together." Then he laughed and enjoyed a nice big grin before he pulled himself together to relate the details of his experience less emotionally."

Maryl paused in her story, a smile on her own face at the memory of Reete's words.

"Reete's no longer with us. He died not too long ago. But those of us who've done mynie Transferences understand his words. "A perfect fit." It's comfortable. The separateness, you might say, the otherness, is still perceived. The mynie's presence is there and very much felt, but we mold to that presence, share it."

Teesh interrupted. "Hold up. We're just going to check back a few minutes to be sure the audio level didn't dip. Hiri, come over and help."

Maryl relaxed as she waited. The section on distance Transference had originally been planned as her next topic. But that had been cut.

CHAPTER 13

Bly Goodin distractedly prodded the space in front of his monitor, pointing fingers, flipping hands, each movement flicking Earth images across his screen. He stopped and looked carefully at one vivid view. He first scanned the blue skies and a green landscape that matched the green of his eyes. Familiar. Then the white clouds, devoid of Kisa's violet accents. Alien. The green of Bly's eyes disappeared as closed them, leaned back, and tried to steady his breathing. Earth. Amazing. Someday he would do a DT there so he could solidify the knowledge; make it first an experience, and then a memory.

But he didn't have to.

Life was pleasant enough in his cream-colored apartment, sparsely, softly, expensively, furnished. Money for the trip, or for anything else, for that matter, was not a problem. Money in lieu of family.

Still, he probably did need to experience distance Transference first hand. Of course, Earth existed. Of course, there were creatures, like him, living their lives, losing their families, struggling to get through the day. Just like him. The kernel of doubt about the existence of Earth exasperated and embarrassed him, and he needed to be rid of it.

He knew he wasn't alone in his inexplicable doubts, though he felt he was at the more rational end of the disbeliever spectrum. Some felt that Transference of any kind was a drug-induced deception. To what purpose? To push radical ideas that could only emerge in the face of a universe they were not alone in.

Bly felt his own struggle with belief of life beyond Kisa was more benign, more the result of his personal grieving. His was a fear of even more strangers in a life that had, until a dozen years earlier, been filled with familiar faces. He'd grown up with the unfamiliar being something that was introduced slowly and carefully. Until everything changed.

Bly shook himself from his thoughts, contemplating his legs stretched out in front of him on the firm cushions of the chair's leg supports. His shoes were on. He should just go now.

He'd told Sumee he'd go at the first opportunity. Days, weeks, had since passed. It was true that the new door knocker designs he'd created had been inspired during this time, his creativity surging to better justify his procrastination. Even now he thought of opening a blank hovi screen to see what ideas were waiting to take shape.

His RT song, a bland choice from the stock menu, broke his reverie. He checked the preview. It was Sumee, plump, radiant, beautiful. Bly shook his head, embarrassment seizing him. He wouldn't answer it. She'd just ask if he'd yet done the DT and he'd have to say no. He felt like a kisling, but he couldn't face it. Instead, he'd consider this call as the final push. He'd go now.

The messages on the entrance signs of Beyond the Clouds Travel Center were concise.

TICKET HOLDERS: RIGHT. TICKET PICK-UP: LEFT. TICKET SALES: CENTER. LOCAL AND DISTANCE TRANSFERENCE: ALL STATIONS.

Bly moved toward the left of the hall, having managed to secure his last minute DT reservation via a hovi offer from a kisan unable to travel that day. They connected via RT to finish the transaction.

"Have a great time," his seller said, before he uploaded the ticket to Bly's hovi. "You travel often?" he asked.

"Never," said Bly.

Bly bid the seller a quick goodbye, watching the kisans open mouth melt in the RT space before he could say what Bly expected, which would be a comment along the lines of "You're kidding, aren't you?"

Talking about his novice travel status wasn't something Bly yearned to do with yet another stranger. Yes, he'd done a few local Transferences in controlled environments. But never, as this travel center boasted, "beyond the clouds."

Bly thought of his local Transferences, all in mynies. Like most new travelers, the otherness of the physical abilities of the host had fascinated him. The feeling of ears moving in strange ballet-like swivels at the will of the mynie, easily pulled into play by the dozens of unfamiliar muscles. An awareness of just how loud, shocking, and at times, even painful, noises could be. An equally strong understanding of how many sounds unknown to the kisan ear were a constant to the mynies, and the reason for their hunting prowess. The nearly-beyond-hearing squeak of a tiny creature meters away, and the distinct whoosh of displaced air as prey hopped from one patch of ground to another.

Bly turned his thoughts back to the present as he approached one of the cheerful young attendants, one stationed at each of six low-gated entranceways to the travel rooms beyond the hall. A short tisani kisan, with calico tufts peeping over his shirt's neckline, greeted him as he approached.

"Welcome, sir! Your ticket please?"

Bly handed him the ticket which the attendant scanned with a palm-attached apparatus. The attendant peered at the screen on the device, nodding.

"All right, I see this is your first time doing a DT." The attendants' voice had risen in pitch to match his rise in wonder, and he quickly composed himself, realizing his proclamation had caught the attention of others in line. He continued at a lower volume and pitch. "I see you've been through your orientation so everything's in order. You can come right in."

The attendant stopped short as he peered at the screen.

"Hmm. Well, actually your orientation was – is this right?"

He shared the screen with Bly, showing him the date. Bly nodded. The attendant whistled.

"That was some time ago. But, things are pretty much the same. Well, there are a lot more web colors to choose from, and actually it's a smoother ride now. You ok with your orientation being so long ago? Yes? Ok, then please validate right here to indicate you understand I offered you a delay in your travel date, and a more up-to-date orientation? Which I'm doing now. Anyway. You ok with that, sir?"

Bly nodded again and pressed his thumb against the proffered screen.

"Thank you, Mr...., um," he looked at the screen, "Mr. Goodin." The attendant swept his arm and hand behind him. "Please follow the indigo smoke trail. Down the hall, make a right, and then about halfway down that corridor. You're in Room 3-2-3. It's got a glowing blue door. You did request the blue webbing, yes?"

"I said it didn't matter."

"Right, ok. Blue is what you've got. That's 323. Indigo smoke, sir."

Bly tilted his head toward his destination but didn't move.

"Sir?"

Bly nodded again at the attendant. "Thank you for your help." He started slowly forward, turning to smile briefly when the attendant called "Are you all right, sir?" The truthful answer would have been "Feeling faint, actually." Not the answer they wanted to hear, and an answer that would have delayed his trip, so another nod would do.

Though it had been some time ago, Bly clearly recalled the orientation. He and fourteen other would-be travelers had reclined in soft enclosures meant to simulate the Transference experience. The orientation teacher, hands clasped, earnest as she strolled the classroom, talked about the need to relax the muscles of the body, and to concentrate on pleasant thoughts as the Transference began. Bly unconsciously shook his head as his teacher wandered, knowing he possessed a mind that strolled like his teacher, constantly touching ghosts of problems; new, old, real, imagined.

He'd been the oldest person at the orientation. Generally, the only people at distance Transference orientations were those who had come of age and were allowed to finally have the experience.

He'd left the training wondering if he could manage to clear his mind sufficiently for the process. He had. He had accomplished local Transference. He saw similarities between the Transference and using his Reader abilities, since that also involved sharing thoughts with others. So perhaps this would work out.

At home, he'd prepared for the DT. He projected a moving image of lavender clouds on the ceiling and watched them ebb and slide, letting their beauty and motion fill his mind. He'd also done the same exercise outside, with real clouds. He could now conjure the relaxing image at will. Though the decision to make this trip was spontaneous, he felt ready.

Now the trip was imminent. He passed doors of different colors as he walked through the knee-high indigo haze, the vaporous lines interlacing with other colored smoke paths. Some of the tiny rooms were occupied, some being tidied. The variously colored, shimmering doors were closed, but glimpses of each interior could be seen through O-shaped windows. A flash of reddish hair in a room of green light. The face of a balding traveler, smiling broadly, cheeks twitching, eyes closed, enveloped in flickering strands of lemon-colored illumination.

The blue door was slightly ajar to Room 323 and he entered. The white-walled space was bare except for the observation instrument, suspended from a corner. Kisans in a central monitoring room, unseen to the travelers, watched through the telescopic tube dubbed "the eye.'"

From the orientation he knew he should shut the door and wait.

"Welcome, Mistah Goodin! Ah you ready for your trip?"

It was a disembodied voice, also expected because of the orientation. What was unexpected was the lilting accent of the woman on the speaker. It was pleasant, a voice from the Central Islands, not often heard locally.

Bly's reply was confident, disguising, as he often did, the truth of his feelings. "All ready."

"Please allow your body to relax. We don't want you comin' back all achy. All rahty now, jes' be calm, and loose, and we'll begin wrappin'."

Bly tried to relax but knew he felt, if anything, quite stiff.

Bly heard the "click, click, click, click" sound Beyond the Clouds employed to signal the process was beginning. He breathed in deeply. "Lavender clouds! They're so lovely, so peaceful! They're so…"

Fine strands of baby blue light extended from the room's corners, reaching like tentacles toward him. More threads emerged at an increasingly rapid rate from ceiling, floor, and walls, wrapping Bly with spider-like expertise.

The strands, strong, held Bly, making only the faintest indentation on his skin as he was enveloped and lifted. Soon, only Bly's head remained unwrapped, an odd incongruous bump in the mass of pulsing blue.

"There you go! Now, the eye is trained on you and will be monitorin' your trip. If we notice any unusual movements that indicate your discomfort or fear while travelin' with your host, we'll disconnect you and credit you for the balance of your trip. If you do transfer successfully and land in a sleepah, you will be refunded half the cost of your trip."

Sleepers were animals who slumbered during the entire Transference process, a not unusual occurrence.

Geenah clicked off the sound to the observation room for a few seconds while she turned to her co-worker, just entering the booth, and shook her head. "Ah don't know about this one." She clicked the sound back on. "Just to confirm, Mistah Goodin, you've chosen "squirrel" for your visit, is that raht?"

Bly nodded his head. Squirrel was all that was available at such late notice. At least he didn't have a luck-of-the-draw ticket. Although Transferences could miss intended destinations, those who paid for a certain animal would get a refund if they didn't reach the host they'd chosen. L-T-D ticket holders had to accept the trip results. They did pay significantly less, but there were L-T-D horror stories about spending entire visits running inside a hamster wheel. Some enjoyed the wheel visits. Visitors felt the hamsters' euphoria while running, and the jiggly scenery made more than one visitor, secure in his web, erupt into giggles.

Like everyone else, Bly had wanted a cat, but cat visits by the general public were limited. He read in the promotional copy that a squirrel, especially at the time of year he was visiting, should be mindless fun, like a joy ride. It had been that or "small dog" and he wasn't in the mood for that bumpy, noisy, mind trip. Another plus was that the squirrel visit had a better chance of being human-free, which sounded fine to Bly.

In the observation area Geenah and Perrin made small adjustments to the web. "Personally, I can't stand squirrel visits," said Perrin. "Too much dashing around."

"Don't ah know it, darlin'? Ah'm glad this job gives us choice of host."

In the glow of blue light, the web's strong, flexible strands moved easily with Bly's slight movements. Since the body in the web could react in a manner similar to the host body, the web needed to withstand vigorous twitching and jumping.

"All raht. We're all set then, Mistah Goodin. You jes' relax now and get ready for your trip beyond the clouds. Have a great one!"

"Will do."

The lights dimmed slightly, not because it had anything to do with the process, but, like the "click, click, click" sound before the webbing, this particular travel port thought staccato sounds and lights fading added to the romance and excitement of the experience. The words "Enjoy Your Trip Beyond the Clouds!" appeared in smoky lighted letters on the wall opposite Bly. A low hum began, reverberating through the cocoon. "Lavender clouds," thought Bly. "Lovely lavender clouds..."

In the monitoring room, Geenah shook her head. "Ah'd say he's a no go. Look at the way his eyes ah all screwed up."

Her companion, Perin, frowned.

"I dunno, Geen. I know you're good at spotting them, but I say this is a go-go. Look, he's relaxing now. The no-goes are rare lately, and we just had one yesterday. What're the odds?"

The monitoring room crew liked to make bets on which travelers would turn out to be groundlings, kisans unable to do distance Transference. Many believed groundlings were shackled by the feeling, sometimes consciously, sometimes unknowingly, that the enveloping virrius gasses in their skies sheltered their planet from nothingness. Or from the heavenly Baata, the latter definitely a place they should not, while alive, attempt a visit.

"I'll go 20 on this. And I'll take payment today."

"You mean you'll *make* payment today," said Geenah.

"You're on."

Geenah smoothed a patch of the exotically spotted fur at her neckline, a home dye job. Perin, himself kyan through and through, looked admiringly at Geenah's multi-colored mane, and scratched his own furless neck.

They continued to observe Bly through the eye, while also keeping watch on four other travelers displayed on their monitors.

"Blue room's a good looking one," said Geenah. "Even looks strong. But ah still say he's a no-go."

Bly, suspended in the web, closed his eyes against the pulsing lights. He focused on his breathing. While being wrapped he'd felt excited and agitated, so he was surprised to feel drowsiness begin to overcome him. He heard sounds like those heard in the subterranean roadways. Hollow sounds of speeding over countless miles in what seemed like endless space. But why would he be hearing anything? His body wasn't actually, physically, soaring anywhere. Was this right?

He felt weightless, bodiless, unanchored. But no, he was still aware of the web around him. He had to admit that being in the web was comforting, like being held by those in his Group, those who had loved him, those who were now gone.

He heard a loud, long, moan.

He gasped for air as he experienced the feeling of plummeting, and then all was still. His eyes twitched open. He was still wound in the pulsing web, suspended in the room's center. The moan had been his own.

In the monitoring room, Perrin groaned. The orange dots of light, indicating where on the Transference spectrum Bly Goodin had traveled, had brightened encouragingly, but then hadn't budged.

"If you can't pay me that 20 today, ah could wait until tomorrow." Geenah smiled at him and winked. "Of course, ah also accept in-kind reimbursement."

CHAPTER 14

Lena tapped the drum stick on the overturned plastic bowl. Not bad really as a practice pad. She was about to head off to find the matching stick when she stopped herself, talking aloud.

"Stop it, girl! What are you doing? A little drumming, ok to get the creative juices flowing. A lot, not ok. Not right now."

Mooshie, squeezed next to Einstein on Lena's desk, lifted her head, annoyed to be awakened by Lena's chatter. Her yawn was enormous. Lena caught the flash of pink, and the quick snap of Mooshie's jaw closing, hiding all signs of the sharp teeth behind the cute nose, and innocently blinking green eyes.

"Good God, Moosh. How can such a pretty girl have such vicious fangs? What do you do with those things, anyway?"

Einstein, awakened by Mooshie's movement, lifted his head and stared at Lena.

"Sorry, sorry. It's your own fault for sleeping in my work area. You know I talk to myself, and read my stuff out loud to make sure it flows ok. OK? You know all this, you cute little monsters. And you are sooo cute."

Lena's admonishment had quickly morphed into high pitched cooing, as the two cats flipped on their backs to show their tummies, and hit with a bull's eye the pleasure center of Lena's cat-loving heart. The cats, both calicos, seemed to blend into each other, creating a two-headed, eight-legged creature.

"You're little beasts. Of course, I know that's your job, being irresistible." Lena gave a quick rub to both tummies. "But take a break, would you? It's distracting."

Einstein righted himself and turned his gaze to the animated bird Lena programmed to flit at random times across her tablet's screen, along with the occasional mouse, squirrel and rabbit. All there for the enjoyment of her cats, since Lena barely noticed them anymore. As Lena settled more comfortably in her chair, and readied her hands to type, Einstein laid his gleaming white paw on Lena's wrist. The cat tilted his head as if to say "Why not just nap? Or watch that bird in your machine? It may fly out one day, you know, and we should be ready."

Lena sighed as she gave Einstein's head a quick pat. "All right. Where was I? Yes, the magic of filking. Guys, attention please. Tell me how this article is flowing. The title is "Filk Music: No, That's Not a Typo."'"

She read aloud.

While Donny and Marie Osmond billed themselves on their musical variety show as "a little bit country and a little bit rock and roll," filker Glen Mitchell might call himself "a little bit sci-fi, a little bit fantasy."

Those are the roots of filking," says Mitchell. "Science fiction and fantasy literature and media. It's a kind of music that was born in the amazing minds of writers and fans at conferences that focus on science fiction, speculative fiction, all that stuff. Some is parody, really high quality parody, and some is original music inspired by, let's say, worlds beyond our own.

Lena paused in her reading. Worlds beyond our own. She loved that quote. It could mean so much. It was amazing how it almost always worked out well when she interviewed someone for a freelance piece. Just about every time, the person she was interviewing came up with statements on the article topic that surpassed any she could have made up.

During their interview, Lena had pegged Glen Mitchell as the classic unpopular-kid-in-high-school, who grew up to slam shut the high school chapter of his life, and start fresh. Now, he was probably no cuter than he'd been as a teenager, but he was more appreciated in the wide world for his creativity, humor, and smarts. She admitted to herself that she wouldn't date him, but then, she also acknowledged her long, wide, shallow streak. Glen had great gals galore to choose from without her.

Lena scrolled through the web site on her screen, "Filk Classics," knowing she still hadn't narrowed down her list of music snippets to include in the article. She'd probably go with Benjamin Newman's hilarious "I Think I've Contracted a British Accent."

Lena jotted down her notes, found where she'd left off her recitation, and continued reading aloud.

"Ok, guys, heads up. The masterpiece continues."

Lena's next words were lost to the sleepy Mooshie who also could not hear the urgings of her unknown visitor.

"Stay awake, girl, come on. Lena's saying new things we don't know about and we want to know more!"

Lena's habit of speaking aloud as she wrote was more appreciated than she imagined. Though this time, the prose couldn't keep the drowsy cat awake.

"Baatadom! Why *does this mynie sleep so much?"*

RT || Saras Lyder

Saras's image flung itself down impatiently onto what must have been a chair in the RT recording area, her long legs extended and crossed in front of her, her arms doing the same. Her body language and slim figure bespoke a young woman. Her worldly air, the color of her hair and fur, and the deep lines on her face, revealed the true age of the oldest researcher at the VRC. She spoke through gritted teeth.

"Another frustrating Mooshie trip! I know, mynies... cats... I know they sleep a lot. It's understood that we spend much of our time in *search* of a creature that's actually awake. But some, like Mooshie's brother, Einstein, for example, are up and about more often. So. Once again, I ask. *When* shall the placement accuracy program begin?"

Saras sighed quietly and closed her eyes for a moment before showing signs of regrouping.

"All right. I'll admit, I actually did get a smattering of new information before Mooshie went comatose, so here goes. Apparently there's a kind of music called 'filk'...."

CHAPTER 15

RT | | Maryl Tymin

No. Distance Transference, fraught with its theoretically unsavory implications, wouldn't be a topic on this latest RT destined for ears on Earth. That would wait. Who knew how long?

The calamitous outcomes predicted if those on Earth learned about DT's were only speculation. But none of the VRC decision-makers were taking a chance. Not Braelind Carsinsen, not his boss, the VRC head, and, after discussions with sober researchers involving explanations of group reactions to unfamiliar and uninvited visitors, not her research group.

Maryl sighed, her mind brimming with the details she'd be sharing related to local Transference, never mind the distance process. The scent images. Scenes of the Baata. The mynie dream deserts. And the first encounters with physical unfamiliarity, like the startling realization that a tongue could shape itself so precisely into the shape of a spoon.

Of course, those listening to her were likely as interested in kisan bathrooms as much as anything else. Everything said would be alien, fantastic.

She heard Teesh's hands. Clap clap clap. "Ready?"

Maryl nodded.

Hand and finger pointing upward, Teesh gave a last glance around him. He pointed to Maryl. "Go!"

Maryl heard the quiet starting "tick", indicating she was being recorded.

"The mynie Transferences were by far the most successful. Our travels, or "visits," as we also call them, are done under controlled circumstances. We don't just show up in random mynies owned by anyone."

At least that's how we do it here, was the censored phrase that flitted through Maryl's mind.

"We travel with the consent of owners who allow random Transference visits of their pet."

"Both the inner life and outer life of the mynies proved to be of great interest. By outer life, I mean just simple physical perceptions. The first time you experience a sensation you'd be utterly incapable of experiencing in the body you're born in, believe me, it gets your full attention. It took us time to begin to sort through and isolate each of the unfamiliar feelings, each as intense as a plunge into icy liquid, though generally more enjoyable, I'm happy to say."

"There's a time of transition in the Transference process. We're relaxed, cocooned, as the process begins. But when the change happens, it's sudden. First is the sensation of soaring ahead, and then it's as if a giant hand thrusts you into the host. A catch of breath in your throat is the last awareness of your own body."

Maryl paused at the memory of that thrilling transformational moment, thinking those listening on Earth would now try to imagine the experience.

"So, what's it like? To inhabit a body that's not your own? Well, paradoxically, despite the fact that the typical mynie weighs about a tenth of the typical kisan, an awareness of *strength* is usually the first thing a visitor notices. Mynies may be small, but either no one's ever bothered to tell them that, or they refuse to believe that size has any bearing on the damage they can do if they put their minds to it."

"That strength, that energy, feels always ready to assert itself. In the right circumstances, which occur pretty frequently, mynies do relax completely. But any noise, any movement, can engage the cogs, ignite the fluidity of movement, the readiness to defend."

"I realize I'm waxing poetic. And I'm definitely not a poet. But, it's hard not to. Especially after the first time you feel what *seems* to be yourself sailing through space, almost vertically, to a spot at a distance three times the length of your body."

Maryl's eyes followed the finger she'd angled upward, pointing to the remembered point in her memory of her first mynie jump to the top of a tall shelving unit. She remembered the mix of terror experienced by her distant web-wrapped body, and the more potent feeling of calm and confidence exuded by her host.

Maryl caught a glimpse of Teesh, moving in his rocking horse way to a different area of the room. Teesh walked with the jagged movements of one who didn't have full control over his limbs. And he didn't. His legs, paralyzed since youth, strode with the help of inner tubing that allowed his unfeeling legs to convey him where he needed to go. For Teesh, and others like him who could not jump or move quickly, Transference was a particular joy. The quick smile on Maryl's face was for Teesh.

"Let me tell you more of what we feel when we visit a host. Fluidity. Body parts moving in ways they should not logically move. The head turning easily around, past the ear, past the familiar stopping point, bobbing down to clean a bit of dust from our fur. Ears, easily under the host's control, one or the other swiveling at will when it seems the host is trying to better understand his surroundings or situation. A jaw

86

opening, opening, beyond where you feel it should and then snapping closed with a strength you know could do some damage."

"Another aspect of the startling new "outer life" that Transference allowed us to experience, was the enhanced ability to detect scents. We now joke that kisans experience smell in about the same way a chair experiences smell. I imagine human senses are on par with ours, so I'll tell you, compared to mynies, and probably cats, you and I might as well be walking around without nostrils."

"A tree branch that seems virtually odorless in our kisan form is suddenly, experienced through a mynie, a palate of odors, each with meaning, potential taste, and substance. Scent becomes central to survival, with each falling into two major categories: safe and unsafe. "Good," safe scents may trigger a feeling of warmth and security; "bad," unsafe ones bring the urge to flinch or flee, until free of the odor."

"Sometimes, a "bad" odor will also act as an attractant, tempting the mynie to more fully investigate a possible problem, like a territory infringement. Figuring out potential trouble is sometimes preferable to outrunning it, if you think what's causing the trouble could be an ongoing problem."

"Everything I've told you might not seem surprising if you've watched cats. You've seen them pull back from sharp scents, or share a nose touch with another cat whose smell they recognize. No, what took us by surprise were the images; what we've come to call scent images."

Maryl hesitated a moment, her thoughts flashing to the recollection of her first scent image. Her host had been sniffing one of the dense, tiny wreaths of leaves common to Kisa foliage. The sniff triggered a realistic, though ghostly, image of a distinctly different mynie, sniffing at the same leaves.

The first kisans to experience scent images through their mynie hosts, found themselves thrust back to their home bodies, back in their web, gasping for breath, startled by the unexpected apparitions.

It was eventually determined that the ghostly visions, triggered by smell, represented events of the near past, usually within hours or days.

"We think the scents gathered by the object hold enough information to recreate full-blown moving pictures, almost as clear as a real life experience. But less substantial. You can tell a scent image that's older when it's vague and shapeless."

"The snippets can be anything; as varied as any activity in day-to-day living. Did a kisan spend an evening in conversation over dinner out with a friend? When he comes home and his mynie sniffs his hand, the pet gets a quick-time view, bits and pieces, of his owner's night out. A mynie dragging herself home after a fight? Another mynie, with a welcoming sniff, will know the gory details."

"It takes a tiring effort on the part of the mynie to perceive each scent image, and the ability is used only a handful of times each day, sometimes skipping a day. They do regularly use the ability by trees or shrubs, to see who the latest visitor has been. They'll do it at the hand of a stranger, though sometimes a sniff is limited to pure scent only. We still don't know how such scents are interpreted, but we do know a strong feeling of interest or disinterest usually follows that sniff."

"As stunning as the scent images were, our next revelation equaled or exceeded this discovery."

Maryl paused because the next statement deserved a pause.

"Through Transference we learned that mynies, like corasans, are historians, keeping memories alive. Recent memories, memories of the ages, and memories before the ages. They relive the past when they sleep."

CHAPTER 16

Rob and Lena pulled into the dust-filled Faire parking lot, the festival itself still a half mile walk away.

"I'm psyched."

Rob looked at Lena in the passenger side of the car, her blonde hair tucked into the revealing web of her knitted and beaded black snood, her green eyes enhanced by contacts with a tint of the same color.

"Welcome to Larkspur," he said. Want to walk, or wait for the shuttle? You should be warned that dust will now be your intimate friend, no matter where you walk around the Faire."

"Let's walk." Lena crossed her leg, waggling a sandaled foot on her knee, displaying slim strips of leather crisscrossing her exposed foot.

"Admire these faire white toeseys while ye may. Soon they shall be naught but dust. Well, dust-covered."

Rob leaned over and kissed the side of Lena's foot.

"You." Lena put her arms around Rob's neck as he looked up. "How about one here, for the road," she said, indicating her lips.

They kissed, Rob's hand feeling the wealth of Lena's hair beneath the snood. Lena pulled away gently.

"Ok, that's it for now, shining knight. Otherwise we'll need to take a few hour stopover in ye olde Larkspur no-tell motel."

"Hours? God, that sounds promising. Forget this lame festival thing. Let's go."

Lena grinned, but shook her head. "How about tonight, ye olde sex fiend? I'm finally within a mile of the damn fair. Use that energy," she tapped his upper thigh, "for fiddle playing."

Rob answered by grabbing Lena's fingers, giving them a quick kiss on the tips, releasing them, and swinging open the car door.

Climbing out, Rob walked to the car's hatchback. Lena met him as he opened the hatch and handed a round black bodhrán case to her. Next he pulled out his fiddle, nestled in its fiddle-shaped case.

He offered her the fiddle. "How about you carry the music-making stuff, and I'll carry the noisy girl."

The plan was to do some limited busking to earn the cost of grog and turkey legs. The Faire's music coordinator didn't think the combination of fiddle and percussion, with no other accompaniment, was ideal, but had, in previous years, noted the popularity of little Matilda, blinking in the sunlight, purring amidst the chaos.

He gave Rob his annual caution. "Remember you need to keep it low-key when you take the cat out of her cage. Her wandering around is not strictly kosher, if you know what I mean. Keep her in that harnessy thingy."

Rob reached into the hatch for Matilda's cage, peering in at the sleeping cat, already trussed into her specially sewn harness, altered to keep the agile cat secured within. The original design had kept Matilda captive for less than the time it took to say "get back here, cat!"

"It's good weather," he said as they walked toward the Faire's entrance. "It can be Death Valley hot sometimes."

"It's still early."

A man in breeches and a balloon-sleeved white shirt checked their entertainer passes, and nodded them in through the false castle façade that marked the festivals' entrance.

"Wow," said Lena. "We're not in Kansas anymore." Her head tipped to Matilda's carrier. "At least we've got Toto."

Lena and Rob were surrounded by the festivals' village of faux medieval architecture harboring trinkets, weapons, and winking shopkeepers. Ersatz paupers roamed, teeth blackened, clothes ragged, swapping jibes and puns for tips. Women glanced at passersby, bodices low and smiles broad. One of the few trees in the opening area sheltered a flute-playing minstrel who lifted his eyebrows in greeting, as his fingers danced, and his lips caressed his instrument.

Rob peered in the cage at Matilda. He loved the idea of cats living in different ages, including the Renaissance age. Around them swirled political upheaval, changing attire, the creation and demise of great civilizations. But cats, whether painted on the knee of a young monarch, or described as a barn monster, were still just cats. The domesticated ones in search of soft-fingered pets, the wild ones attuned to scurrying rodents.

"MEOW."

Rob broke from his reverie. "What is it, Tilda girl? Too hot and dusty out here at the entrance? Of course, it is. We'll find a comfy place for this princess."

"Not to mention this princess," said Lena.

"Yeah, right. Come on this way. I know a spot you can usually rely on for shade. It doesn't earn as many tips as some places, but you don't sizzle and burn."

"MEOW."

"See? Tilda knows."

Zig zagging through the crowds, Rob tried to hold the cage steady. Leaning her head over to Matilda's cage as they walked, murmuring soothing words, Lena turned her head to Rob in surprise.

"This little nut is actually purring. How could a cat enjoy this atmosphere? Not possible."

"Ah, you still don't know my little love, my big love. Matilda's lack of hearing makes the whole thing palatable. And there's nothing wrong with her nose. She knows this is the place where she gets some killer turkey leg. That's not something she gets at home. Plus, she seems to enjoy snuggling into some of the ample bosoms around here. Can't say I blame her on that one. Hey!"

Rob scurried to the side as Lena lifted instrument-filled arms menacingly in his direction.

"I was about to say that the most delightful ample bosom in the countryside, and beyond, is residing in that dress you're wearing, but you didn't let me get that far."

"Yeah, yeah. Is this the place?"

Rob put Matilda's carrier down near the crook of three small trees blessed with abundant leaves. "This is the place."

Lena looked around. "It is kind of out-of-the-way. Is anyone going to find us?"

"Believe me. When I play this fiddle, and you go crazy with percussion, they'll come and they'll stay."

"Really?"

"Probably not if that's all we had. But the cutest cat in the world is with us, so we'll be good to go once we get her out of this carrier, and word spreads about the Incredible Renaissance Kitty."

Rob placed the carrier gently on the shaded ground. He opened the door and Matilda emerged, resplendent in belled collar. Rob attached the harnessed cat to a generously long leash which he looped around a tree trunk. The cat sat and yawned. She'd done this before.

Lena pulled out a tiny collapsible stool stored in her percussion bag and placed it on a flat and shady area. She reached again into the bulging bag, and chose a large tambourine which she shook with vigor. Behind her, Rob tweaked the violin's tuning pegs, head cocked to the instrument as the bow traveled the strings.

He looked down at Lena and nodded. "Yes?" she asked.

"Yes."

They played. Matilda lounged on her restraint. Word spread. Tips clanked and rustled into the beckoning opening of the pewter tankard set in front of the musicians. Matilda sniffed the hands of her loving admirers, who caressed her soft fur, as others around them jigged and swayed to Rob and Lena's music.

Cavnee smiled in his webbing as he considered the ghostly show. First there were two men swinging tankards as they pranced on a stage. Next up was a mud-covered woman with a comical expression. That was followed by a view of multi-colored ribbons, woven into the raven hair of a beautiful girl.

As far as VRC needs were concerned, the little troupe could stay right where they were, comfortable in their shady enclave. The scent image snippets Matilda was picking up as she sniffed outstretched hands were enough for a day's worth of RT's.

CHAPTER 17

Bly remained still, breathless. The lights came up and he felt the supple strands around him simultaneously disentangle and lower him to the floor, the invisible spider turning herbivore, releasing her prey. He reached for the single sturdy strand which dangled from the ceiling before him to steady himself.

"Mistah Goodin?"

The lilting voice.

"Mistah Goodin, it seems this particular trip didn't work out for you. Don't you worry about that. This happens." Geenah rolled her eyes at the comically exaggerated expression of pain on Perin's face, glad that clients couldn't see inside the monitoring booth.

"Mistah Goodin, if you'd please exit the room and head to your raht, a representative will see to it that you ah given appropriate monetary credit, and will inform you of options for future travel. We truly do thank you for choosin' Beyond the Clouds for your Transference. Bah bah, Mistah Goodin. You come back again real soon."

As the last blue string retracted and disappeared, Bly straightened his shirt and gave a quick nod to the viewing apparatus, as he turned and left the room.

Halfway down the hall he was met by an older kisan, his mien not nearly as cheerful as those employees who'd taken his ticket at the entrance.

"Mr. Bly Goodin? Hello, I'm Nemr Keet." Keet offered no palm or fingers in greeting, only a perfunctory smile.

"Mr. Keet."

"Yes. Well. Come this way, please. And please don't brush against any of the doorways, since Transferences are going on all around us, and we don't wish to disturb anyone."

Nemr Keet began walking, indicating with head turned over his shoulder and raised eyebrow that Bly should follow. Bly followed, a vague guilt rising.

Keet led Bly into a tiny room, made to feel tinier by the profusion of wall images. On each was an artistically rendered sight a traveler might see after a distance Transference, including one with the absurdly large leaves and flowers of Earth, as seen from an animal's perspective, a glimpse of whiskers and a portion of snout included in the view.

"Well, Mr. Goodin." Keet's auto-smile activated briefly, followed by a quick sigh. Nemr Keet had been weary of this work since day two, and disgusted with those he spoke with since day one.

"Yes. Well. Your trip just didn't work out." Because you're an idiot, Keet thought. Broad-shouldered, no doubt seen as outrageously handsome and confident, and you can't accomplish Transference. Probably some conspiracy theory swirling around in a little brain in that big head. Pathetic.

"Mr. Goodin, after one unsuccessful attempt, I'm authorized to return 85% of your payment. At this point we recommend that you *don't* try again until you've gone for professional conversation."

Keet nodded at the expected surprised look on Bly's face. Didn't these people read? Did they just traipse in here with heads full of virrius gas? Thank Baata, thought Keet, that I refrain from saying all this out loud, since I need this ridiculous position.

"Yes, Mr. Goodin, professional conversation. It's recommended after an aborted Transference attempt." He loved describing it that way. Just the right amount of disapproval, almost always causing an obvious flash of shame in the client. And they should be ashamed. Who couldn't do Transference? His idiot brother was capable of Transference.

"I see."

Yes, Bly did see. Being told, as he had all those years ago, to get professional help. Well, he was getting professional help. He wasn't always as forthcoming as his Listener might wish, but at his next appointment today's adventure would be the main topic of conversation with Danyin.

"Seeking a Listener is not a requirement. But if you try to travel again, and the attempt is halted again, you're only given a half trip credit. After a third try that doesn't work, no credit, nothing. So it really is in your best financial interest to get some guidance, as it were." Keet emphasized the word guidance as if recommending that Bly needed to learn to dress himself and check his face for bits of food after eating.

Emerging from the disappointment of the Transference failure, Bly began finally to absorb the unpleasant nature of the kisan across from him. Unconsciously, he'd been reading the barbs and jabs of Keet's thoughts, but not acknowledging them, his own thoughts occupying him. The unspoken insults of the travel center representative flooded his conscious mind. "Pathetic."

At the harsh thought he stood. He was done here. There was no need to waste his time responding. At least this small-minded kisan hadn't yet articulated his rude thoughts, though he screamed them through his demeanor. Bly's Reading abilities only confirmed the obvious.

"All right then. I assume I go to the cashier's window."

Keet was disappointed. No complaining? No tearful questions?

As Bly turned to leave, Nemr Keet rose.

"You know, Mr. Goodin, DT is real."

Bly turned, surprised at the unexpected perception of the unpleasant kisan.

"I've been there," said Keet, "and I can hardly wait until I'm able to be there again. In fact, I'm partly in this job, which does not pay a princely sum, or allow me any mental challenge, or provide the company of intellectual equals, because of the excellent travel benefits I receive. I've even had the opportunity to travel in a cat. Just for your information," he smiled again, this one smug and genuine. "If you don't want to be a groundling forever, you'll want to take some steps to address your, ah, problems."

Groundling. An insult. But Bly wasn't going to bite. "Thank you, Mr. Keet."

Keet sat down, bored again. He waved a hand as he looked down at a hovi.

"Yes," he recited. "And we at Beyond the Clouds, thank you for your business."

CHAPTER 18

RT || Maryl Tymin

"I've been doing Transferences for a long time. I know, I look young. It's the luck of mixed breed types. We don't live longer than anyone else, but we make for a nice looking corpse when the time comes. I'm probably somewhere in the middle of the human age spectrum -- maybe a little more. I'm old enough to have had more Transferences into mynies – our cats - than almost anyone on my planet, since I was part of the research from the beginning."

"So far I've touched on the purely physical aspects of the process, including the scent-triggered images. Now, let me tell you more about the mental parts."

"There are two aspects. The waking thoughts and the dreaming thoughts. We're not certain if we merge with the minds of our hosts; if we reach their inner essence. There's just no way of confirming it."

Once again Maryl could detect the up and down bobbing of heads in the room, the silent spectators nodding their agreement with her words based on their own experiences.

"The mynies waking thoughts are fleeting. More like flashing images. Some show things, such as the chair they're about to jump on, the strip of sunlight outside the door, their water bowl. Mundane stuff. No complexity. Until the mynies sleep."

Maryl recalled the progression of learning related to the sleep-time of the mynies. Had the discovery of their rich dream life been a surprise? Maybe not, since surely there was a reason the animals enjoyed sleeping so much. But some of the content had been unexpected. And some had been a shock.

They already knew, from observing eye movements of sleeping mynies, that the animals dreamed. They learned that the dreams varied in tenor. They could be nothing more than a vision of a cushion being enjoyed as fully in sleep as it might be in life. And they could be nightmares. Dreams of mynies in crisis situations, such as a crevice catching a leg; gravity doing its nasty job during a plummet from a great height; the feeling of being lost, yearning for food, among a thousand tiny forest leaves; being bitten, the pain searing, and life ebbing.

All these heart thumping episodes didn't seem unusual. After all, most kisans had themselves, at some time or another, experienced nightmares based on fears, imagination, and real-life incidents. The shock occurred when research notes were compared and the phenomenon happened time and again: different mynies sharing dreams. And not at the same time. The visions could be weeks or months or years apart.

After one mynie, inhabited by the mind of a researcher, had been flattened by a rolling tracktrain, the definitive connection was made. The incident was so violent, so unique, it could be mistaken for no other.

The researcher who'd transferred into the doomed mynie had barely made it back to her own body. She'd been luckier than her mangled host had been.

Immediately, dreams began appearing through mynies who should have known nothing of the incident. Word spread like a giant vine weaving its leaves through the dreams of one mynie and onto the next. The rumble of the train. *Just one more minute and I'll catch this bug on the track.* Too late. Piercing pain and the air crushed out.

The definitive incident gave rise to the Mynie Dream Theory.

"The mynies appear to dream their history. Important, memorable, and shocking occasions are shared and passed on, perhaps forever. We know certain dreams are repeated over time among all mynies we've studied."

Not only mynies, thought Maryl, and nearly every other kisan in the room. Also cats on Earth. During distance Transferences they discovered the same phenomenon of shared dreams between cats. But this knowledge wasn't to be voiced yet to those on Earth.

"The repeated dreams must represent exceptionally important events. Though it's not always apparent why some dreams are important."

Two dreams were most frequently shared by mynies. One was nothing more than a peaceful vision of an open vista, desert-like, with a few scattered structures that appeared to be dwellings made of rocks and clay. The beings in the vision were engaged in domestic activities. There were kisans in the dream, all of the kyan variety.

Before distance Transference, and before knowledge of Earth, there was never any reason to believe that the dreams of kyans in primitive homes and stark surroundings represented anything but an ancient Kisa, geographically unfamiliar, but perhaps representing a time before memory. Now there were other possibilities. The beings in the dream could be humans. The setting could be Earth.

And then there was the other dream seen over and over in mynie minds.

"Ultimately the most startling aspect of the mynie dreams wasn't understood for what it was for quite some time. Not until a corasan, one of our historians, saw the same dream during a Transference, that she had dreamt hundreds of times during her lifetime, also being dreamt by her mynie host."

"The dream was one that corasans are born knowing. It's a dream of the kisan heaven, Baata, representing the accepted spiritual womb of our culture. The scene is of many kisans and mynies in repose on raised platforms, dark angels walking among them. The only difference in the mynie dream? It was from the mynie perspective."

They'd later learned that all mynies had this dream at one time or another, just as the musical corasans did. Later, they learned another creature, well beyond the confine of the virrius, also dreamt of the vision of Baata. The cats.

CHAPTER 19

That night, restless, Maryl watched Danyin asleep beside her, his expansive chest rising and falling with his breathing. Ever ready to smile when awake, a hint of a smile showed even while he slept. Absent of any of the delicate features of a tisani, Danyin's face was squarish. His eyes, when open, were the lightest of blues. It was his smile that enlivened his eyes, and added vibrancy to his face. Her breath caught just considering how her love for him had grown, and how it now filled her.

It was chance and luck that they'd connected on an intimate level, even considering both were selected for Earth work, and that there'd been a professional relationship between Danyin and her best friend Sumee. Though she and Danyin had first seen each other during a VRC meeting, they'd never worked together. But they did, eventually, attend the same class that taught the Earth language English.

English had been one of three Earth languages Maryl could have been assigned in those early DT days. She'd been hoping to be chosen for Chinese language studies. She'd never felt she was a strong language learner, and Chinese sounded more like her native tongue than English. But English, chosen for her by Braelind, based on specific VRC needs, had been an interesting challenge.

The process of kisans learning Earth languages hadn't been simple. The initial language specialists would take rapid, successive trips to feline host bodies to memorize and report on the words they'd heard and, when possible, managed to see. It had been, and still was, difficult to become proficient in the written word, since their hosts, the cats, spent little time staring at items with writing on them. The written transcripts broadcast via the RT's to Earth, would no doubt be fraught with errors.

Maryl leaned on her elbow, reacting to Danyin's sleeping smile with one of her own. She reflected on the ridiculous words, spoken in the graceful tenor of that endearing Robee accent, that had launched their intimate acquaintance.

"Hello cutie!"

Holding a hovi inches from her nose, Maryl had been leaning against the hallway wall, waving through the newest English phrases, constantly updated at a most annoying pace, when Danyin joined her.

Her mind had been deep in English studies despite the class break. She wanted to excel. The class aimed for near proficiency in the spoken word, and ridiculous combinations like "TH" mangled the mouth, unknown as they were in day-to-day Kisanon, or even Baatanya, the ancient kisan language. Those who had strong, language-learning capabilities, like Danyin, were quickly sought.

Though Maryl's progress was slow, the VRC was willing to push her along because of her other abilities and experience.

Maryl looked up at Danyin. He was biggish around, like one of those bear-like bondins, Maryl thought. Not fat. Just big. The smile on his face, the one she would come to expect and love, triggered one on hers.

"You know," she said to Danyin, "I don't think you'd walk up to an Earth female and say "Hello cutie," unless you wanted to give the impression you were a pretty uncouth character."

"Really. And I usually hide that part of myself so well."

His smile turned jokingly rueful and Maryl laughed. She lowered her eyes, and looked again at the hovering English words on the device's screen in her hand. She'd been reading about the word "catnip," a substance she hadn't yet experienced through a host. From the description, it sounded like mendo, the syrupy liquid kisans enjoyed when relaxing that made sensibility roll away and giddiness slide in. That she was familiar with.

"Please allow me to try this again," said Danyin, still standing before Maryl.

Maryl pulled her focus from the hovi, looking up at the grinning kisan. She felt the last wisp of irritation ebb in the wake of that contagious smile and lilting voice.

"You know, I wouldn't ever use such a greeting as "cutie" in our language. I'd probably say something like..." he paused and held out his hand to Maryl. "Good afternoon. I recall seeing you across the room when the Earth team was first formed, and I believe, after all this time, we're now in the same class? May I formally introduce myself? Danyin Mesterdide." His hand was extended out for the brief fingers to palm touch common among new acquaintances.

Maryl's fingers touched Danyin's palm gently as she looked closely at his broad face. She took in his edge of dishevelment and thought "quite appealing," almost laughing aloud at her thought. How long had it been since she'd looked at a male colleague and thought something beyond "I wonder what his specialty is?" Danyin's caress, and it had been a caress, left her palm tingling. Amazing. The first time in quite a while that Maryl found her researcher's brain focused on, and intrigued by, a member of her very own species.

They made a date for that night.

CHAPTER 20

Lena sat in bed, propped up by pillows and covered, as usual when in that position, by both a blanket, and two calico cats. She petted one, then the other, as she watched Rob, wearing only green boxer shorts, standing beyond the foot of the bed, arm encircling an upright bass, locking his eyes with hers, as he pulled a bow across the bass' strings.

She frowned. "Why did you put on those shorts?"

Rob stopped bowing and tapped the front of his boxers. "You don't want anything dangling when there's a big hairy bow around. Trust me."

Lena laughed and nodded. "Understood. But what made you grab the bass, instead of coming back to me?"

"Well, it seemed as if your body was taken over at this point." He used the bow to point at first one, then the other cat, draping Lena's abdomen and legs. "So, I grabbed the closest thing around shaped like you."

Lena laughed again, as Rob stashed the bow in its pocket and used his fingers to pluck a jazzy tune.

"These guys always appear about a second after we've finished making love. Do you think they have any inkling of what we're doing? Or does the whole thing just annoy them because our hands are too busy with other activities to give them pets?"

Rob plucked two notes then answered. "I choose door number 2."

"Yeah, me too. Though I do think cats are smart." She settled more comfortably into the pillows. "How about you? Do you think they're as smart as humans? I mean, putting aside for the moment, all the incredibly stupid things human beings do all the time. But, you know, native intelligence."

"Are you going to make me send your cats to college? I've barely begun paying off my own loan. And we've got to send you first."

"Seriously," she said. "Have you thought about what's going on in these cute triangular heads? Or do you just like petting them?"

Rob's fingers plucked thoughtfully, then twanged a string and let it reverberate.

"I wouldn't answer in terms of smarter than, not as smart as. Compared to us, to humans. They're different. They evolved a different skill set, a set that matches their physicality, their needs."

Rob leaned forward against the bass, his long arms wrapped around it, as if around the waist of a woman with low slung jeans, and belt loops at just the right height for his hands to relax in.

"If a cat could talk," said Rob, "here are some of the things I think she'd say. I think, at the beginning of the day, she'd jump on the windowsill, look at you, look out the window, look back at you and say "Day." Then she'd proceed to let herself be involved with, if only visually, the day, and everything she was noticing in it. Then, an hour or so later, she'd jump down and turn to you and say, in a weary voice, "Nap." She'd processed a lot while looking out that window, and her mind would need to rest with it, turn it around for a few hours."

"So, you're saying cats are hideously boring."

"No! True, it might seem that way, outwardly, to us. But their inner life. I have a feeling that's what's rich. Even when they're sleeping."

"Hmmm." Lena's eyes narrowed as she lifted first one, then the other, annoyed cat from her body, placing each in the bed's center, where each lingered only a moment before pushing off the bed, thrusting harder than necessary to show their irritation. Lena sprawled forward on the bed, her head now closer to Rob as she spoke.

"Well, sometimes I look into those big, round kitty cat eyes, and it feels like they understand stuff. Maybe at a primal level. I like it. I feel extra connected to the fluffer nutter when that happens."

She shimmied closer to Rob. "On another topic, I think if you had one of those cool electric upright basses with the barely existent bodies, I'd be getting a better view of those Wizard of Oz Emerald City shorts than I'm getting now."

"Oh!" Rob grabbed his bow and slashed back and forth a few times, creating the background sound of a dramatic film moment.

"Here I think we're having a deep philosophical conversation about our beloved four-footed companions and what?" He pulled the bow across the strings slowly, pulling out a deep tone. "Her mind is in the gutter!"

"Hey. At least it's in your gutter, right?"

Rob executed a final slash of sound before dropping the bow and leaping, cat-like, on the bed.

CHAPTER 21

Maryl rolled onto her back on the bed, edging her hip closer to Danyin. Why all the nostalgia tonight about their early days? Maybe because of the perfect sense of security she felt. This rare stillness. A moment to reflect on the thousand moments that led to now.

Maryl recalled exactly how she felt before Danyin arrived the evening of their first date.

She'd stood in her bedroom, holding a mynie toy in one hand and, in the other, a shoe whose partner had apparently disappeared into the virrius. Claudi stood at her feet. No, on her foot.

"Myow."

Maryl looked at her. "What? Were we playing? Oh, I've got to clean. I told you, I have a date. All right, Claudisune, I've got to focus."

She dropped the toy at the mynies paws. Claudi sniffed the toy, shook her mane of fur, and huffed away. Maryl pitched the shoe she was holding beneath the bed, and arranged the bedclothes to conceal the mounds of possessions piled underneath. Of course, they could be seen, outlined under the covers. She sighed.

"It's ok," she said, speaking to both the clutter and the play-deprived cats. "He won't be in this room tonight. Maybe another night, but not tonight. At least I don't think so. But then again, why not? Oh Baata, thinking about this is not helping me get ready."

She hurried to the kitchen and surveyed the surfaces.

"There is no way to get this all under control. Why in the world did I make a date for tonight? I couldn't wait a few days?"

As she pushed bowls down into the dishbox, not quite managing to clip the top shut, she thought, no, maybe I couldn't wait a day. How long had it been since she'd had a date? She squinted. Oh, yes. That catastrophe what, eight, nine months ago? It had been foolish to try when she was so busy. She sighed. When wasn't she busy? Never. And time whirled along. Not that she felt desperate for company or stimulation.

She thought of Saras. She could think of worse lives than her aged colleague had. Intense involvement in her research most days; relaxation in the evening with a mynie. She'd always had a vague sense her life would follow a path like Saras's, though perhaps with a touch less class.

But then she thought of her parents, now gone. Each also a scientist, both had lived half their lives with only brief, awkward romantic encounters. And then they met each other and had no regrets about less time in their futures than their pasts. "Don't worry about finding love quickly," they'd told her. "Chances are you'll find it. Or it will find you. If we'd compromised earlier, we'd never have had each other." Maryl herself only regretted that she'd had limited time with her parents, already elderly when she was a young adult. But if that was the price for the contentment she witnessed, then the cost was fair.

And now she'd met Dan. He stirred feelings in Maryl that had been dormant, feelings that went beyond her work, her friendships, her jigsaw puzzle mind. And he was kyan, like her mother. Devoid of those territorial urges tisani's worked to keep at bay. Putting the two types together could be a problem, but her parents had worked through it.

111

Maryl had emerged from her reverie, finding herself pressing the dishbox hard with both hands. It still wasn't quite closed, but there was no time for rearranging. She pulled a wrinkled red dot-patterned cloth from where it half-extended off a shelf, and laid it across the top of the box, pulling it slightly over the front gap. She half-heartedly pressed once more on the top of the container and neatened the towel. Fine.

She moved quickly around the apartment, applying the dot-cloth method of cleaning to the rest of her home, pushing items under furniture, and covering others while the mynies looked on. Did they seem amused? Maryl glimpsed Valin's half head, peering around the corner at her, one ear twitching.

"You mynies are no, and I mean no help at all."

As Maryl straightened and sighed, feeling almost ready for a guest, she glanced in a nearby full-length mirror and let out a shriek.

"Oh, please!"

A small section of her hair was cinched up straight in a decades-out-of-fashion hair holder; her shirt was decorated with the ghost of a spattering of a long ago meal that had turned the shirt into casual wear; and she had no covering on below her hips, her abdominal fur, and all that went with it, cheerily on display. Danyin was due in 20 minutes. She wished she could cover herself with a dot-cloth.

Jamming open the door of her clothes area, she surveyed the field of brown, blue, and gray. Where was it? Sumee had pointed out to Maryl some months earlier that her friend was often so darkly clad, she had to fiddle with her RT settings to fully see Maryl. Sumee had been kidding, but her meaning came through: Maryl had become a fashion nightmare. Sumee reminded her that marching ahead in years and responsibilities didn't mean falling behind in grooming and sex appeal.

"Color, Maryl, color. Would it kill you to wear something brighter than deep blue? Every night after suns-set you disappear!"

She'd forced Maryl to go shopping with her. With much prodding, Maryl purchased a skimpy red dress that was carried home, and promptly stuffed out of sight.

Ahh! A tinge of red. That was it. She dressed quickly and fluffed her now-loose hair.

Her hands smoothed the crimson skirt of the dress, as she checked herself in the mirror. The dress was short, showing her thighs and calves to advantage. The hints of brown and white fur on her neck and bosom gleamed in soft contrast to the material. She sometimes forgot her looks weren't bad, not bad at all.

A rap on the door, and glance at the time, had shown Danyin arriving at the agreed upon hour. Taking a breath, she kicked a last mynie toy out of the way which squeaked just once in protest. She walked to the door, opened it, and there was Danyin, and there was that smile. He handed her a small bag.

"A gift for your kislings, so they won't be too mad at me for taking you out tonight."

Maryl had told Danyin about her pointy-eared brood, and he'd told her of his own furry twins Mally and Dally.

"A bribe?"

"Indeed."

Maryl leaned in to place her cheek gently, quickly on Danyin's, pulling away as quickly as she'd leaned in.

"That's so thoughtful, how nice," she said, unfurling the bag. "Oh, they love these things, and I haven't gotten any in such a long time."

The bag contained bumpees, little balls with springs that made them jump as if tiny lightning bolts assailed them at irregular intervals. Irresistible to any mynie alive.

"I'll drop them just before we go. Would you like a drink? Have a seat." She paused. "Anywhere."

"No need to be so polite. Where would you prefer I sit?"

Maryl was pleased with the response. At times it could be uncomfortable with kyans, since, overall, they were mystified by the territorial sense ingrained in most tisanies.

"Since I'm part kyan, I'm not intensely territory conscious. But, you're right in guessing my tisani side does exert itself. The couch is a very comfortable shared area for me. Thanks for asking."

Danyin settled into a sitting position on the ample pillowed couch, extending his legs onto the cushions meant for their comfort. Maryl moved into the kitchen, a room almost an extension of the living room, with no wall between.

As Danyin spoke, Maryl again thought of how much his almost musical accent delighted her.

"I've known some painfully aggressive tisani," Danyin admitted. "Well, painful to my poor rear, after I'm subtlety nudged off a seat, and land on the floor. So, I've learned to respect the nuances of territorial needs, and find out as quickly as possible what those needs are in honor of peace and the good health of my rear."

Danyin bowed his head in playful respect toward Maryl, as she prepared drinks in the kitchen.

After pouring the thick liquid that was the base of the two drinks, Maryl glanced back at the couch to see two furry faces examining their guest. Claudi sniffed Danyin's outstretched hand on one side, and Willo, planted at Danyin's feet, and delighted with the decorative wisps dangling from his shoes, helped herself to a pleasant gnaw. As Maryl walked to the couch, the mynies scattered and fled.

Danyin reached for his drink as Maryl settled beside him. The glasses were generously filled with a fruity mendo concoction.

"I think the mynies aren't used to much company lately, so I hope you'll excuse their manners."

"What? They're great! I had no idea these tassels held such snacking potential. My own kids haven't even noticed them. Now, there's at least one more around here, right?"

"Right. Claudi's the one with the brown pattern, and Willo's the gray. Little Valin is more retiring. He's my orphan mynie. I found him, abandoned, and I still don't know much about his past. But he's sweet."

"Have you done any Transferences to get some ideas about his past?"

"I have. But I learn nothing beyond the day to day whenever I visit. Maybe he's suppressing some bad past memories. Nothing like on Earth, of course."

Danyin nodded, his usual smile receding. He'd been unlucky enough to experience, through hosts, some of the horrors possible on Earth for cats.

"No. It would never be anything like that. But, there are, unfortunately, some idiots around here, too."

"I know."

Danyin glanced around the room, sipping his mendo, his smile returning.

"This is a very comfortable place you've put together."

Maryl looked around, and fully saw her apartment for the first time in perhaps a year or more. She closed her eyes and sighed.

"Oh, dear. I'm sorry it's such a mess. I really did try to clean up. And when I realized that was going to be futile, I tried my best to hide things. If I'd had a little more time, well..."

She paused, looked at Danyin and chose the route of honesty.

"If I'd had a little more time it would look exactly the same way, because time gets away from me when it comes to my personal life."

Danyin smiled the smile, as Maryl continued.

"At work I'm the Organizational Wonder. At home, I don't know. I just spread out I guess."

"No complaints from me. If there's a couch big enough for me, I can be comfortable. But, if you don't mind, I don't think I'll fully investigate what you have covered by a blanket under the table over there." He pointed, a mock uneasy expression on his face. "There are just a few too many bumps under there for me to even imagine what's creating that shape. And if it moves, you may hear a squeaky shriek from me."

Maryl's eyes followed Danyin's finger and grimaced.

"Wow. Pretty bad. Hey! I'll bet that one bump is my missing shoe!" She sighed. "I'll be honest. I've never had a knack for creating either an orderly or beautiful home interior." She gestured around the room. "You can see my decorations are varied. If someone I like gives me something, I display it. I guess I appreciate the sentimental value of ornamentation. Even if what they've given me is ugly, I only think of them when I look at it."

"Ah...your friends are ugly?"

She laughed. "You know what I mean."

"Yes, I do."

"So," Maryl said, "part of your work has been in groundling counseling at the VRC, right?

"Right. I still have my Listening practice, but I've cut back over the years to work with people who have difficulty with distance Transference. Now VRC's been tapping me to do more and more DT's, since it turns out I'm a genius at English. With all due modesty of course." The grin. "As you know, cutie."

"Yes, I know, you, uh, oh, what would be the equivalent to cutie for a male? Stud? Is that it?"

Danyin paused mid-grin, and then realized Maryl didn't quite know the meaning of stud.

"Close enough for the moment," he said.

"You know, I realize I've seen your name on the RT lists, when I've recorded my impressions after a transfer visit. We work from the same cluster of labs, I think."

"Really," said Danyin. "Maybe you'd consider a co-DT sometime. I've been visiting a household that's been very useful to the linguists. A writer lives there. My host, Einstein, has a lovely habit of facing toward the words on the writer's computer screen. You know those things that are like hovies? I think Einstein is actually watching a bit of fuzz, or a reflection

117

on the screen. But that works for what I need to do. Of course, like most of the hosts, Einstein only stays awake for so long. There's also another cat in that house, and I've already done a few co-transfers. With colleagues."

"All right. I'll plan on it. Let's talk more about -- Einstein, did you say? -- at the restaurant. I'm hungry. Shall we start making our way to a place that will feed me?"

Danyin downed the last of his drink and nodded.

"Sounds like a delicious idea. Let's not forget to put the bumpees out first."

"Oh right. Hey mynies!" Claudi and Willo appeared as Danyin, with much show, dumped the contents of the bag. The balls lay silently on the floor for a moment. Then one took off, as if startled, shooting up straight, then bouncing about the room. Soon others started bouncing at different intervals, each seeming to be a creature that would startle awake and fall asleep just as quickly. As the two kisans shut the door, they spied two furry bodies dashing and jumping in pursuit of the springy prey. Valin had extended his entire head around the corner, bobbing in time to different bumpees, deciding whether or not to join the hunt.

Their meal that night had been delightful, the meat perfectly undercooked, tinged in red.

Conversation, laughter, flirting. Listening to Danyin's marvelous accent. Maryl couldn't remember the last time she'd been so engaged. Or at least so mesmerized by a creature that could speak her language. She silently thanked Sumee for the forced visit to the clothing shop, and for selecting the outfit Danyin had complimented more than once. She wondered if there was time for some quick shopping the next day. Danyin invited her back to his apartment for dessert.

Maryl remembered she had reigned in her desire that first night to skip up the four flights to Danyin's apartment, as she would have liked, three or more steps at a time. Danyin was in good physical shape, but lacked the tisani variation in bones and muscles. As they entered Danyin's dwelling, Maryl's jaw dropped. Ambient lighting. Contoured furniture straight from the latest hovi design mags. Combinations of tile, rug, and wood artfully connected as flooring. And not a dot cloth in sight.

"Danyin, this is lovely. Just gorgeous. And embarrassing! I'm never letting you into my home again!"

"Oh, don't say that. Interior and exterior design are passionate hobbies of mine. Not to mention my profession. But your place has its own voice. I like it." He led her to a plush seat wide enough for two. "Now come. Sit. Relax. Let me go get our treat. I got it from the local sweet shop. I think you'll like it."

The small couch had artful indentations in the leg extensions, making it easy for Maryl to quickly climb onto the seat and enjoy its comfort.

"Brrrippp?"

They both turned their heads at the seeming question. There, looking like mirror-images of each other, sat two mynies. One began to walk toward the couch, its tiny body clothed in luxurious black fur. The second followed quickly, rushing to keep pace with the first. They stopped a few strides from Maryl and Danyin, sitting together like bookends and staring at the two kisans. Danyin suppressed a smile and tilted his hand toward the twins.

"How rude of me. I haven't introduced you to my roommates. Maryl Tymin, please meet Mally and Dally." Both mynies meowed in response, and walked up to Maryl.

"That's quite a trick," she said.

"No trick." said Danyin. "They're just very sociable. Like their dad."

One of the twins jumped into Maryl's lap.

"Mally, no!" said Danyin.

Maryl put both her arms around Mally. "No, no problem at all," she said. "I love mynies. Now, how in the world do you know this one is Mally instead of Dally? They look exactly alike to me."

Danyin sat next to Maryl and rubbed Mally's ears with both hands.

"A parent knows these things. You'll begin to see a difference in them over time, too." Dally saw the opportunity and took it. The couple now had a mynie per lap each, and not an inch between them. "Hey, fella'. I still need to get our guest her dessert."

"Oh no. I couldn't disturb these sweeties. Look how comfy they are! I'm not hungry."

"Not at all?"

"Well, not for anything you'd need to move the mynies for."

They pet the twins and leaned into each other, laughing, talking, whispering, and finally quieting, nuzzling, touching, through the lavender twilight, and on into the aubergine night.

That night had started it all, and it hadn't ended yet. Maryl thought nothing would end it now. She hazarded a small kiss on Danyin's sleeping head. Had his smile broadened just slightly? She thought so.

CHAPTER 22

"What ...?"

Teesh's off-kilter amble around the lab halted abruptly as the alarm from his monitoring board, now well behind him, across the large room, began to whine.

A quick look at Saras, body engulfed, head at ease in her web, revealed no trouble there. Cavnee. Turning his gaze to the web opposite Saras confirmed that the keening sirens were justified.

Cavnee's body writhed, and intermittent moans escaped his throat. The sounds were barely audible over the alarm and more imagined by the opening and closing of the kisan's mouth. Teesh swore as he willed his legs to increase their hobbling pace to get him to Cavnee.

There should always be two monitors present. Why had he let Hiri leave? Because all had been quiet. The rare disasters seemed almost mythical at the moment Hiri asked Teesh if it was all right to join the gawking throng for the so-called "event" on the floor below them. Everything had been so quiet. Teesh inwardly cursed himself. Of all people to be such a fool. He, who lived by the words, "Do not relax. Something can happen anytime." And this time something had.

Teesh stopped short before Cavnee, taking a breath before slowly extending his arms. Teesh knew better than to touch him suddenly. Jolting back a traveler had consequences ranging from headache to death. He'd seen the entire range, though the latter, thankfully, never caused by his actions. He heard the running feet of someone entering the room.

"Watch the board," he barked, not turning to see who would be assisting him by watching Cavnee's vital signs while he worked to gently coax the kisan back from the host. The noise of the alarm slowly lowered, then disappeared. The emergency wasn't over, but the quiet would help with the next steps of the rescue attempt.

"I'm here," Hiri spoke in a subdued tone from his place at the monitor. "I'm with you."

Teesh worked his hands into the webbing around Cavnee's shoulders, slowly expanding and retracting his fingers, gently tugging the fibers that embraced Cavnee.

Hiri called from the board. "He's still tight in that host. Not a molecule moving toward us."

Hiri watched the flickering pulses on the monitor that indicated Cavnee's body was in the room before him, but his essence completely elsewhere.

Teesh swore quietly as he removed his hands from the areas in the web where he'd first placed them, reinserting them even closer to Cavnee, repeating his web massage movements.

"Elevated pulse. Body temp hot, really hot."

Hiri drew in sharp breath. Some of the orange dabs of light on the monitor left their motionless cluster, jumping into the middle of the screen, like the bumpees that so delighted mynies.

"He's sensing us, or something. We're getting indications of consciousness."

"Yes," said Teesh. "I see it happening." He leaned in to Cavnee, speaking quietly. "Come on, you pretty idiot. We want you back with us. I know you'll just snicker at the idea, but I miss you. I want you back. We all do." An image of the smiling face of Cavnee's partner flashed in Teesh's mind. "Especially Linny."

Hiri grabbed the edge of the instrument panel in surprise, as the dancing orange lights on the monitor defied their usual slow, steady return trek across the screen. Instead, in a flash, the pulsing mass streaked from one end to the other.

Teesh watched as Cavnee's eyes shot open, and he seemed to choke, moving his jaws as if to scream, then, not finding the air for it, gasping. He stared at Teesh but didn't seem to comprehend what he saw. He clawed at his bindings.

"Help us! No!"

"It's ok," said Teesh, as he tightened his hold on Cavnee. He called to Hiri. "Unweb!" Hiri slapped the control. Cavnee fairly tumbled out of the quickly retracting threads, falling heavily on Teesh who struggled to keep hold of him, failed, and fell to the floor with Cavnee grasping him, hugging him, crying.

Teesh pulled his head back, startled at something Cavnee had said, quietly, as he cried. Hiri ran forward. "Is he all right. What did he say?"

Teesh cradled Cavnee's head. Cavnee. The one kisan Teesh could be sure would trade playful barbs as sharp as his own. The only one who Teesh had never seen flustered after a Transference. Had never seen cry.

Teesh pulled Cavnee close to his chest, playing over what Cavnee had said.

"Teesh. They burned us. Baata save me, they burned us."

Cavnee had arrived an hour earlier for a DT. He called to Teesh, seated at a table near the monitoring board. Teesh's eyebrows knitted as he read something on his hovi.

"What's up?" asked Cavnee. "Why's the lab so empty? Is there a VRC party and we weren't invited? Seeing as how we're by far the cutest kisans in the place, I find that hard to believe."

Teesh had pursed his lips as he seemed to come to a stopping point in his reading. He put the hovi down and turned to Cavnee.

"Yes, something like that. Although, we are indeed invited if you want to go waste your time. The self-proclaimed marvel of DT travel is on the premises, and, of course, everyone, including Hiri, just had to go see him."

Cavnee had heard the tirade before. He'd tried to keep his comment neutral. "Oh, is Mekkel around?"

Teesh moved to the monitoring board and picked up a mini-hovi, focusing on the tiny screen's output, not looking at Cavnee.

"Yes. The great Mekkel Sord."

Cavnee walked to the webbing area.

"Mekkel's not so bad. Granted, he's not deep. And most conversations you have with him do seem to gradually move back to the oh-so-fascinating tales of himself. But he's harmless. He's a good VRC promo face, you know that."

Teesh had slapped down the hovi.

"It's pathetic that we need to have that insincere dolt representing our work, our strides. That kisan is about as deep as a puddle. Have you heard the verbal miasma he records after his DT's? Please. My mynie would be more coherent. Of course, when the whole planet is watching him do an interview, he suddenly remembers how to speak. Or, after a nighttime visit to *Abigail*. Oh, then he's full of detail after detail."

Teesh, one of those responsible for finding connections between information the returning travelers recorded, shook his head thinking about the unnecessary minutiae Mekkel added to RT's when discussing his visits to the host cat Abigail. The cat lived with a female human who had a dwelling large enough for ten kisans. Though the woman lived alone, she was decidedly not lonely most nights in her bedroom.

Mekkel spent an extravagant amount of time describing visits involving his host lingering by the woman's active bed. In-depth, and Teesh had to admit, appropriately, he described the human male and female anatomy, and what they did with it together. What Teesh found distasteful, were the examples Mekkel included from his own experiences to, as Mekkel said, "fully support his comparative conclusions between kisan and human behavior."

"You've got to admit he's quite the talker when he's webbed. A pretty unusual trait. And we look for that."

Cavnee had been referring to the rare traveler who would speak almost continually during a Transference. Though the talk was a mixture of babble and observation, it was a real-time way to gather information.

Teesh snorted. "Yes, he's a noisy one, all right. Except he spouts almost nothing but pure nonsense."

Cavnee laughed. "You don't give the guy a break, do you? Not that he needs one. But ok."

Cavnee stopped speaking and, going for dramatic effect, jutted his finger at Teesh.

"You must admit …. you must admit…."

"What?" asked Teesh, annoyance ringing in his tone. "*What?*"

Cavnee lowered his voice and leaned into Teesh. "You must admit he's quite the good-looking fellow." Cavnee waggled his eyebrows, one of the more charming habits learned from humans.

The joke and the waggling broke the tension.

"All right. I'll admit he's my type looks-wise. But I need to have my handsome kisans filled with brains, so he most definitely does not fit the bill. And I've already got someone better looking and more talented and..." Teesh flung his hands in dismissal. "All right then, enough wasted time. Are you ready?"

Cavnee made a little bow, hands palms up, indicating his readiness. He straightened and folded his hands over his chest in what he knew was his ideal Transference position, as the stringy fibers began rapidly encasing him, far faster than the threads at the public Transference centers. In the center, the process was slowed to allow amateur travelers to position their bodies for comfort.

Wrapped tightly, Cavnee winked at Teesh.

"All right, you," said Teesh as he'd made last minute board adjustments. "Have a pleasant trip. Though I hope not too sensual a visit, since it took me *hours* to clean the drool off the web after the last trip."

And Teesh had activated the Transference.

Cavnee could see through what looked to be the mesh of a container...a loosely woven basket? Yes. He was wedged tight, the fur of other cats pressing his hosts back, sides, even below him. He felt the bruises of the kicks and scratches of the other cats, finally slowing, one by one, all movement stopping.

127

Chance placed his head pressed to the basket, allowing his eyes to see through the cracks, his breathing less stifled than most of those around him, whose consciousness seem to be waning or gone.

Through the slats he saw nothing but sky, and what appeared to be the occasional lick of an orange flame. He heard voices, human voices, dozens, maybe more, yelling. He struggled to recognize the language, which seemed like only so much babble.

All right, I should go, he thought. This can't be good. But... let me stay long enough to hear some of the words, to report what I've heard. What language are they speaking? I thought I'd transferred to an English-speaking country.

His hosts heart was pounding, throat raw, breathing labored. His eyes began to sting as the basket, which had begun to sway, moved in and out of smoke.

He picked out a word from the shouts, chanted over and over.

"*Brûlez! Brûlez!*" And then, from others, "*Brûlez, diable!*"

What did it mean?

Cavnee realized it was past time to leave and he tried to move himself out.

It wasn't working him. He felt panicked. Of course he knew that a feeling of stress or danger would sometimes thrust the visitor out of a Transference. And sometimes it did the opposite. It prevented a return. But Teesh and Hiri should quickly see the stress signs. They could be relied on.

The basket was swinging furiously. Cavnee could now see it was attached to a wire or rope, its movements under control of a person. The crowd broke into screams of approval.

Cavnee, through his hosts blinking, stinging eyes could see nothing but smoke. The cat, perhaps the only conscious one in the pile, began crying piteously. He felt his hosts' terror and it became his terror. Having access to oxygen was now his hosts misfortune.

"*Un!*" shouted the crowd, responding to some signal that made them all shout, more or less, together.

"*Deux!*" screamed the crowd, and the basket swung more, almost overturning, Cavnee's host still conscious and howling.

"*Trois!*" was the last yell, as Cavnee felt the basket, his host, the other cats, himself, hurtling through the air. Cheers erupted from the crowd. Weak mewls of fear came from all sides, some of the other cats reviving, as the smoke thickened and the basket flew. Then the heat, and then just as immediately, the pain that couldn't be borne. His host shrieked, and he shrieked.

CHAPTER 23

The mild roar in the rear VRC lecture hall was comprised of a hundred murmured discussions, in two's and three's, comprised of guesses at the reason for being so suddenly called together. They had a good idea why. A VRC alarm activation was something all would know about, though only some would know the related details.

Cavnee wasn't in the hall. After the incident the day before he'd been checked, coddled, and, at the insistence of Braelind Carsinsen, sent home in the arms of his partner, Linny, with advice to rest, and call if help was needed.

Hiri jiggled instrumentation on the side wall, finishing the setup of the tri-RT for Braelind, enabling the group's research leader to establish his presence in person and in three simultaneous RT images around the room. It allowed both real and simulated eye contact with every kisan in the assembly.

Hiri nodded to Braelind, seated on a platform in the right front corner. Almost simultaneously the tri-RT flickered into life, establishing three life-like floating Braelind Carsinsen's, his narrow chair unseen, one image front left, a complement to the real Braelind on the right; two others midway into the audience, one on each side.

The RT images and Braelind himself, at least one image or reality in the line of vision of all present, silenced the group.

Danyin and Maryl, seated together toward the front of the hall, hips touching, looked at the real Braelind, the real scuffed platform his chair perched on, the real chair of dull metal he sat on.

Maryl had known Braelind half her life. He'd been the one who hired her and guided her in her early years. Though now removed from day to day work together, she knew that on those occasions she did go see him, when Braelind looked up from his work to see her, a half smile would form on his face. That smile was absent now.

It was Braelind, with a home life filled with a beloved family, who time and again had reminded her there was life beyond work. It was one piece of advice that Maryl had once largely disregarded. She looked at Danyin and resisted the urge to lean her head against his cheek. Instead she took his hand in hers.

From his chair, Braelind pursed his lips, and waited. Waited for each stray cough in the room to settle, each seat shuffling to still. Then he spoke, his liquid voice, as always, deliberate and unrushed.

"I don't like it when I'm left with a body in a web."

Whispers began, and kisans glanced at those around them as Braelind paused again until all was silent.

"All the times I've been left with a body in a web, we've generally been able to figure out the reason. Though, not always, as you all know."

The hush remained, but the minds of all present filled with details of the handful of deaths that had occurred over the years at the VRC. The cause was usually a host who was suddenly killed, whether in life, or a dream, shocking the visitor so severely that the body in the web also died. A few times the traveler seemed to have just lost the way. The flashing orange monitor dots faded, and no amount of coaxing brought them back. When the body would at last be disconnected from the web, it did not survive.

"Today, I almost had a body in a web. Why? Because of a break in protocol. Because it's all starting to seem easy, routine."

His lips pursed again, as Braelind reached up his hand to briefly massage his own weary temple. He turned his head to survey his audience, four of him turning, sweeping the crowd. Even the most distant viewers felt the weight of his stare.

"You know me. I don't yell. I don't rant. Each one of you is here because I trust you. But," and here he leaned forward, continuing his deliberate speaking, "we can't get lazy."

To the far left, Teesh sat with his eyes fixed forward, his nose reddening as he fought back his shame. Others glanced his way, a movement Braelind noticed.

"The kisan who allowed only one monitor on hand was not in any way unique. This happens all the time, every day. Teesh Vindin is no guiltier than most in this room, those who just happened to be lucky when they chose to monitor solo. Today, not only did the traveler, Cavnee Rith, experience a violent dream, a grotesque memory, he also experienced extreme physical pain."

Murmurs gained volume, and Braelind raised his voice to silence them, before returning to his normal tone.

"As we extend our travels, try new hosts, we're going to experience more and more of the cats' communal memories. As we all know, the collective shares what's most unforgettable, and a small percentage of what's memorable for Earth's cats is, at times, barbaric, unspeakable."

"We want those memories. We want to know exactly what we're dealing with when it comes to Earth."

Someone spoke.

"The burning memory. That wasn't from present day Earth."

132

"No, thank Baata. It was from the past. The far past. Check the updates for a few more details."

There were more exchanges of whispering from the audience. Some shifted uncomfortably at the thought of their own memories experienced through cats, of flames, shrieks, the feeling of near suffocation. The dream memories featured identifiable places like England, Spain, and Germany. Other locations and time periods were as yet unknown, the dreams too brief and infrequent to yet glean all the facts.

"I know it's impossible to keep up with all the updates. This burning incident was a centuries old memory, one of the ones from a country called France, related to the religious belief of the time that cats were evil."

All in the room knew that any preserved traumatic incident seemed to be shared by only a small percentage of their cat hosts. It appeared there was a mechanism that continually moved the harshest memories among new dreamers; no single disturbing dream haunting one cat forever. The drownings, beatings. Some in the past; some in the present.

"It's true that the majority of what we experience through our hosts isn't painful or dangerous. In fact, it's blissful. Every one of us has had a "sleeping in the sunshine" dream. Or the "tumbling, playing" scenario."

Braelind was lightening the mood of the room.

"Thank goodness those kittens are in better shape than I am," said Braelind, patting the curve of his stomach.

A few laughed and most in the room smiled, though not Teesh, who kept his serious expression, as he imagined that Braelind locked eyes with him, even if it was only through his replicated image.

"But we can never forget, never, that any trip, any time, can be the far end of bliss." Braelind clapped his hands on his knees and straightened in his seat. "Understood?" He looked around the room. "Questions?"

A few murmurs rose, then faded to quiet.

"All right. Then that's all for now. You all be careful." Hiri switched off the tri-RT, and all but one image of Braelind Carsinsen faded.

The night was slow at the VRC. Only one DT so far, and with only a few hours to go until morning, it didn't seem like another researcher was likely to appear. Jobe had time for filing.

He'd been skimming follow-up RT's from the distance Transferences done by VRC scientists, then moving them to their appropriate place in the taxonomic structure created for their classification.

The bulk, as usual, he filed under the major heading DREAM STATE, using any number of sub-headings, including Baata Scenario, Hunting Prey, and Comforting Human Interaction.

Jobe had begun to skim Cavnee's latest RT but slowed down, rewound, and watched the entire recording. Though the account had been documented days into Cavnee's recovery, the traveler gave the experience immediacy. Jobe had heard about the incident, and read the transcript of the meeting with Braelind he'd been unable to attend. He'd had to close his eyes after viewing the tape, breathe quietly, and remind himself that he would not be doing the kind of research Cavnee did.

Eventually he'd be moving into language research, involving no work-related Transferences. And that was all right with him.

He examined the major heading he needed, MALTREATMENT AND ABUSE, and skimmed the subheading possibilities. He involuntarily squeezed his eyelids together, memories of the RT contents in that category asserting themselves. Bodies infinitely smaller than that of the attacker flung and kicked. Barely born kittens left to starve, overwhelmed with fear, hunger, meowing for mothers. Jobe found the category he needed for Cavnee's experience at the pillar of fire. He placed it in ATROCITIES.

CHAPTER 24

As Maryl stashed her belongings before joining Danyin in the lab, she reflected on Braelind's words. He was right. Though it still wasn't unusual to return excited from a host visit, DT trappings were rote. Prep was like drying off after bathing. The mind went on autopilot, and thoughts meandered everywhere, except on the task at hand.

Maryl and others at the VRC had now experienced the inner lives of a stream of Pussywillows, Fluffys, Blackies, Tigers, Simbas, Gingers, Sylvesters, Maxs, Garfields, Felixes, Johnny's and Muffins. Some for a flicker of a moment, some for hours, and some, in sequential visits, day after day. A multitude of ghost images, dreams, and stray sights captured before yet another cat nap.

In addition to random DT visits, specific cats were visited regularly, based on their unique observation advantages. Maryl, Danyin, and the rest of the dozens who comprised their extended research group, knew about the "top" hosts.

Among the recent favored, was a Chinese male named Qing Yuan, who sat peacefully for the few hours he was half awake each day, in a bustling marketplace, absorbing the kaleidoscope of scents, words, and images, passersby regularly stopping to pet the cat, and converse with the seller in the stall where his skinny pet lounged. Over time, kisan visitors learned Qing Yuan was lucky to be a scrawny old cat, no longer considered a potential meal.

A farm cat had been of initial interest, its roaming of twilight fields and midnight crevices revealing just what cruelties could befall sleepy cat prey.

There was the kitten, now a cat, on what seemed a small island nation. He lived in an earthen structure filled to capacity with people young and old, whose comings and goings kept all DT travelers busy, trying to remember all they'd seen and heard.

Archer, a lovely white-furred, long-haired cat, referred to as an American Bobtail, also offered a window on the outside world, albeit one frequently seen through a cage with unsmiling men and women peering at him, occasionally taking him out to examine and gently stretch to full length. Archer seemed to enjoy the attention, though abhor the interruption of naptimes.

Matilda, the cat who lived with the musician, was among the remarkable ones visited. Danyin had earned first choice privileges for visiting Matilda because of his capacity for lip reading; a useful skill when hearing through ears of a well-traveled, but hard-of-hearing cat. Danyin sometimes ceded his spot to Maryl to allow her, too, to experience the emotional vibrancy of the world of two that was Lena and Rob.

Visits to Matilda led to the discovery of two more members of the "most favored" group of cats. Lena, Rob's lover, also owned cats. The interest in Rob and Matilda was obvious. Through Matilda's atypical wanderings to music performances, the kisans observed groups involved in what were assumed to be typical human ritual gatherings. Lena's value was observed through her computer.

The girl earned her living through writing, the profession's name identified through her muttering "writing sucks," or an occasional happy cry followed by "I shouldn't get paid for writing. It's too much fun." Lena's cats, Mooshie and Einstein, balanced on the side of the computer desk, often stared abstractedly at the results of Lena's key-poundings, becoming living cameras for the kisan visitors who struggled to memorize the images of words and symbols glimpsed through the wandering, distracted gazes of the calicos. DT travelers were grateful when Lena read aloud drafts of articles to her cats, asking, she kidded, for their feedback.

Over time, with advances in understanding English, some of Lena's articles supplied scraps of information on political and scientific topics, while others revealed what seemed to kisans a not unfamiliar weakness for mulling over relationships, physical appearance, and the state of one's health. The articles bore titles like "Voluptuous and Healthy," "Don't Say It: First Date Destroyers," and "So, What Vegetable *Aren't* Good for You?"

Lena's company offered another advantage. Often she spoke at a middling high intellectual level to her cats. Fretting and postulating out loud, Lena made her unknown guests privy to thoughts that would normally have been hidden.

More than once, with either Mooshie or Einstein as host, VRC travelers had been unnerved as Lena leaned in to ask "So, whataya think?" Lab monitors reported that at such times the researchers mouth flopped open, only to clamp back shut. Webbed travelers unconsciously reacted to the urge to reply, before the sheepish realization that, of course, they couldn't. Mooshie and Einstein were not expected to share ideas and supply answers. They were supposed to purr, sweetly nuzzle their person, clean themselves, and fall asleep. All of which they usually did in short order.

Maryl and Danyin were in the lab, the night half gone, having tramped out on a whim. Though less enthused then Maryl about these overnight jaunts, Danyin was willing to join his love occasionally. Especially since he usually reaped the benefits of Maryl's nocturnal energies when they returned home.

Maryl considered tonight's DT. They were going to a random end destination, host unknown. Nearby, Danyin put down a hovi he'd been examining. "All right," he said to Maryl. "What's say you, and I, and some webbing get together, my Marylsune?"

As if responding to Danyin's invitation, Saras moaned in ecstasy from across the room in her white web of light. Of course, thought Maryl, if anyone else would be at the VRC while Kisa slept, it would be Saras. Despite being fully tisani, she was the kind that seemed to thrive on a nap here and there, her long nights happily filled with the work of Transference.

Though hidden under the thick strands of webbing, it was obvious that Saras's back arched. At the sound of the moan, Danyin's usual resistance to temptation crumbled, and he motioned for Maryl to walk with him to where Saras was webbed, to get a closer look, noting the sheen of perspiration on the exposed skin above the tisani's collar.

"Mmmm – yes," moaned Saras.

Danyin and Maryl looked at each other, smiled, then started giggling.

"Shhhhhh!" said Maryl, clapping a hand over Danyin's laughing mouth, and stifling her own giggles. She whispered, "What, have you been hanging around with Cavnee, and picking up his nasty habits?"

Danyin held Maryl's hand over his mouth with his own hand, trying to suppress his laughter, nodding in agreement at the appropriateness of Maryl's chastisement. A traveler responding to a sensual petting was common. The lab monitors looked over with sleepy disapproving looks.

Despite her years, Saras fairly hummed with sensuality, though no one had known her to have a lover. She was either fantastically discreet, or truly what some guessed: someone who took her physical enjoyment through keen senses that naturally heightened the delight of sensory input and stimuli unnoticed, or little appreciated, by those less sensitive. The same talent mynies had. And cats.

Danyin glanced again at Saras, who was now making a sound somewhere between a moan and a whimper, a contented smile on her face.

Maryl and Danyin looked at each other again. As Danyin moved his hand off Maryl's hand, and Maryl moved her hand off Danyin's face, Danyin whispered. "Now that's what's I call a good petting." The giggling erupted again.

The two travelers quickly walked back to their own webbing area, adjusting clothing and body positioning in readiness for the trip. One of the young monitors looked up from the hovi she'd been eyeing. "Hey, Mr. Mesterdide. Do ya' know you're scheduled tomorrow? That's kinda' tight, traveling now and then again tomorrow."

Maryl let her hands rest at her waist where they'd been smoothing folds of clothing. She looked at Danyin.

"You're transferring tomorrow? Or, I should say, today? Dan, that's exactly the kind of thing Brae was talking to us about. Overextending, getting lazy. Or in your case, not being as lazy as you should be, for safety's sake. What are you thinking?"

Danyin raised his palms to Maryl, as if to fend off her words.

"Hold on, my sune. Yes, I'm scheduled, but not for a DT. I'm going to be in the lab, hopefully sipping something warm and invigorating, just keeping an eye on a client. Someone who needs some help with accomplishing a Transference. I'll just be there so the client can look over and see my cheery face."

As Maryl pursed her lips, Danyin pulled out his trump card, knowing the further explanation would earn forgiveness.

"Actually, it's Bly who's coming tomorrow."

Maryl blinked. "Bly? Our Bly? Sumee's Bly?"

"Yes. Our Bly has had the typical unsuccessful DT that most Group Kisans have. And he's got other things going on that I think are inhibiting his ability to transfer. So, I've set up a joint trip. And actually, Bly's kind of lucky, or at least some would think so. Guess who his co-traveler's going to be?"

Maryl shrugged. "Sumee?" she guessed.

Danyin laughed. "Yes, that would be Bly's first choice, probably. And hopefully that's in his future. But no. It's the VRC's star traveler who will be escorting our friend's consciousness."

"What? No, you're kidding. You don't mean Mekkel, do you?"

"I do mean Mekkel. Yes, there's a push to decrease the so-called "groundling" phenomenon, and Mr. Glittering Personality is just the fellow to play the hero as this campaign gets rolling, talking about how, with infinite patience, good humor, and skill, he's helped his fellow kisans break the bonds of their fears. Anyway. It's all quite dramatically worded, but in truth not a bad idea. Mekkel's actually quite capable when it comes to dual travel. He's been able to move a few kisans who'd been unable to travel before."

"And how does Bly feel about all this?"

"He wasn't thrilled, at first, to know that Mekkel was going to be his co-traveler, since he's seen Mekkel's antics, and, let's face it, Bly's got more class than Mekkel. But, I give Bly credit. He seems determined to shake off some fears he's been trundling around for years now. I think Sumee, both as his corasan and his partner, deserves some credit, too. She's been terrifically supportive. So, a few hours from now, I'll be here. No, correction. I'll be about six meters away from this webbing spot, and Mekkel and Bly will attempt a DT."

Maryl sighed and nodded. "I guess that's all right. Just don't end up doing a DT at the last minute, please? If Mekkel doesn't show, just postpone the whole transfer, all right?"

Danyin grinned.

Maryl asked again. "All right?"

The grin remained as Danyin answered. "Allll right."

Maryl turned to call to the monitors. "Send us on a mystery trip tonight. Any region. Your choice." She turned back to Danyin. "All right?" Dan nodded his agreement. She sighed. "Hopefully, whatever we face tonight will be enough of an adventure for you, so you'll stay put tomorrow."

Lena couldn't believe it. Rarely had her fetching ways failed her, but they had this time. Godammit. She couldn't pin down any experts for this story. One dud after another.

She stared at her screen, randomly calling up pages with her right hand, while her left hand, on automatic, petted Mooshie.

Not one physicist she'd interviewed had yet managed to put the idea she was tackling into understandable terms. Her hand rubbed Mooshie's white stomach. Unconsciously, though deep in thought about her problem, Lena heard and enjoyed the cats deep purring.

The concept Lena was trying to write about, supposedly a revolutionary one, was applicable to communication that would involve the creation of 3-D images. Still only theoretical, she was told, but causing a stir among project insiders. The "3-D image" part was intriguing, and lent itself to easy comparison to innumerable sci-fi stories, or just the day-to-day musings of the average imaginative 6-year-old. Now, if she could only find someone even remotely related to the project who spoke "laymanese" when describing the proposed mechanics of the damn thing.

The weird thing was that the first scientists she'd interviewed seemed to imply that the technology existed. Then, in her last few interactions, every scientist insisted the application was decades away, and that the technology was so theoretical as to not warrant a story. They said she'd misunderstood.

Lena wasn't quite ready to let the story slide, though ultimately, like many leads she'd been assigned, she might have to. Her right hand cradled her jaw as she scanned a website that looked like it might produce some interview prospects. Her left hand made her cat roll its head back in delight.

In her web, not knowing it, Saras murmured, "I think I love this woman."

"Whashesay?" The tired young assistant called to her co-worker, closer to Saras than she was.

"Dunno. But her vitals are perfect. So she can tell it to the RT later."

CHAPTER 25

Lying together, knees touching, Danyin gazed at his sleeping partner, admiring the light fur that sprinkled the inner curve of her breasts and hugged her midsection, disappearing just before it reached that delicious spot between her legs. Their quiet bedtime reminiscing of that evening's Transference into playful kitten hosts, had morphed into a reenactment that first mimicked the visit in its warm, tumbling intimacy, and then moved blissfully beyond innocence.

Danyin loved moving his fingertips along Maryl's velvety fur path, until reaching the destination they happily explored to his lovers' delight. The thought made his hands want to venture yet again, but he knew he had only a few hours to sleep before needing to return to the lab. There was always tomorrow. He smiled. And hundreds of tomorrows after that.

His thoughts moved from the pleasure of the moment to the day ahead of him. It was happening because of a long ago referral from Sumee. Back then she'd asked him to meet, in his capacity as a Listener, with a kisan who was having difficulty with Distance Transference.

"This case could definitely be more interesting than some," Sumee told him. "He's a GK. And he's living on his own."

Danyin knew it was rare for a Group Kisan to seek a non-GK Listener. The communally-oriented Group Kisans didn't shun outside professionals. Typically, they simply had no practical need to seek such services beyond their household circle.

"Wouldn't it be more comfortable for the client if he talked to another Group Kisan? I don't really have experience..."

"*Dan.* He's not any GK. He's my GK."

That's when Sumee told Danyin that the client was the special lover she'd come to realize she could be with for a lifetime.

Sumee and Danyin had become more than business acquaintances who shared referrals, once they learned of the mutual love they had in common: Maryl.

"So, I'll meet Bly on a professional basis, before I meet him on a personal basis? Is that good for all our relationships?"

"Danyisune, I really think that will work out just fine. GK's see absolutely no difference between so-called business, and so-called personal relationships. It's all relationships."

By coincidence, some days before Sumee's call, Danyin had been flipping through a favorite hovi mag realm, and noticed a feature on innovations in home design for those kisans born with the desire to share a common space.

The Group homes were magnificent. Some images captured only a small design feature, such as one of the ornate bells that had become trendy additions to house fronts. Others showcased the GK spreads in their entirety, including the massive outdoor recreational areas common to such houses.

Danyin nodded approval at the images of the forested outdoors with their sun-filled niches created here and there for relaxing and socializing. He envied the expansive exterior of the GK's homes, if not their shared interiors. Inside, he'd rather have a partner, some mynies, and that was that. He did enough interacting with others in his work as a Listener and, for the last few years, with researchers at the VRC. An uncrowded home life suited him just fine.

After Sumee's referral, Danyin searched for Bly's name in the design mag realm, and had been rewarded with results that could have occupied him for hours. Bly's house adornment designs, including door knockers in choice of hue, were popular planet-wide, with both GK's and non-GK's.

Danyin had agreed to meet Bly and set the appointment day and time with Sumee through an RT chat.

"You will love Bly. And I think you can help him, too."

"Sumee, for a kisan as cute as you, I'm happy to give it a try. Even knowing your natural prejudice against handsome kyans, such as myself."

Sumee laughed. "Danyisune. We all have our aesthetic preferences. And you wouldn't even know mine if Maryl hadn't told you. And you know," she added, lowering her voice in a playful way, "that I find you exceptionally attractive. For a kyan."

Danyin shook his head. "You just don't know what you're missing, Sumee."

"So Maryl keeps telling me. Well, happily, my loss is Maryl's gain." Sumee's RT image had bowed its head toward Danyin. "Baatani's blessings on you. See you soon." And then her RT had melted in its usual magnificently manipulated way, Sumee fluttering her hands to make her tri-colored gloves form slashes of lines, and streaks of color as they faded.

Memories dissolved as he shifted in bed and turned to his side. Danyin faced the wall, with Maryl, still deep in sleep, inches from his back.

He sighed, scenes of the past still elbowing out sleep. He thought of his preparation for that first meeting with Bly.

He'd spent the better part of a day, in the week before seeing Bly, puttering through his hovi to both refresh and update his knowledge of Group Kisans.

The communal attribute was a given. Also, the fact that they welcomed both "natural" GK's, and those who'd had an inkling later in life that the GK lifestyle would work for them. Some of the converts lasted, some didn't. Sometimes one large, extended family related by blood filled a dwelling, other times kisans of no familial relation dwelt together, and most often the Group was a mix.

The GK's pooled money, chores, everything. Since Groups weren't concerned with having large indoor areas of personal space, the homes could fit dozens of GK's comfortably.

Danyin browsed stories of GK homes where Groups worked together to earn money, and others telling of members who went their separate ways most days, but returned to the shared space to enjoy their leisure hours.

Though the GK's valued their home situation, they weren't insular. They welcomed visitors, and mixed seamlessly in the world. And despite their love of Group closeness, partnerships within the Group settings were much like those on the rest of the planet: two kisans, GK or not, forming a special bond.

There was only one attribute, found only in GK's, and only in a some GK's, that Danyin had formally studied when learning Listener skills decades earlier. Though nearly all GK's possessed a high level of empathy, so-called Readers could also "hear" the thoughts of other kisans. Sometimes complete thoughts came through; other times just emotional impressions, rather than words. Readers gave thanks to Baata, for allowing them a sane life, by also giving them the ability to tune out their gift as needed.

Hours of mag realm reading, watching, and listening had brought Danyin little new information on the GK's that he didn't already know, but the refresher was helpful. All right. "So, why would a GK like Bly choose to live alone?" he'd asked Sumee. "I think he should tell you himself, Dan," she said.

He'd found some generic answers to the question in his research. Group Kisans generally left Groups because of a tragedy. Though not always. Sometimes, the lure of love with a non-Group member would entice a GK to suppress his normal inclinations. And some GK's needed the comfort of a Group less frequently than others. But, clearly, in most cases, it was a trauma that moved a GK to live alone.

So, Danyin had been ready to hear what Bly had to say. Why did he, a Group Kisan, live alone?

Danyin became suddenly tired. The memory of Bly later, blandly, recounting the tragic family story now replayed in Danyin's mind. He adjusted his legs so that his feet now gently touched Maryl's. She didn't stir, and he drifted into what he knew would be a brief slumber.

CHAPTER 26

Danyin took a sip from his steaming cup and sighed with contentment. He thought of the similarity between those on Earth, and those on his planet, when it came to an affinity for a morning pick-me-up drink. He remembered, with a smile, the scent memory of an Earth cat's owner murmuring with pleasure, as she lowered a morning beverage. Was that a commonality all species, galaxy-wide, with the dexterity to grind up the appropriate beans, leaves, or seeds, would be found to share? Maryl had guessed they'd share that, and a love of bad jokes.

Danyin allowed himself a few s moment to enjoy thoughts of the Transference, just hours before, with Maryl. It was a shared DT, and they found themselves peering through young kitten eyes, feeling crackling sparks of energy percolating through them. They both tried to focus on the learning aspect of the journey, but their laughing, giggling, bodies back in the lab knew better.

In their hosts they'd tumbled, hopped, and given each other pinprick scratches and bites that were more exhilarating than painful. Danyin remembered the feeling of his heart, which was really his hosts heart, beating, beating. The force of pure youth and health sped through the body, accompanied by a feeling of invulnerability, and a delirium like that of first love.

It had been unbelievably fun.

"Ow!" Maryl had yelped during the trip. The lab assistant barely stirred, correctly interpreting from the board's indicators that no danger was imminent, and that Maryl's cry was likely the result of any number of cat activities – a jump from a too-high spot, designed to impress onlookers; a swipe from a passing cat higher in the pecking order; a shoulder kink being acknowledged after an extended nap under a fading sunbeam. Nothing harmful.

Upon return, Maryl and Danyin unwebbed and tumbled to the floor, cuddled in each other's arms in a mirror position of their distant hosts. They'd disentangled and pulled themselves up.

Walking toward the follow-up recording area, they'd passed Saras, ecstatic some hours earlier, now unwebbed and relaxed-looking in one of the austere lab chairs it seemed no one should be able to relax in. Saras stretched her long, mynie-like body, yawned, and waved.

Danyin had stopped by to greet Saras. "Hi there. You're looking peaceful. I wouldn't be shocked to hear a "meow" right now."

"Meow, my dear," she said.

"We couldn't help but notice, before our DT, that your trip looked like it was a pretty enjoyable one."

"Yes. Enjoyable." She paused, as if considering other possibilities. "Yes. You're not being revolting, dear Danyin, like some would be. Now Cavnee, that Jewel of the VRC, was once sitting in front of me after my return from an "enjoyable" journey, as you say. Apparently he took *quite* the pleasure in the show at my expense and had *quite* a bit to say about it." Saras brushed an invisible fleck from the arm of her tunic. "It's lucky the kisan has his true charm, or he'd regret his occasional vulgarity."

Danyin and Maryl stole a shared guilty look and Maryl replied.

"Oh, Cavnee's always fooling around. Just young. Not quite ripe, as they say."

"Yes, not *quite* indeed." Saras inhaled and exhaled with deliberation. "Well, my RT is done, my heart rate has subsided, so it's time to leave."

Saras stretched her way off the chair and nodded her good night to the pair. Danyin and Maryl completed a quick follow-up RT and made their way to Maryl's home and bed.

Danyin had risen early to once again return to the VRC for that now unforgettable morning.

Danyin sipped from his cup, and lowered it just as Bly Goodin strode in from the far side of the lab. As usual, he was impeccably dressed, looking youthful, possessed, and appealing. If Danyin wasn't Bly's Listener, he wouldn't have a clue that inside his client and friend roiled with uncertainty. Though Danyin knew that Bly suppressed his Reader abilities during their therapy sessions, Danyin still willed himself to blank out the image that often asserted itself when he saw Bly. It was the vision created when Bly had finally told him why he lived alone. It was an image of Bly's past, of his family slowly suffocating, one after another, until almost all the major figures in his life were dead.

Danyin called to him. "Bly."

Bly tilted his head in greeting as he approached. Danyin understood that Bly's look, little changed to the casual observer, was one of relief at seeing a familiar face, the pleasant demeanor concealing the unease. Teesh moved from the monitor he'd been manipulating and intercepted Bly. He held up a finger to Danyin, indicating he needed a moment with Bly.

As Danyin watched the two talking, he reviewed the events that had led them to the lab this morning. Bly's failed

DT attempt. The discussions of Bly's many fears, all entwined with the fact that a disease had squeezed the breath from his loved ones.

Bly's tragedy had started with the virrius. One of his brothers had flown near it on a sarpac, brushed its wisps, and plummeted. But he had survived. He didn't know he'd been infected. He hadn't been checked, just hurried home by his fellow Group Kisans, forgetting the possible consequences, forgetting that a virrius infection wasn't immediately apparent. Later they remembered, and lived the worst case scenario. The rare instance of contagious infection had become the family's hundred percent certainty.

Danyin was encouraged that Bly had made it to the lab that morning, a semi-smile, however manufactured, on his face. He felt confident Bly's trip would be therapeutic. Mekkel, despite his shortcomings, was expert at dual travel, and Danyin believed that a successful shared trip could be just what Bly needed. It might be the only way Bly could do a DT, but he'd do it, he'd know DT's were real, and he'd know there was life beyond the beautiful murdering virrius.

Danyin saw the conversation between Teesh and Bly ending, Teesh's eyebrows rising, and Bly nodding. "Good," he heard Teesh say. Teesh see-sawed toward the control board and Bly walked toward Danyin. Danyin turned on his infectious grin and watched its twin appear on Bly's face. "You're starting to look ready now."

Bly nodded at him. "With you, and your charm, and your lovely accent, and that goofy smile? How could I not feel good?"

"Goofy? You've been learning Earth words *and* associating with that Sumee again, haven't you? What has she got you saying about me?"

As the two grasped hands, fingers to palms, in the quiet bustle of the lab, a deep voice bellowed.

"Suns are up and here we are!"

All heads turned toward the new arrival, Mekkel, striding into the lab. Charisma flowed from the kisan, tall, large-framed, fully kyan, from a long line of kyans. His hair was thick and blonde, his face smooth and pink, his eyes the blue of the Kisa sky.

Danyin reflected, not for the first time, that Mekkel could be the prototypical "celebrity" type they'd identified on Earth. Both planets had some overlap in their choice of "stars." Part looks, part ineffable quality – magnetism, allure – or whatever it was. Not everyone loved Mekkel. But it was difficult to ignore the spell of his presence; a truly bewitching person who was lucky to have missed being born across the universe, in another time, in reach of stakes and flames.

Bly turned to watch Mekkel approach. Stopping in front of the slim kisan, Mekkel turned on his dazzling grin, extending his hand for the expected fingers to palms greeting.

"I know who you are. You're Bly Goodin, our groundling. I'm Mekkel Sord."

Bly offered his hand to Mekkel. Danyin put a hand briefly on Bly's arm in reaction to Mekkel's artless "groundling" comment.

A well-groomed male tisani kisan who'd followed a few steps behind Mekkel leaned in to the large kisan and spoke quietly, though all in the lab could hear the words.

"Mr. Sord. We just talked about that."

"What? Oh, right Timm." Mekkel's laugh, with its theatrical edge, was one that could be produced without

153

thought or sincerity behind it, though the same sound erupted when Mekkel was genuinely amused. After years as a popular public figure, even Mekkel wasn't sure if he'd engineered the reaction or not at any given moment.

"Hahaha. No offense, Mr. Goodin, I assure you. You know, the word "groundling" has sort of become the vernacular. I forget it can be construed as an insult, which my good assistant Timm has just reminded me. Again, my apologies! I can just be a bumbler sometimes, hahaha."

Mekkel wrapped his arm around Bly's shoulder, Mekkel taller than Bly, who was himself tall. Pulling Bly slightly away from Timm and Danyin, he lowered his voice an iota.

"You need a hand, and my hand is here. I think highly of you, Goodin." Mekkel squeezed Bly's shoulder. "Did you know I ordered those colored door knockers of yours right after they came out? Forty identical knockers! Of course, I realize now the advice the seller gave me was smart. Should've bought a variety. Sometimes I don't know which door I'm heading for. House is too big, but, the partner says we need it, so who am I to argue? Still, love those knockers, hahaha!"

Bly swayed a few inches under Mekkel's friendly slap of his shoulder, the big hand returning to Bly's shoulder to help steady him. Bly replied to the compliment. "Ah, well, thank you."

Mekkel abruptly lifted his arm and turned from Bly to his assistant.

"We ready to get this going? A lot going on today."

"Yes, as always."

Timm called to the board where Teesh stood frowning, and Hiri stood smiling and nodding his head at Mekkel.

154

"Ready?" asked Timm. "All right. I'll be back soon, Mr. Sord. RT me if you need me sooner."

As Timm left the lab, Hiri hurried forward and gestured to an area a few feet away.

"Yes. This is the webbing spot you'll be using, Mr. Sord." Mekkel walked over, first tapping Bly on the elbow, and indicating he should follow. "This is us, Goodin."

Hiri spoke to Mekkel. "Anything special you need, Mr. Sord? Seats? Web shirt?"

Mekkel used both hands to slap his strong, broad chest. "Got everything I need right here. Enough here for this fellow, too, right, Goodin? You rely on me, and you'll be telling the family about your DT in no time."

Danyin involuntarily squeezed his eyes shut and caught his breath in reaction to Mekkel's ill-chosen reference to Bly's family. Well, he might be insensitive, but in this case his callous words were unintentional. He didn't know about Bly's losses. Danyin retreated a few steps as Mekkel steered Bly to the webbing area.

"Good luck, Bly," said Danyin. "Just so you know, I'll be here."

Bly pasted on a quick smile and nodded at Danyin as Mekkel once again pulled Bly close to him, this time positioning him for the dual webbing. Bly gave a sigh, though even he, as nervous as he was, was not immune to the ineffable Mekkel appeal.

"Ready to web, and I mean now," said Mekkel.

Hiri, back at the control board, called out. "And here we go, Mr. Sord!" Teesh rolled his eyes and whispered to Hiri as the young man released the threads in the webbing area. "If

155

you're really lucky, maybe that dunce will drool on you. Oooh. Real Mekkel Sord saliva!"

Hiri took a moment to give Teesh a squinty glare before both went back to observing the webbing process.

Teesh silently acknowledged that Mekkel at least knew what he was doing when it came to dual DT prep. Mekkel's firm grip on Bly would assure secure webbing of the two travelers, and keep the necessary contact points in place. Each traveler, chest-to-chest, one pair of hands surrounded by the other. Each head was turned, one pressed to the other, side to side. Perfect positioning, really. Well, the idiot had to do something right besides grin broadly and chuckle.

Hiri gave Teesh an inquiring look, his hand ready to activate the webbing. Teesh gave a small nod. Hiri knew what he was doing by now, so he didn't really need Teesh's go-ahead. But after the fiasco with Cavnee, they were going by the book.

Danyin saw Bly flinch as the webbing rapidly tangled around him and Mekkel. He saw Mekkel's lips moving, presumably, hopefully, forming words of comfort. Bly did, in fact, seem to be calming. His raised shoulders lowered, and he sighed audibly.

In only moments, the speedy webbing complete, the two travelers were ready.

Hiri looked again at Teesh, and saw the slight tilt of Teesh's head, the pursing of his mouth, that indicated Hiri should continue.

Danyin heard and felt the slight vibration radiating from the webs perimeter, indicating the beginning of the DT process. No blinking lights, no color fluctuations, no clicking sounds, but the vibration and hum were real and always sent a thrill through Danyin, whether he was in the webbing himself or, as he was today, a nearby observer.

He watched as the intertwined figures seemed to melt into each other as their muscles relaxed and, he knew, their consciousness blurred.

Danyin spoke softly aloud, knowing neither Mekkel nor Bly could hear. "It's working. Bly's doing it this time."

"With help from Mr. Sord," said Hiri. He tapped the screen in front of him. "Yeah. Definitely on their way. It's a little slow, but that's how it is sometimes with a double."

Danyin walked to the back of the control desk to see the activity on the screen, as Hiri continued watching and Teesh leaned in to join them.

Danyin felt a tinge of worry as he watched the lighted dots almost imperceptibly moving forward. "Seems awfully slow."

Teesh moved in more closely. "Yes. Slow."

They were all silent a few moments as the red lights conglomerated mid-screen, pulsing. A few moved forward.

"Ok, there's something," said Hiri, hope in his voice.

More moments passed, and Danyin and Teesh looked at each other.

Teesh nodded at Danyin and turned to Hiri.

"Bring 'em back."

Hiri balked. "What? They've barely left? Mr. Sord has, like, never, messed up. I mean, another few minutes wouldn't hurt. I mean, he could be mad if we yank them back too soon."

"Move over." Teesh activated the help alarm as he brushed past Hiri, jabbed him aside, and leaned over the monitor's controls. His mind filled with the words he'd use with Hiri later. "A few minutes wouldn't hurt? Have you had a brush with the virrius? Has your brain melted? A few minutes, even a few moments, can fry a traveler if something is wrong."

"Baata." Teesh muttered as he left the board and rushed in his awkward gait toward the travelers. "Now Mekkel's vitals are going berserk." Danyin first followed, then hurried past Teesh.

Neither face of the travelers could be seen from the angle of the control board. Crossing the short distance to the web, Danyin gasped as he approached. What he could see of Mekkel's face was drenched in sweat, the famously smiling mouth clenched.

Perhaps more shocking than the grimace on Mekkel's face, was the contrast of Bly's expression. Bly looked peaceful, a gentle smile curling his mouth. It was a look of relaxation Danyin had never seen on Bly.

The alarm brought four kisans rushing into the lab. Hiri pointed them to the webbing area, still frozen in the spot he'd been pushed to.

"All of you healing trained?" asked Danyin. The kisans nodded. "Good. You two. Stand by this one," he said, pointing to Bly. "As the web retracts, catch him and untangle him as quickly as possible. We'll move him out fast. Try not to let him get a look at Sord as you move him, for Baata's sake, please." Danyin knew he need not explain who Mekkel Sord was.

Danyin turned to the other two kisans. "You both stay near Mekkel. Be ready to grab him and be ready for anything."

As the webbing loosened its grip, flickering in front of Bly's face, Mekkel's face, and his own face, Danyin saw that Mekkel's hair looked damp, the side of his neck flushed. Danyin called out. "Hiri, get over here to help! Mekkel's a big guy."

Hiri looked inquiringly at Teesh who nodded impatiently indicating yes, Hiri should be the one to help, not Teesh with his stick-like legs and slight upper body. Teesh hurried, teeter-tottering, back to the monitor.

Danyin walked to Bly's side of the webbing. Bly's eyes opening slowly, his beatific look meeting Danyin's quietly panicked one. Danyin gave a silent thank you to Baata that Bly had become accustomed to masking his Reader talent when near Danyin. That should also prevent Mekkel's thoughts from intruding on the calm tisani's mind.

"Dan."

Danyin spoke to Bly as the helpers gently removed Bly's hands from Mekkel, blocking his view of the big kyan kisan as they worked. "Hello, Bly. We needed to bring you back a little early, but you're doing great. As the webbing loosens completely, I'll be walking you right over there, to that room. These kisans are going to come too, and we're going to stay with you for a follow-up talk."

Danyin hurried the helpers and Bly to the nearby room, all of them quickly entering and closing the door, Bly's delighted chatter now just a murmur to those in the lab.

In the webbing area, the two kisans supported Mekkel, while Hiri eased a chair under the nonresponsive traveler.

"Mekkel's still not fully back," Teesh called, his eyes on the monitor. He muttered to himself. "I've never seen anyone come out of a DT like this."

At that moment Mekkel's eyes snapped open and remained fixed, like wooden eyelids revealing the painted pupils of a toy figure.

"Mr. Sord." Hiri spoke quietly, leaning over and placing his hands gently on Mekkel's arms.

The sound of a door opening and closing was quickly followed by footsteps, as Danyin approached the group around Mekkel.

Hiri moved aside at a touch from Danyin, who kneeled to be closer to face level with Mekkel. "Mr. Sord? Mekkel?" Mekkel's mouth was slack but his eyes seemed to begin to focus. Though his face was only inches from Mekkel's, Danyin still couldn't hear any words. He saw Mekkel's lips move, trying to speak.

The kisans checking Mekkel's vital signs murmured calming words and told Danyin they'd need to move Mekkel soon to do a thorough physical check.

"Mekkel, how are you holding up? Can you hear me?" Mekkel's vacant stare cleared, like a streak of virrius floating over, then beyond, the face of a cloud. His eyes locked with Danyin's and welled with tears. There was no "hahaha," no meaty hand reaching to give Danyin a slap on the shoulder. Instead he crossed his arms around himself and leaned slightly forward, toward Danyin.

"So sad," he said. "So sad."

CHAPTER 27

Bly was pleased with the look of the VRC lab when he'd walked in that morning. It was nothing like the bright and image-festooned "Beyond the Clouds" travel center. That was a relief to Bly. The lab was practical. It appealed to the designer in him to see the basic product, unadorned, the "before" that existed prior to someone like him smoothing its edges, and making it visually and sensually appealing to those who wouldn't feel comfortable with raw materials.

He'd been advised of the larger-than-life personality he'd be encountering that morning, but still felt a quickening of his pulse, and a sheen of perspiration rising, as Mekkel strode across the room to him, enormous hand outstretched to swallow his own real-life-sized one. Still, the touch, surprisingly, turned out to be a comforting one.

Bly understood, from Mekkel's touch, that there was an underlying empathy in the kisan. Buried, perhaps, under time constraints, years of real and perceived expectations of others, and a healthy measure of self-love. But the empathy was there, real and pulsing. Bly could perceive those things, even with his strong Reader qualities politely reigned in.

Bly was happy Mekkel didn't share his own level of empathic ability. Mekkel might perceive Bly's worry, but not necessarily, and not in an intimate way. Just as Bly was sure of his talent for empathic sensing, he was sure of his talent for pretending. Pretending he wasn't worried. Pretending he was just a sought-after designer with no more concerns in life than imagining the next household ornament, and catering to his clients' desires.

By the time they'd entwined in the web, Bly was calming. The feel of Mekkel's head leaned into his, the energy pulsing from the large hands, Mekkel whispering *you're doing great*. It all calmed him. Bly could sense Danyin on the sidelines, concerned on his behalf. "It's all right," thought Bly, not quite saying the words aloud before, suddenly, the DT began.

The comfort Bly found in Mekkel's nearness abruptly expanded. The kind of elation he'd once felt with siblings during play was the kind of joy that flooded him. The carefree feeling of strength of body, the security of loved ones near, the pleasure of a spontaneous moment of delight, all mixed freely. The sensations grew stronger and deliciously complex.

Images, known and unknown, blossomed to match each feeling. The known included glimpses of his home in Posloq, the touch of his first mother, the smile of his second mother, Wilina, all revealed at times when they'd brought the most happiness to Bly. The unknown images were just as numerous, but fleeting, and each brought a strong emotional reaction. A smile that imbued a feeling of pleasure; one hand caressing another, bringing a sense of accomplishment; the sound of a crowd cheering followed by a welling of pride; the first sight of a newborn that he sensed was his kin.

All too soon the images receded, though Bly was still infused with a feeling that had been alien to him for so long, a feeling of happiness untainted by guilt. The feeling remained even as he opened up his eyes to Danyin's anxious expression. Why was Danyin worried? Everything was great.

CHAPTER 28

The group Braelind gathered in the days after Mekkel and Bly's trip was small. Maryl, Danyin, Teesh, Cavnee, and Saras were now settled around the niches of the flower-shaped table in his office.

Braelind spoke. "You three," he said, pointing in turn to Maryl, Cavnee and Saras, "know the bare bones of the situation. Mesterdide and Vindin know more, since they debriefed both Mekkel Sord and Bly Goodin."

Danyin and Teesh nodded their agreement. The others shifted eyes, glancing at each other.

"A few of Mekkel's hangers-on got involved after the DT, didn't they?" asked Cavnee.

"Hmm," said Saras. "That Timm Whoever was fairly hysterical. Not concerned his employer might be unwell, mind you, only worried they would miss their appointments of the day."

"Yes, a few others were involved, some VRC, some Sord's group." Braelind waved his hand dismissively. "For now, you five, and me, of course, will be the core group in this first follow-up phase." Braelind leaned his head and shoulders in the direction of his clasped hands, drawing himself nearer to those at the table.

"As you know, there was one DT with Sord and Goodin. They traveled together because Goodin couldn't previously accomplish a DT, so Sord was assisting. They traveled at the same time. Made the same trip. Came back with two very different stories. Vindin. Talk about Sord."

Teesh, looking tired, ran a hand through his pale hair, moving the strands from their accustomed spot on his forehead, where they would soon return.

"The talk with Mekkel Sord wasn't long. Well, it probably seemed long to him. I'd say we badgered him longer than he would have liked."

Teesh paused, reflecting that previously he'd never felt sympathy for Mekkel Sord. That was before.

"Mekkel was largely unable to communicate the details of his experience. His first words were…Dan?"

Danyin remembered Mekkel holding him, and then, with what seemed like great effort, whispering words to him, Mekkel's face inches from his own.

"He said "So sad." And repeated it. That's it." Danyin nodded to Teesh to continue.

"And those were the only words he used at first," said Teesh, "though eventually we got more out of him. Here. I've put together a montage recorded after the trip. The aborted trip."

All heads turned to the hovi screens set at various angles at the core of the tabletop, each filled now with the image of a haggard Mekkel Sord faced toward Teesh and Danyin both seated.

Mekkel slumped forward in his chair, repeating the two words a number of times, as if not realizing he'd ever said them once. "So sad." The lifeless look he'd worn following his return was gone, replaced by a look of gentle sorrow.

Cavnee shook his head at the image. "Baata. I don't think I've ever seen Mekkel without a grin plastered eyeball to eyeball."

164

Danyin's screen image spoke, his hand resting on Mekkel's arm.

"Mr. Sord. Mekkel. Can you tell me what's so sad? I think it would probably help you feel better if you'd tell me."

Mekkel first tilted his head down, and then raised it to face Danyin. The image showed tears sliding down his face.

Mekkel waved a hand in the air to accent each listless word. "How can I put it into words? There was the family. The sickness. Mother, kislings, everyone. Just...so..." Mekkel stopped and put his hands over his face, the tips of his fingers pressing into his forehead, as if trying to stop the images he could still see in his mind. "They're all dead now," he said.

Danyin spoke to his companions watching the hovi recording. "He's talking about Bly's family. They were decimated by a virrius infection."

Teesh spoke as he stopped the hovi and the images blurred. "You can watch more of the early interview on your own, but there's not much more to see. Basically, Danyin asks Mekkel, in different ways, all very persuasive, to give us more details on what he's seen, and why he feels the way he does. And Mekkel answers by looking off into the distance and saying "I don't know," or "I can't explain it." Later, after Mekkel rested, ate, washed up, we had this interview."

Teesh forwarded the hovi to a new blurred image and set it in motion. The characters were the same, Mekkel, Danyin and Teesh together, but this time all three looking more refreshed, especially Mekkel, who seemed almost normal, exuding his signature bravado and, though subdued, his usual cheer.

"Sorry I was such a mess before guys. My brain was fogged I guess you'd say. I'd say I've snapped out of it now."

He snapped his fingers but his shoulders suddenly sagged, as if under the weight of the mammoth falsity of his statement. He lowered his voice to share his next insight. "It's going to take a while to feel – right again. During that DT, I felt things I've never felt before. Sure, I've felt unhappy before. But this. This was grief to the virrius and beyond. If you'd told me, right after that DT, that my life was ending, I'd have said "Praise to Baata." Me. Ha. I really think I would have."

"You had strong feelings about ending your life," said Danyin. "Is that the kind of idea that would normally occur to you?"

Mekkel's laugh started with his stock "Hahaha" and then moved into another laugh, a gentle one.

"No, no. The idea of my life ending being a pleasant event is something that never would have entered my mind before and, if I can help it, never will again. And to keep that promise, I'm thinking no more dual DT's, ever. Solo DT's, yes. Co-DT's maybe. Dual, never."

He spoke the last word firmly.

"Since it's the dual DT's you'd like to stop, I'm assuming you think the negative feelings you experienced were a result of your travel with Bly Goodin?" asked Danyin.

Mekkel winced at the sound of Bly's name but quickly regained composure.

"I guess I didn't make it clear. Yes. That blackness came from that tisani, the groundling. Goodin. He was in me, or I was in him, or something. We weren't sharing one of the squirrel or cat hosts at the other end of the universe like we were supposed to. I had no urge for an acorn, or a saucer of milk. I told you what I had an urge for." Mekkel pressed his lips together.

166

"Believe me, I know what I'm saying. I know Transference between kisans hasn't been possible in the past. I know this is really something, and I'll be happy to be in the hovi records from now until Baata descends." He shook his head. "But I'll never do it again. And if anyone does do it again, well, may he or she not go through what I did."

"Now that you're less "foggy," said Teesh, "can you elaborate on some of things you saw in your mind?"

"Some of the things you felt," added Danyin.

Mekkel stood.

"No can do, fella's. It's all forgotten. The memories are a wisp of a wisp of a shadow of a shadow. I just know I didn't like it, didn't like it one bit, and now it's time for me to move on. I've missed I don't know how many appointments, and now that Mekkel feels like Mekkel, thank Baata, I need to leave. I leave it to you geniuses to take over." Mekkel glanced around him. "Where's my assistant?" Mekkel called to the outer hallway. "Timm?"

Mekkel walked out of the hovi's recording view, leaving the image of Teesh and Danyin sitting together, but not looking at each other, each considering his own thoughts.

The group was silent as Teesh stilled the image.

"You heard him" said Teesh. "The blackness came from that tisani. His assistant told us Mekkel won't talk more about the subject, and will not be available for contact for an indefinite period."

"And we can't compel him to talk more with us," said Braelind. "But we can continue to work on understanding what's happened. OK. Vindin. The Goodin hovi next, please."

Teesh changed the blurred hovi image again.

167

Danyin and Teesh appeared on the screens, as disheveled as they'd been in the first Mekkel hovi. They sat in chairs while Bly stood, occasionally strolling to different parts of the room.

Bly needed no more prompting from Danyin than "Bly...." before excitedly speaking.

"Danyin, you know I have Reader abilities. Mr. Vindin..."

"Call me Teesh."

"Teesh. You probably know that all GK's have an enhanced empathy level. Me, I'm a GK, and I'm *also* what's considered a strong Reader. My Reader abilities allow me to perceive a thought here and there with those I don't know, and the ability to receive directed or strong thoughts from family members, including my extended family, which includes good friends like Dan. But this," Bly shook his head while smiling, "this experience with Mekkel Sord cannot be equated with *anything* I've ever experienced."

Teesh spoke quietly. "Maybe this can't be equated with anything anyone has experienced."

Bly saw the empty chair near Teesh and Danyin and settled into it, some of his energy spent.

"It was extraordinary. I was in Mekkel's brain. I intimately perceived what he experiences as certainly and surely as anyone who goes to a Transference Center experiences the inner life of a forest rundy, or a cat on Earth." His smile, never having quite left his face, widened slightly again as he relived his feelings of an hour earlier.

"I was lucky. I went into a kisan who is content to his core. Who is confident. Unless everyone is walking around with such contentment in their innermost being? Could it be? Then I want to go again. I can learn from this. So." Bly looked from

Danyin to Teesh. "Did Mekkel also experience... me? I was too starry-eyed after the trip to notice anything, so I don't know."

Teesh exchanged a glance with Danyin and nodded. "Yes," said Danyin. "We think he had the same experience you did; we believe he experienced your mind. I don't feel at liberty to give you details now."

Bly nodded. "That's understandable."

"For now, we did want you to know what we think occurred. You came to the same conclusion we did. We're hoping you'll be interested in continuing to tell us more, maybe work with us more."

"Absolutely. Especially if I can repeat the experience I had."

Teesh shook his head. "It's not going to be possible to continue work with Mekkel." He saw Bly's worried reaction. "No, he's...fine. For reasons we can't elaborate on right now, we don't think Mekkel will be part of this work."

The real Teesh brought his on-screen self to a blur. "There's a lot more, but I believe that's about all Brae wants me to show right now."

"That's right. I'd like you all to carefully watch the full sessions on your own. Now. Mr. Mesterdide. Please share your thoughts with the group you shared with me earlier."

Danyin nodded. "It's clear that Mekkel and Bly guessed it right. During a nice, innocent, DT, where the intent was to move two kisans to a distant host, an intra-species Transference occurred."

Braelind held up his hand to fend off the questions he knew were at the ready.

169

"Hold up. Let him say more." He nodded to Danyin.

"Thanks. All right. I do think what happened was a result of Mekkel traveling with a GK with Reader capacity. I checked back, not a thorough look yet, but a quick flip, through intra-species experiments. Looks like we did try to do them with GK's, thinking they would, in fact, have more of a capacity to enter a same-species host. Different combinations were tried. One GK and one-non-GK. Two GK's. Nothing worked. But I think the researchers had the right idea. This time we stumbled on the perfect combination. And we'll need to figure out what that was."

Cavnee gave a short laugh. "You think this "worked?""

"Obviously Mekkel had a less than stellar experience. But, it wasn't the same, not even close, to the reports of other intra-species Transferences. In those cases, no one came back with any discernible emotion or image. Those attempts were nothing but unidentifiable, physically painful, sensory input. This was vastly different."

"True." said Cavnee. "Co-DT's are done pretty regularly by researchers and this roaming in each other's brains hasn't happened. So, I guess one question is – was this a fluke?"

Saras had been sitting quietly with elbow on table, and chin elegantly perched on the back of her hand. "I suppose we'd better try again to find out then, shouldn't we?"

All eyes turned to Braelind who regarded them all. He knew they grasped the implications. Could the GK's be used, and the technique evolve, that would allow easy "travel" into another kisan's mind? Maybe GK's wouldn't be needed once the missing key, unknowingly supplied, was understood.

"Lyder, Rith, Timin, Vindin. Get together and decide which of the mechanics you'll each be working on. Keep me

170

posted. Mesterdide. You'll be a traveler, if you're willing, but first things first."

Danyin knew what Braelind would say, so he said it first. "Sure, I'm willing. But you think first I should help Bly lose some of that inner darkness. Otherwise, we can't use him as a volunteer."

"Right," said Braelind.

Danyin leaned back in his chair, hands on the edge of the table. "I've been Bly's Listener for a while, and I'd thought we'd made great progress in improving his life outlook. Now, it's embarrassingly obvious there's more close-to-the-surface pain than I realized."

"Yeah," Cavnee snorted. "Just ask Mekkel. He'll give you a mindful of reasons why Bly needs a major infusion of happy."

"All that blackness," said Maryl. "I hate to say it, but I don't know if anyone could wipe that away. I think you could throw some "happiness layers" on top of it all, and I think Bly's done that. Both Dan and I know his partner brings him all kinds of joy. But sadness from the past? I don't think that will ever completely go away."

"I don't think it needs to go away," said Danyin. "In retrospect, I think Mekkel was about the worst person to have been with Bly. Mekkel has some qualities the VRC uses well, but he's not, shall we say, a deep thinker. I think most of us here could do what he did, and come back and talk about it."

Braelind cut in. "Maybe so. Let's learn more. For now, be Mr. Goodin's Listener. Everyone else, do what you need to." Braelind slapped the table as he moved to stand. "Too many times, in this father's life, I've had to tell my kislings a new world was dawning, yet again, because of what we'd discovered at the place I work. Not that it's been bad news. But I think

171

I'm getting worn out with all these proclamations. Somebody else say it."

Each in the group looked from one to the other. Saras tilted her head back, and enjoyed a deep inhalation and quick exhalation of breath, followed by a short laugh. As she stood she said "We've done it again." She began walking toward the door and swiveled back to face the group. "Or, soon we shall."

As Saras exited, Cavnee nodded his head in approval. "Nice. We should let her make all our announcements."

CHAPTER 29

Lena's eyes flew open.

"What the hell?" she thought.

The dream was at the edge of Lena's memory, ready to slip into waters of forgetfulness. She took a deep breath. Sometimes if she lay still for a moment, yes, there it was. She remembered. In the dream she'd been talking to her mother on a park bench near the Brooklyn Bridge, Brooklyn side. Her mother was assuring her that, yes dahling, she would get married some day and who knew? With any luck, praise God, maybe it would be a Jewish boy. And then Lena saw the streak of light, as if God himself was saying "it *better* be a Jewish boy, young lady."

The light in the dream was intense and surprising, and had awakened her.

Talk about messages, thought Lena. Luckily, I know these things come from my own weird and abstract thoughts, so I'm not listening. She turned her head on her pillow to look at Mooshie, pressed against her side, and Einstein, just beyond, pressed against Mooshie. At the first touch of Lena's hand, Mooshie began to purr. Lena felt a calm sensation seeping into her; the contagion of her cats' serenity.

"Thanks for the good vibes, Moosh." She scratched the cat's right ear, Mooshie's favorite spot, followed closely by her second favorite, the left ear, which Mooshie obligingly turned toward her.

Lena turned her head to see the glowing numbers on her clock showing two minutes before the time her alarm was set to go off. Not bad timing, she thought, if you've got to have a dream wake you up. She switched off the alarm. "I think I've had enough alarms for one morning."

She sat part way up and buried her head first in Mooshie's stomach, planting a kiss, and then stretched to Einstein, bussing the cat on his side. She sat full up and yawned. As she swung her legs over the bed, cats scattered and the mobile rang.

Lena spoke before Rob did. "Hey, gorgeous. Wake up thinking of me?"

"Sorry I didn't make it over last night," he said. "The gig lasted past one, and then I still had the hour ride home."

"In that case, thanks for not stopping by and disturbing my beauty sleep. How was the birthday party?"

"Good. The guy turned 60 without a hitch, and was still standing when we packed up. Barely though. A bottle of booze seemed to be the gift from every guest."

"So if you got home a mere," she peered at the clock "6 hours ago, what are you doing up already, for God's sake? Crazy man."

"You guessed it. Thinking of you. Thinking of downing some coffee in some over-priced breakfast joint, knowing it's worth the price because you're there."

"Oh, get over yourself, Romeo. Yes, we can meet if you'll stop spouting so much sugar. I've got a waistline to think of."

"You've got time this morning? No 18 straight hours of work required to meet a deadline?"

"Actually that might have been true if my assignment, originally due two days from now, hadn't been yanked from me yesterday. That whole "new mode of communication" piece is dead. All the experiments failed, and the PR folks are sending out apologies. Some big R&D fiasco. Which I suggested would be a story in and of itself, but the site guy says forget it." She yawned. "Oh, sorry. I just woke up a few minutes ago. Anyway, it's good to know when a story has fallen down and can't get up. At least I get a kill fee for what I already wrote."

"That's too bad. But, at least it leaves you available for breakfast this morning."

"Yeah." Lena remembered her jerk to consciousness that morning. "Hey, before I forget, I had a dream just before I woke up I wanted to tell you about."

"About me?"

"Not exactly. Maybe indirectly. In this dream my mother was encouraging me to hook up permanently with a guy. However, she hoped it would be," and here Lena adopted a Yiddish accent, "a nice Jewish boy." Lena dropped the accent. "And then a dramatic streak of light hit the horizon."

"Huh. Well, being a nice Jewish boy could be tough for me. Since I'm an atheist. And I never was Jewish. However, I would like to say, here and now, that I do enjoy Woody Allen movies."

Lena laughed. "That's a start. Maybe my mother will work with us. And, of course, I can vouch for the fact you're circumcised."

"Yes, you can. You know I was wondering where you wanted to eat breakfast, but now I think I know."

"Don't tell me," said Lena. "I can see where you're heading. You're going to say we should go to either East Side Kosher or Zaidy's Deli."

"Exactly!

"My mother would be so proud, boychik!"

CHAPTER 30

Bly slept as Danyin relaxed in the seat next to him, occasionally adjusting the transport settings, but mostly paging through hovi notations, and letting his thoughts drift. The gritty, flat overground provided maximum traction for the vehicle's three wide wheels.

They were headed to Posloq. When Bly climbed in beside him hours earlier he'd barely managed a "good morning" before falling asleep. He didn't have to tell Danyin his night had been restless.

Danyin understood. He was taking Bly to a home that had been devastated, and now housed ghosts that few but Bly could see. Bly's Group house had been long since repopulated, though few remaining flesh and blood family members were still there. Bly just hadn't made the trip back in a long time. Those now gone, and the manner in which they lingered and died, were clear in his mind's eye. Part of him hated the thought of once again acknowledging their suffering and absence by visiting the home they should be in.

Danyin had suggested the trip home during a listening session. "Those images won't completely disappear," he'd told Bly. "But you can add new, important ones to your memories. The gorgeous images of Sumee you're collecting are a good start, of course. But seeing some of the family you grew up with, and getting to know some of your new family, I think that will be a help to you."

Bly had nodded as Danyin spoke, smiled at Danyin's rib about Sumee, and opened his mouth to speak. Moments later, no words coming, he shrugged.

"Listen," said Danyin. "If you'd like, I'll go with you. I can make the arrangements. I could use some time away. And I'm

176

dying to see those door knockers you designed up close and personal."

Bly smiled. "I have a dozen at my place. I can give you one. Two if you want."

"Bly ..."

"Just kidding." Bly looked at his hands clasped in his lap, then lifted his head to face Danyin. "Let me think about it. And no matter what, you can still have a knocker."

In the end, Danyin's offer had been the key, Bly admitting the trip sounded appealing if Danyin would be along. By this time the two kisans had spent substantial time together, their bond now teetering between that of professionally connected acquaintances, and that of close friends, both aspects constantly blurring. Each gladly imagined a day when professional expertise would no longer be necessary, and their friendship could fully blossom.

As Bly slept, Danyin glanced at the countryside streaking by all sides of the vehicle, patches of bright and dim color made elongated and anonymous by their speed. The front held a more realistic view Danyin had already spent time enjoying on the trip. They sped through relative wilderness, the kind of scenery he rarely experienced anymore.

Danyin looked again through his hovi, both reading and remembering his first encounters with Bly, who had come to him on Sumee's recommendation. He remembered the handsome young kisan entering his office and recalled his first thought. "Sumee's joking. He needs help? She probably sent him to gossip with me about what a great catch his sweetheart is."

He'd just as quickly caught himself, knowing the talent some had for masking almost anything, including shyness and

177

sadness. Vulnerable to Danyin's warmth and skill as a Listener, it wasn't long before Bly revealed what his mask did not.

Their first session started much like any session with someone who'd been unable to do a DT.

"I thought it was working," said Bly. "I felt as if I were leaving my body. And then, just as suddenly, I was a dead weight in that ridiculous web, hanging there."

The feeling of an aborted DT was predictably the same. It was the reasons for the failure Danyin needed to uncover; the psychological or emotional impedances. The way to uncover them was through talk, interaction. The answers usually, eventually, became evident.

Danyin spoke in his lilting tone, the calming effect of his brogue obvious on Bly's face.

"Let's plan on spending some time together. Let's figure this out. I think you'd like "visiting" Earth, as it were."

The story of Bly's life had emerged after a few sessions. An almost ideal life as a GK in Posloq, living with a close-knit Group in a house and neighborhood much like the ones Danyin saw in the mag realms. It was an enviable life until the disease they called Grett's, caused by the brush with the virrius, settled in his home and slowly, agonizingly, stilled the breathing of almost all those he loved.

Danyin had silently acknowledged the enormity of the tragedy. For a Group Kisan, someone who craved familiar close companionship, to lose his family, was tantamount to death of self. Recovery would take effort.

"I'm truly sorry."

Bly had nodded slightly.

Danyin continued. "So you left your home?"

Another nod.

"And you found a new Group home?"

Bly shook his head as he spoke. "No, not a Group home. A small space. I live there myself." A forced smile appeared on his face. "Very comfortable. And I'm not entirely alone, really. There are others in adjoining spaces."

Danyin had stayed silent, allowing Bly to collect his thoughts with no prodding.

A sigh. "I know what you think. It's uncommon for a Group Kisan to ever really adapt to being alone. All I know is, the thought of being with so many others again seems unthinkable. At least for now. I interact with my neighbors. I work. I hire a corasan to sing with me twice a week. And of course, you know who that corasan is, and I don't need to hire her anymore."

Danyin nodded and grinned in response, yes, he knew the corasan was Sumee.

"Living alone feels right, for now. I know it's not what I'm "supposed" to be feeling. I'm a traitor to Group Kisans everywhere," he joked. "But right now, living alone makes me feel safe. I'm not even sure I want to ever resume my GK life. I mean, the main reason I'm here with you is because I don't want to be a groundling."

Danyin once again allowed a momentary silence to fall between them. He picked up a hovi on a nearby table, and looked at the notes he's made earlier. He resettled the device on the table and turned back to Bly.

"Bly," he said, "I do need to ask a personal question. Would you tell me if you're a strong Reader?"

179

There'd been no pause in Bly's response, as if he was eager to get on neutral ground, away from thoughts of death, and his own peculiarities as a GK. "Yes, I'm fairly strong. I'm told I have a high level of empathy. Thoughts do come through, and especially from those I'm close to, in terms of personal relationship. But it's inconsistent, and so far I've never learned anything embarrassing about anyone. Or at least nothing that embarrassed me." He smiled. "In your field, as a Listener, you probably know that the myth about Readers is more exciting than the reality. It's pretty bland stuff that filters through."

Danyin's thoughts returned to the present, in the transport, as Bly shifted in the seat beside him, turning his sleeping body so that his fine features, framed by his black wavy hair, now faced Danyin. Considering the face of his resting friend and client, Danyin became aware of his own weariness. They had more than a day of travel still ahead of them. He set the auto-drive to a more sensitive and slower setting, and curled up in his own seat to rest.

They arrived the evening of the second day. Despite the circumstances, Danyin was excited at being able to visit the magnificent Posloq homes. As they pulled up to the home of Bly's youth, Danyin drew in a sharp breath. He leaned over Bly, and stared through the transports window at the homes' façade.

"This is magnificent Bly. You had a hand in this design I'm guessing. Unless others in your Group have a talent for design, too?"

Bly, who'd been looking straight ahead, and had not yet turned to face the house, nodded. "I'll plead guilty. Others contributed, but it was my passion from, oh, I can't even remember. Started playing around with how the house looked since I was a kid. I was lucky to have a family," he paused for a moment, but then quickly picked up his thought and turned to Danyin, "yes, I was lucky enough to have a family that let me indulge my creativity. Some of it a little unconventional, too. But they supported me."

Danyin caught his eyes. "That's great." As Danyin looked past Bly, the tisani also turned and looked at the home of his past.

"It does look good, doesn't it?" He laughed. "You should have seen some of my early experiments." He pointed to different spots on the house. "Stone mynie tails curling around doorways, there and there. Colorful eyeball shapes dotting those two windows up there to the right. With eyelashes glued on, I'm afraid to say."

Bly turned to Danyin and smiled. "But I improved."

"Yes, you did," said Danyin.

They were expected, so it wasn't a surprise to see the front door, a gay shade of red, and adorned with one of Bly's signature knockers, swing open to reveal an elderly female kisan. She squinted toward the transport, smiled, and strode out the door and toward them with a youthful step. Another Saras-type, thought Danyin. Those tisani keep their energy over the years.

Bly opened the transport's door and rose to meet the approaching figure. They embraced and Danyin heard their murmured single word exchange.

"Blysune."

"Mother."

The sun caught the older kisans shining green eyes under their slightly drooping eyelids. She let go of Bly and looked around his shoulder to Danyin, still in the transport.

181

"Mr. Mesterdide?"

"Yes, call me Danyin," he said as he hurried to leave the transport and approached the pair, a bag of travel gear clutched in one hand, "Wilina?"

Wilina smiled with pleasure. "You're right, that's me. You must be a good Listener with your patients. You were able to associate my name with me after our RT talk, even though visuals were off, and I inundated you with chatter and a dozen other household names."

Danyin shrugged. "Good guess?"

Bly put his hand on Danyin's shoulder. "Don't listen to his modesty, mother. Dan's a genius, but you need to pull a whisker or two to make him admit it."

Danyin put up his hands in mock fear. "Hey, I thought the GK's were a gentle folk. And," he plucked at various places on his face. "And, no whiskers, I'm afraid."

Wilina and Bly laughed.

"I guess we're not ferocious," said Wilina. "But when you live with a Group, you learn to be plenty assertive to get a decent share of every meal, and maybe, sometimes, less than your share of the chores."

"So, Group Kisans are like the rest of us, then?"

"In most ways," said Wilina. She paused, and she and Danyin stayed silent a moment, Danyin enjoying the older kisan's slight smile.

Wilina turned again to Bly, and gathered him into a second hug. "You. It's so good to see you. Come."

Wilina motioned them to walk toward the house.

As they entered the front room, Danyin reflected that he knew Bly wasn't Wilina's son, though she was, in fact, a blood relative. The term "Mother" was a common endearment, though not required, for any older female in GK settings, just as sister, brother, son, and daughter were. They all considered themselves family, blood in common or not.

Wilina turned to the open door and called "He's here!"

As Danyin walked in the house behind Bly and Wilina, he watched as Bly was hugged on all sides by kisans who'd been waiting inside the door. Even more started gathering, rising from pillows, chairs, and lounges they'd been relaxing in; descending from the two stairways in the enormous living space; and a few hurrying in from adjoining rooms. An almost equal number of mynies of various furs and shades also scurried by, though most were exiting instead of approaching.

Wilina leaned in and said something to Bly, who nodded and smiled first at Wilina, and then craning his head, at Danyin. The nod and smile weren't a surprise. Once the trip had gotten underway, Bly had been uncharacteristically upbeat, talking excitedly about seeing his family. It hadn't been the reaction Danyin expected, and he'd wondered if the anticipation Bly exhibited was all show. But Bly had sensed Danyin's skepticism and said no, he was, for the first time in a long time, yearning to see his home. And he believed it was because of Mekkel, and what Mekkel had unknowingly shared with him.

Wilina hooked her arm through Danyin's. "Bly says he's fine for now. Why don't I show you where you'll be sleeping? You'll meet everyone over dinner. They're too excited now to be civilized."

As he and Wilina walked together, Danyin silently marveled at the home's size. It was comparable to the space his entire living complex encompassed, but that space was parsed into units that held one or two kisans each. This home somehow reflected the comfort of a smaller space, while easily accommodating the more than a dozen kisans Danyin had glimpsed.

There were varying colors throughout the home, muted, elegant, and plentiful. In contrast, thought Danyin, to Bli's current home, painted in beige hues.

Passing into a courtyard open to the sky, Danyin disengaged from Wilina to walk to the raised pond located off-center in the square.

He leaned over the rock wall, tightly bunched violet-colored blossoms sprawling over its sides, and stroked the strong neck of one of the white birds gliding on the water. The bird gave a pleased trill, and nudged its beak into Danyin's hand, encouraging more pets. The creature's two companions, spotting an opportunity, gathered around for their turn.

Wilina shook her head. "You don't know what you've started. Those girls will turn their full charm on and you'll find yourself in a trance in no time."

Danyin smiled as he stroked each bird in turn. "Oh, I love thallies. I had them growing up. When I travel, I try to stay in places that have them." He leaned over and gave one of the birds a kiss on the head, receiving a pleased trill for his efforts. "They're such loving creatures." He turned to Wilina and lowered his voice. "I should tell you I'm one of those kisans you've heard of who claims to have especially nice dreams when thallies are singing."

Wilina raised an eyebrow. "A tad erotic, perhaps?" Danyin nodded with feigned guilt. Wilina leaned in to Danyin and said "You're not alone. Which is why my room is on the other side of the house. I do need to get some uninterrupted sleep, after all." She paused and smiled. "But, I enjoy, occasionally, taking some naps in the vicinity."

Wilina pointed to a doorway a few yards from where they stood. "Your room is quite close to the girls, here. So if it becomes too distracting, let me know. Usually, though, they don't sing for too long at night. Why don't you settle in? The evening meal won't be too long now. Come out any time, or we can come get you when everything's ready."

"May I help?" asked Danyin.

Wilina waved her hand dismissively. "No. GK's routinely make big meals." She turned as if to leave, then turned back to Danyin. "By the way, I think you should know. Bly told me that meeting you and the corasan Sumee were among, and I'm quoting here, "the most important events of his life.""

The grin that Maryl so loved appeared for Wilina. "Really," said Danyin. He stood thoughtfully. "What a great thing for him to say." He shrugged. He looked toward the door of his room. "A nap right now would be perfect. And maybe if I wish hard enough, one or two of those thallies will start singing."

"I'll bet we can make that wish come true." Wilina nodded and turned to walk across the courtyard. Danyin entered his small room. A rich rainbow of colors painted in a stripe along the ceiling contrasted with the solid blue of the rest of the ceiling and walls. A sleeping shelf dominated the room; a small table with a chair the only other furnishing atop the plush floor covering. Drawers were inset into the walls and when Danyin opened one it was empty, ready for guests' belongings.

As he put down his travel bag on the table, and began to unpack, he heard Wilina talking soothingly to the thallies. In a moment, they began to sing. Danyin climbed on the sleeping shelf and reclined, sighing with comfort. Too bad Maryl wasn't with him.

CHAPTER 31

Maryl entered the VRC from a clouded black night, the contrasting illumination transforming the building into a mystical gateway to a realm where dark was banished.

With Danyin away in Posloq, Maryl's sleep was more abbreviated than usual. Without the familiar bulk beside her each night, her bed seemed like foreign territory she didn't want to explore alone. Though she understood the importance of Dan's trip with Bly, she hoped his stay wouldn't be too long. Meanwhile, she was trying to use the time practically, to the annoyance of the mynies who had gathered to stare at her resentfully, as she left home at what should have bedtime.

"Hey!" said an energetic voice, as Maryl walked into the lab, the perky tone seeming mismatched to the time of night.

The voice belonged to a young night monitor, biding his time on off-shifts until he could move ahead at the VRC.

The monitor, a tisani and kyan mix like Maryl, waved from the DT board, and then looked intently at the hovi in his hand. "Just clearing up some stuff from the last trip. Ok." He put down the hovi. "Here to travel? You're Maryl Timin, right?"

Maryl approached the young kisan, and the two touched palms and fingers in greeting.

"I'm Mal," he said. "Jode, the back-up, just stepped out, but he'll be back in no time. Are you pretty much ready? Want to get in position, and when Jode comes back we'll get you," he tapped his fingertips together and grinned, "on your way."

Maryl folded her arms over her chest. "Mal you must be the most wide-awake being on this side of the planet at this time of night. Good for you. You want to tell me your secret to having all that energy?"

Mal gave Maryl a-yes-I've-got-a-secret-smile. "All I can say is my dad loves to jump as a hobby, and my mom, even though she's one hundred percent kyan, loves to run. So, I think it's in the genes. My friends say if they could put me in a cup, and drink me, they'd get twice as much done each day."

"Ok!" Said Maryl. "I'll breathe deeply while you're around, and hope that some of what you've got is contagious."

"I'm happy to share."

As Maryl walked to the webbing area, adjusting her clothing in readiness for the trip, a door to the lab opened and another kisan, this one appreciably more tired-looking than Mal, came in.

"How you doing, Jo?" asked Mal. "We've got a DT."

Jode pushed his hair back and yawned. "I'm ready. I'm a little tired, I admit. But if any alarms go off, I'll be all action, I guarantee."

Mal turned back to Maryl. "I believe him, as unlikely as it looks. I've seen him shift from absolute stillness, to pure movement, in a flash. So, set to go?"

"All set."

Maryl heard the almost-silent clicks from the monitoring board as Mal released the strands that enveloped and held her. In moments, Maryl was covered by the webbing.

Maryl was in the mood to self-position, and so had kept her arms raised above her head as the webbing wrapped her torso. When the fibers stilled, she moved some of the strands around her neck, shoulders, and behind her head, ending with tucking her arms elbow-deep into the cocoon. She felt her eyelids droop and close as she relaxed, and the DT process took hold, her awareness of her surroundings receding, and the

188

sound of wind that was not wind filling her ears. It still made her smile, that she had the sensation of flying madly through the ether as if propelled from a mountaintop, while in reality, her body hung, motionless, in a dull laboratory.

Then she was warm.

Her host's back was sun-drenched. The feeling contrasted with rough coolness on paws and belly. It was Mooshie, on her haunches in the tall backyard grass, the sun's warmth infusing the cat and her visitor with a pure drowsiness; the shaded earth supplying a delicious chilliness. Though on the edge of sleep, an underlying edge of alertness emanated from her host.

Nearby, Maryl saw Einstein through Mooshie's sun-induced stupor, as he stepped gingerly through the grass.

Mooshie seemed to suddenly remember a needed task, her sleepiness ebbing. Chewing on grass seemed the right thing to do. Mooshie's mouth lazily sought some nearby stalks. The aroma was enticing, and Mooshie chewed on the wisps of greenery. "Not bad," Maryl thought.

A ghost image appeared of a largish animal that had, the night before, been in the spot Mooshie now occupied. The cat stopped to consider the vision, pausing mid-chew. Maryl had a notion that Mooshie was considering, not for the first time, that the spot she enjoyed in the daytime held potential danger overnight. Better to lean against Lena and sleep at night. It was a decision made and confirmed, time and again.

The drowsiness that had momentarily decreased, began again to creep through Mooshie. "Here we go," thought Maryl. "Sleep. I just hope there will be some worthwhile dreams."

The content and visual quality of cat dreams were unpredictable. The images could appear gossamer-wrapped, or be in sharp relief, as solid and real as any walk down a street.

189

They could be mundane, and they could be dramatic, ranging from eating, leaping, and lounging, to hurting, fearing, and dying.

As Mooshie slipped into sleeping, and then dreaming, she carried her kisan companion with her. Maryl watched the dream solidify, and saw it was a familiar one. It was the oft-viewed vision she and others had reported in the past. As she watched the dream play out through her host, she thought of watching the pacing Cavnee in the RT he'd made after he'd first experienced the same shared dream.

"I'm not a corasan, but I can only say that what I saw matches what every corasan I know of has ever described, written, or sung about the Baata. And you know what? I used to be a complete unbeliever in the Baata. But what else can it be? It's the dream that's been told, and re-told to all of us, in any number of poetic ways our whole lives. It's those tall tables, beds, whatever they are, spread throughout a walled-in place. Mynies are laying on about half and kisans ...kyan-type kisans only, no tisani...are lying on the others. And then there are those other creatures. Dark all over. Just a few, scattered, leaning over some of the tables."

Cavnee shook his head as he recalled what happened next in the dream. "One of those dark...things...leans over me and does something to my side; the mynies side that is... maybe rubs something over it? Not his hand; it feels too hard. It feels more like the thin edge of a blunt object. I feel movement and pressure. But no pain."

Corasans interviewed by the VRC, including Sumee, had agreed, yes, it seemed the transference travelers were seeing portions of the dream they'd been born with. The religious declared it a vision of the Baata, the origin of all life.

190

Those researchers less spiritual who'd first seen the dream through mynies, didn't have an answer for the shared vision, but they had a theory. They felt the event depicted was a traumatic one for the host animals, and therefore was memorable to them as a group, owing to the enormity of its impact in the distant past. The shadowy dream-kisans were part of a drama whose script non-believers could only guess. An illness being monitored by an ancient species? An age-old ritual unrecorded in more conventional ways?

Hypotheses expanded and multiplied when the same dream was later seen through the minds of Earth inhabitants: the cats. Were the visitors themselves projecting the dreams? Were the cats and mynies communicating over the vast distances that separated their homes? Or was there a past connection between cats and mynies and, the next logical question, a past connection between kisans and humans?

The dream Maryl watched through Mooshie unfolded as if in a haze, as if the power source to the scene was faulty. Cats, unmoving, lay on elevated, soft surfaces, dark figures hovering over them. The tactile and visual perspective of the dream came through one of the cats lying on a yielding surface. Despite the comfortable padding, Maryl felt the unease of Mooshie, and the unease of the dream animal. The vision didn't allow her to sense what the dark figures were feeling. The Baata. Comforting when told as a tale; unsettling when indirectly experienced.

The figures, the tables, and the fear melted as she and Mooshie dropped away from the dream visions, into a deep and dreamless sleep.

CHAPTER 32

The meal with Bly and his family had been a delight of superbly seasoned meats and vegetables, Danyin the fortunate recipient of more of the GK's communal activities: cooking and gardening. Now, Danyin was in his room, jumbling the clothes in his bag even further in his search for something warmer to wear to join the others, gathered in the courtyard, relaxing and digesting.

Danyin tried again, in his mind, to match names to the many kisans he'd met during the meal, but failed. Well, it was a lot of information, and probably not necessary to remember it all. Only two, Wilina and Garin, the latter a handsome male near his own age, were related by blood to his friend, and had been through what Bly had been through. They were the two, along with Bly, he'd arranged to meet with in the courtyard.

Danyin pulled a red shirt from his bag and tugged it over his head and big chest. It would be a lovely evening to sit outside, with only a slight coolness making the extra layer necessary. Danyin left the room, and stopped for a moment near the thallies to admire their beauty.

"You'll do a bit of singing for me later, all right then?" He winked at the closest thallie. The bird blinked both her eyes and gave a quick trill. Danyin laughed. "I'll take that for a yes."

He moved toward the GK's gathered in the courtyard, spotting Bly in a small group in the corner, legs stretched out on a semi-circular seat that held him, Wilina, and Garin. A few kislings leaned on the end of the seat nearest Bly, hands resting on his legs, or teasingly playing with his hands and feet. Bly looked content. The littlest, who Danyin remembered was named Stebinn, tugged Bly's left foot, a mischievous smile on his sweet face.

As Danyin approached, Wilina nodded to him, then turned and spoke to the youngsters. "All right now, the adults need some privacy, so go and play before sleep time. You'll have time to visit with Bly tomorrow." The kislings began to disperse, giving Bly final pats and tugs before leaving.

Stebinn, grin firmly in place, shook his head ferociously as he held on all the tighter to Bly's foot. Garin gave him a mock stern look. "Stebinn. You know Bly needs that foot so he can run around with you tomorrow. Don't you think?"

Stebinn giggled and nodded, but kept his grip on Bly's foot. One of the older kislings walked back and patted Stebinn's head. "Come on, Stebinnsune. We need you to play with us, all right?"

Stebinn looked up at the young GK above him. The temptation worked and Stebinn released his grip on Bly, and transferred it to the hand of his temptress. "Yeah! Play!"

Wilina nodded from her seat. "Thanks, Dev. Have fun," she said as the two youngsters walked away.

She turned to Danyin and patted the ample space next to her on the semi-circle. "Please, join us."

Bly began speaking as Danyin settled into the comfortable seat. "I was just talking to Garin and Wilina some more about my DT with Mekkel, about its effect." Bly looked toward his seatmates. "Both of these members of my Group have kept in touch with me, on and off, via RT." Bly hurried to elaborate. "The "off" part was me. They tried to be in touch more than I was willing to, uh, be touched. But now they're marveling at the change in me. *I'm* marveling at the change in me."

"Count me among the marvelers," said Danyin. "Though, as I've mentioned to you, and I think you don't mind if I speak freely in front of your family...?" Bly shook his head. "I have an inkling your pain is still there, not far from the surface."

Bly nodded. "No. I'm not quite foolish enough to believe my experience with Mekkel was the cure-all. And I honestly don't know how my night is going to be..." Bly's voice trailed off. "But." Bly smiled. "The effect can't be denied. Intimately touching the inner contentment of that -- idiot -- has helped me immeasurably."

The group laughed. "Before now, I can't say I would have disagreed with your assessment of our fine Mr. Sord," said Danyin. "But surely, you think more highly of him now?"

"Oh, yes, yes I do. At first I wondered if I had to be an idiot, too, to experience the happiness that kisan is infused with. But I realized, no. The specifics of Mekkel Sord's external life are not what affected me. It was his internal being that seared and jolted me. How did he come by his confidence, his calm, his...?" Bly lifted a hand in the air, trying to pluck the word he needed from his surroundings. "His joy. How did he come by his joy?"

"Probably dozens of ways," said Garin.

"Hundreds," added Wilina. "And give him as many years as I've had, and the number will be thousands or more."

"Yes!" said Bly. "I don't need to know, exactly, the way he got to that end result. For me," he smiled, shaking his head, "I think I just needed to know that end result was possible. For anyone. I was in a place in here," he tapped his head, "where I wasn't sure such a feeling could exist, like a second skin. I'd forgotten I'd once had that skin. The experience with Mekkel accelerated my understanding. Things were already happening in my life that were helping me remember. Sumee, of course. And if I'd done a dual DT with Sumee, I likely would have had the same experience. Maybe better. In fact, I *want* to do a dual DT with Sumee. Soon."

Wilina and Garin looked at each other, then looked at Danyin. Danyin spoke. "Bly, you know what Mekkel's reaction to the dual DT was."

Bly shook his head dismissively. "A moment ago you all laughed when I said Mekkel is an idiot. You agreed." Bly's companions began to speak. "Hold on, let me finish." Bly paused a moment, looking like a schoolboy who knew his recitation needed to be extraordinary, if he wanted to reap his hoped-for reward.

"Mekkel has a great lightness in his soul. Frankly, I think some of that comes from an essential immaturity. A mixture of a planned avoidance of certain types of discomfort, and luck. He's afraid of, or maybe unfamiliar with, deep emotional turmoil. When he felt my pain, it was completely foreign to him. Sumee isn't like Mekkel. Sumee is a corasan who helps people in pain all the time yet, somehow, holds joy close. She would be fine."

Bly paused again, looking at the concerned faces around him, Garin slowly shaking his head. Bly dropped his head, putting fingertips to his forehead. "Baata, what am I thinking? I'm so wrapped in my own healing that I'm willing to subject Sumee to the same mind-wrenching pain Mekkel went through. Willing to drop my garbage into her." He lifted his head and leaned it against the back of the seat, eyes tracing the stars. "What is wrong with me?"

Wilina placed her hand on Bly's arm as Danyin spoke.

"Look, you know how strong Sumee is, so it's not much of a mind-stretch to guess she'd thrive during a DT with the male she loves. And she might. I'm just saying let's stroll along this path, and not run. My suggestion is, how about a DT or two with me first?"

Garin broke in, getting to his feet as he spoke. "I don't know if that's a good idea either," he said. "I think it should be a GK. And I'll volunteer. I mean, we've already sort of done this kind of thing on our own, us both being Readers."

Bly looked up at Garin. "That's very kind of you Brother, but I don't think so. We Readers think we're getting into each other's minds. I think the reality is that our capabilities actually prevent us from reaching deeply into each other's psyches."

Bly looked at Danyin. "Look, I know I'm the designer. You're the researcher. I'm throwing out ideas here. Unproven. And I'd like to help you learn more, on a scientific level. But Danyin, I also want to do something for myself. And if I can do that, and you and the VRC get something from it, all the better. I'm just asking if you can pave the way. If doing a DT with you is the way to do it, yes, I want to do it. And if you're willing to do one with me, I'd be grateful."

Danyin reached over Wilina and squeezed Bly's arm. "I am willing."

Bly reached up to clasp the hand on his arm. "But I also don't want you harmed."

Danyin held eye contact with Bly as he nodded. "I'll be fine. With any luck, some of your handsomeness will seep into me, and won't my Maryl be surprised?"

Four days later, outside Bly's Posloq home, Bly in the transport, Wilina stood before Danyin, his hands held by hers.

"Danyin. Bly is not as well as when he arrived, is he?"

"Wilina, I wouldn't look at it that way. His euphoria was bound to fade. And coming here, even as welcomed as he was, was a trial. Even baby mynies hold onto trauma, so why shouldn't we? It's normal. And that's good. Hmmm…remind me why that's good?"

Wilina leaned in to hug Danyin. "You'll be joking during your own demise, won't you?"

"It'll make the time fly."

Wilina leaned back, still holding Danyin's hands. "Listen. There's something I do want to say. It may not matter, but it's something you should be aware of when you travel, well, do the thing, the Transference, with Bly."

"Yes?"

"Bly, as he's told you, is a rather adept and sensitive Reader. You should know that when Readers feel distress, even ones less talented than Bly, they may connect at a deeper level than usual with someone they've sought comfort from. They may actually, unconsciously -- tug -- at the mind of the comforter. Under normal circumstances, no harm is done. But during a Transference? I think it's possible your Mr. Sord reacted the same way all others will react in the same situation."

"Believe me, Wilina. Everything you're saying has crossed my mind. And when I go winging off with your son, I will be sure that everyone in that lab is ready to drag us back to our beautiful reality at the least hint of distress. Especially mine."

At the look of worry on Wilina's face Danyin grinned. "Don't you be worrying, Mother. I'll keep an eye on your boy, too."

CHAPTER 33

Maryl laid out the mynies dinner while awaiting the arrival of her friend. Sumee had insisted she required Maryl's in-person attention.

"Not something you want to talk about on the RT?" she'd asked that morning. Sumee's hovering image bristled with impatience, arms folded, mouth fighting, but failing, to find its accustomed smile.

"No," said Sumee. "I'd like to be able to poke you with my finger if necessary."

Maryl now watched her furry trio finish eating as she waited for her visitor; one continuing to lick the empty bowl in search of tasty molecules, one tidily licking a paw and ignoring the remaining few bites in her bowl, and one walking huffily away after having made motions of burying what was so obviously an inedible meal.

Sumee walked in without knocking, treading barefoot from her nearby home, white blonde hair and gray eyes complementing the double-layered transparent dress of vivid blue, ghost lines of white fur from generous bosom to sumptuous thighs glimpsed through the shimmering material. Maryl wavered between judging Sumee's diaphanous outfits as too erotic, and feeling envious of her young friend's bold creativity.

Willo and Claudi performed their duties as house greeters and, in Sumee's case, enraptured admirers, circling Sumee's legs, purring and throwing their gray, brown, and white colored bodies against the swirls of blue. Valin, still shy with visitors, though less so with Sumee, walked a few inches into the front room, and sat quietly.

"Claudi! Willo! And how's my timid mynie boy, doing?" Sumee shared a cheek to cheek greeting with Maryl, then settled on the floor in front a lounger, the two bolder mynies climbing into the sea of dress covering Sumee's lap. One was caressed by Sumee's attentive hand; one turned circles to create a comfortable nest. The third, having slowly approached, sniffed the outstretched fingers of Sumee's free hand that beckoned the reticent mynie to join the party. Valin rubbed his pink nose against Sumee's fingers, then slid the length of his body against Sumee's knee, hidden under dress material. He flicked his tail and exited, as if to say, "All right. I've done my bit to welcome you. Carry on."

Sumee shook her head. "You are a mynie who likes his privacy, aren't you?" she said to the retreating Valin.

"Oh, that mynie. If he can ever get you all to himself sometime, without those other two pests around, he'll give you some proper attention." Maryl had walked back to the kitchen area and pointed to two bottles on the counter. "Some mendo?" She held up one of the containers. "I've got the nasty green stuff you like. Guaranteed untouched."

"Mmmm, sure. The green stuff, huh? Baatasune, you are blessed. Not to mention generous. That isn't cheap these days."

"Thank Braelind. A present. I'm not sure I should tell him I detest that kind of mendo. Danyin hates it, too." Maryl poured two glasses of mendo from separate containers, Maryl's a reddish tint, and Sumee's a murky green.

"Don't you dare breathe a word! Isn't a present that your dear Sumeesune appreciates as worthwhile as one you'd like yourself?" She fluffed her skirts and smiled.

"How thoughtless of me. But, of course."

Maryl brought the drinks back to the lounge, handed Sumee one, and settled in next to her friend. Maryl placed her own glass on the floor, and pulled a pillow from the lounge to put behind her head. Willo defected from Sumee, and crawled into Maryl's lap, her grayness quivering with the storm of her purrs.

"Traitor," Sumee muttered. "Oh, well, I suppose your mother should have one of you. Anyway." She lifted her glass to Maryl, and Maryl lifted hers in reply. "A toast to Braelind Carsinsen. A kisan of infinite taste."

They clinked glasses. "This toasting ritual is marvelous," said Sumee. "Definitely one of the lovelier practices we picked up through Earth DT's."

"I agree. And it's pretty much the norm now. Amazing how a good idea can take off."

"I'll toast to that, Marylsune." They both took another sip from their glasses.

"So, what's up, Sume? What's the emergency? Does this have something to do with the dual DT next week? Has Bly talked to you about it?"

Sumee rolled her eyes skyward. "Hold it. I need some more liquid strength before I answer." Sumee lifted her glass dramatically to her lips, tilted her head back, and swallowed a gulp of the mendo. Her eyes closed, and a languid smile appeared.

"Now that's better. That's really better." Sumee tossed her hair back. "The answer to your question is, yes, *my* darling has spoken of almost nothing else besides the upcoming DT he's doing with *your* darling." Sumee tapped the side of her glass with the tip of a fingernail, pausing. "My question, the question that keeps coming back to me, is "what if?"

"What if? What if, what?"

"What if, something goes *fantastically* wrong?" She sighed. "Of course, Baata knows, the twines of my worries in life could be woven into enough garments to clothe everyone on the planet. And in most cases, these fears affect no one but me, and need not concern my clients or loved ones."

Sumee laid her drink aside and shifted toward Maryl, laying two hands on her friends' hand. Claudi complained with a meow but stayed in place. "In this case, however, my dear Marylsune could be affected."

"Sumee, I think that mendo went right to your pretty head because I have no clue what you're talking about. Enlighten me."

Sumee released her friend's hand, and leaned back against the lounge.

"Have you talked to Mekkel Sord recently?"

"Talked to him? No, I don't really know him."

"Well, you *do* know the outcome of Bly's DT with him?"

"Of course. I've seen the follow-up tapes. Bly was ecstatically happy, and Sord almost suicidal."

"Exactly. And you chose a good word, because I've spoken with the corasan who works regularly with Mekkel. She says she's never *seen* such a change in a client in such a short time. She says he cannot shake the darkness he touched. She told me because she wanted to be sure I wasn't in some self-nihilistic mode, choosing to be with Bly! I had to assure her that little of the pain Mekkel experienced from the inner Bly Goodin, is evident in the outer Bly Goodin. Not that Bly is all smiles these days. You know he's been struggling since his trip home."

"Yes, Sume, I know. And I also know he's excited about the dual DT with Dan, which I think is all for the good. And yes, I have heard about what Mekkel is going through. Dan has shared all that with me. Poor Mekkel."

The sound of exasperation from Sumee brought one of equal intensity from Claudi. "Yes! Poor Mekkel! And will I soon be saying Poor Danyin and Poor Maryl as the one you love starts reeling around in despair after a peek at the inner workings of my love?"

"Sumee." Maryl gave a dismissive laugh. "Is that what you're worried about?" Maryl reached across the billow of blue that was Sumee's skirt, and handed Sumee her set-aside drink. "Here. Take this. I'd like to make a toast."

Sumee accepted the drink, but retained her worried expression. "What? A toast to dark days ahead? May we face them with strength? Please."

Maryl lifted her glass. "I said I'd like to make the toast, please, if you don't mind." She lifted her glass and waited until Sumee lifted hers, accompanied by a dramatic sigh.

"A toast to the kisans we love. One has already released a demon or two and is now working, with a little help, to bid farewell to the rest. The other has, for a large portion of his life, invited the darkness of others to temporarily inhabit him, in order to help them in their internal housecleaning efforts. A toast to the merger of these two worthy and well-matched souls. One is following a new course of renewal, and the other a well-trod path of therapy."

Maryl lifted her glass and clinked it against Sumee's motionless one.

Sumee lowered her glass without taking a sip. "Maryl, you're acting like what Dan and Bly are doing is routine. But

202

it's not. I know Dan works with troubled psyches all the time. But he doesn't enter them. No one does. Not to this extent. Not even the Group Kisans. That's the difference."

Maryl moved her back more comfortably into the cushions behind her, hands encircling her glass. "I won't deny there are unknown elements here. But, if Danyin feels all right and I feel all right, I think you should feel all right. And, I don't want to hear "what if"... no." Maryl put a hand up to silence Sumee's' next words. "Even if something happened, we'd work it out. Danyin. Me. You. Bly. Don't worry."

Sumee closed her eyes, her shoulders relaxing. "I just love Bly so much. So much." Opening her eyes, she looked at Maryl. "And you and Dan, too." She sighed, and pursed her lips. "All right. But just understand this. If anything goes wrong, I may resort to wearing orange for a year which, as you know, will not be at all flattering to me, and could bring angst to all who look upon me. But, I don't want to hear a single complaint about it." She flung back her hair, chin upraised, the hint of a smile appearing.

Maryl laid aside her glass, and placed her hands in prayer position. "To Baata I say: "Whether she dons orange or not, I shall always love my Sumeesune."

Sumee snorted and lifted her glass. "Yeah. Wait until you actually see me in orange. You think these are empty threats I make, but they're *not*."

CHAPTER 34

Lena banged through the front door, carrying all five of the supermarket sacks she'd filled at King Soopers. As the bags started obeying gravity, Lena lunged toward her living room couch, cans and fresh fruit rolling together on the futon seat.

"Just in time. Score!"

Einstein, curled peacefully a moment before at the end of the couch, now stood on all fours, eyes wide, ears erect, nose dipping slightly toward the dropped groceries.

"Sorry, fella'." Lena leaned in to scratch Einstein's head but missed her target, the cat pulling his head back to sniff her fingers.

"That's right. What am I thinking? Sniff first, pet after. Do I smell good? I should."

Einstein backed away from the proffered fingers, and gave a wake-up shake of his head, declining the pet.

"Well, you be that way. You're just mad because I woke you from your nap. What, you didn't get your usual 18 hours?"

Einstein leapt off the couch, anticipating the predictable destination after Lena's arrival home at night. And the cat was hungry. It was later than usual.

"All right, time for dinner. Sorry it's so late," she said as she walked into the kitchen. She looked down and saw that two cats had magically appeared at her feet.

"Yes. It's definitely time for a dinner. And I'll tell you what." Lena turned and opened a narrow cupboard. "Since I made you wait so long, you get a treat." The ears of both cats twitched at the word "treat," and Mooshie lifted her head.

"That's right. Tuna treat. Yum." The cats swirled around and through Lena's legs as she opened the can, and scooped equal amounts of the fish into the bowls resting on the floor. The meowing, going from low to loud as the tuna's aroma increased, changed to the sound of rapid munching.

Lena walked to the kitchen table and pulled out a chair, giving a tired sigh as she sat down and watched her cats eat their special meal. It brought her pleasure, watching the cats enjoy their food, the two mini-behemoths unrecognizable from the starving kittens they'd been when she'd adopted them years earlier from Rocky Mountain Pet Rescue.

There'd been five kittens that day, all from the same litter, eyes still blue with babyhood, retrieved from where they'd been left to fend for themselves on the shoulder of Interstate 70. One, the sixth of the litter, had been flattened by a driver who likely hardly felt the bump, while crushing the small, soft body. Three of the kittens had been quickly adopted, the story of their precarious beginning a heart-tugging encouragement to prospective owners.

Lena spoke her thoughts aloud. "Only two of you scrawny things left when I got there. And I actually went to get puppies!"

Most of her life Lena had bought into the stereotypes about cats, having not known many while growing up. Hers was a family of dog lovers from way back. She thought cats were standoffish. Loners. A bit nasty. Now she knew those stories were rarely true, and cats were now about 50-50 on her love-o-meter vis-á-vis dogs. She'd always need a cat in her home. But she still adored dogs, still felt her heart melt at the sight of floppy ears and a panting tongue. She sighed at the thought. It was another Rob thing. He'd told her he wasn't big on dogs. And that was a problem. Another problem.

The sleep was a good sleep, his dreams filled with scent images of the morning. Damp, uneventful.

His heart pounded, and brain flared, at the dull thumps of sound that awakened him. The split second of fear quickly dissipated as a strong familiar scent permeated the air.

"Just in time. Score!"

Smells rose from the rolling objects, but nothing good. Nothing bad.

"Sorry, fella'." Lena leaned in to scratch Einstein's head but missed her target, the cat pulling his head back to sniff her fingers.

The image from the fingers was immediate and strong. Tall. But not the Rob tall. Another tall. Walking with this one, eating with this one, lying with this one. Unfamiliar. Unpleasant, because it was unfamiliar. Something to be examined slowly, another time. Not now. Now, it was time to walk, then to taste.

"All right, time for dinner. Sorry it's so late."

CHAPTER 35

The music suddenly distorted through the headphones. Damn. This gig demo needed to be mailed the next day.

As Rob took off his headphones, and turned to grab for the phone, he thought: Lena. It wasn't likely, he knew, but in that split second, he'd hoped.

"Gandy, love! How are you, sweetie?" Rob squeezed his eyes closed. Lord help him from hippies with phones.

"Hi mom, how's it going?"

"Great, honey! Your daddy and I are visiting friends in Utah, working on a Burning Man piece."

Burning Man. Rob remembered the gathering of tens of thousands of people his parents had taken him to when he was a kid. The communally-living assemblage brimmed with a creativity that was encouraged to overflow into the creation of objects and antics. It all culminated in the dramatic burning of a giant wooden figure. He never went to the event anymore, feeling like it was a remnant of childhood, even though his parents still attended. He felt a stab of nostalgia. It was actually pretty fun. Maybe he'd go again sometime.

"What are you guys working on? Will it be better than the motorized couch we saw that one year?" That couch. It had been Rob's favorite. People wearing wide grins, as they sat comfortably on a wheeled sofa that rolled through the Nevada desert sands. It was hilarious. It even had an end table with a lamp on it.

"Funny you should mention the couch, because we were thinking of that when we came up with this new transportation thing. We were thinking about how people, at a party, always gather in a kitchen. You know? I mean, you can have the living

207

room filled with cushions, and snacks, and a huge group of people go sit in the kitchen!"

"That's true, mom." Rob smiled, shaking his irritation at being interrupted. As eccentric as his mom could be, after years of meeting other people's mothers, he still admired the enthusiasm she showed for every new project. Would it ever wane? He hoped not.

"So, we're doing a table!"

"A table?"

"And chairs. On a moveable platform. With linoleum! And the whole thing will be very, you know, fifties. Chrome, Naugahide. Maybe you'll come this year and see it. You'd love it, I know. And we miss having you come, Gandy."

"I know, mom. It just gets so busy with gigs that time of year. And that is how I support myself. In fact, I'm kind of in the middle of some important recording right now."

"I know, I know. You're busy. Well, we were just taking a break – we've got the linoleum installed now. And I thought of you, honey. Maybe it was the linoleum. Kind of like the floor at Grammy's house you used to play on."

Rob's mother sighed. At least in that way she was like every other mom, Rob thought. Worried about her child, and nostalgic about the past.

"So how is your girlfriend? Lorna? Is that her name?"

"Lena."

"Lena, of course."

Rob hesitated. Did he need to say anything right now? Maybe a joking reference to Lena's "why can't you be in one real band, instead of ten temp bands?" question. But it hadn't been funny when she said it. And it definitely hadn't been funny when she'd become less and less available over the last few weeks.

"Yeah, she's fine. We've both been crazy busy so we haven't been doing much lately. You know how it is."

"You know, honey, I don't know how it is. Your daddy and I have barely had a day apart since we've met. Almost thirty years now. But. Maybe young people are different now?"

"Yeah. It's different, mom." Rob knew that the conversation, unchecked, could go on indefinitely, one topic flowing into another. "Well, it was great to hear from you. I'd love to see some photos of the table piece when it's done."

"All right, Gandy." She laughed at herself. "I mean Rob. I'm trying to call you that, hon."

"I know, mom."

"All right, then. Talk to you later. Love you, sweetie."

"Love you too, mom."

CHAPTER 36

Danyin relaxed in his office chair, the RT he faced fading along with the memory of his sister's concern that her three newborns were still not walking at the age of 6 months. Danyin had comforted her, assuring her it was perfectly normal for young ones of only partial tisani background to totter uncertainly until the age of 7, or even 8 months. Though the kislings looked wholly tisani, his sister was forgetting that she, herself, was a fairly undiluted kyan.

His mind went back to the issue he'd needed to stop thinking about for a few minutes. The reason he had welcomed his talkative sister's call.

His concerns were real. He was stepping into an unknown vista. Maryl, Cavnee, Saras, and especially Teesh, had done what they could to prepare him, to anticipate experiences and outcomes of his DT with Bly. No one was discouraging him from going, though. The potential for increased knowledge was too compelling.

His parting from Maryl that morning was casual. "It'll be fine. Remember, I'm not Mekkel. And if you think I am, I may have to throw a bit of a jealous fit, because what are you doing of thinking of that dim-brain when you should be thinking of your charming Dan?"

He'd left himself time this morning for this side diversion; a stop in his office, a talk with his sister, time to view some mag realms that had nothing to do with Transference, nothing to do with his vocation.

But, now it was time to leave. He smiled to himself at the gravity of his own thoughts. Chances were, things would be fine. Was he so averse to potential emotional upheaval?

Apparently, yes, since he still felt agitated. He switched off the mag realm, and readied himself for the short walk to the VRC.

"That tisani is excited. Looks like he's on the verge of getting married, winning a prize, and solving a medical mystery all at once. If he doesn't stop breaking out into grins every two seconds, his face will be killing him later."

Teesh grunted assent, nodding his head distractedly at Cavnee's prattle, as he jostled the board controls. Cavnee was sprawled in a nearby chair, doing nothing but watching Bly circle the webbing area, the tall kisan occasionally standing dead center in the area, or perching on a nearby stool.

Cavnee called to Bly. "How you doing, Bly?"

Bly turned his head toward Cavnee and left the webbing area, walking toward the control panel.

"I'm fine. Probably making you nervous with all my stalking around. I'm early. But, I could barely sleep last night, so I thought I'd just get here and get a start as soon as possible after Dan arrives."

"Yes, so you mentioned before. Excited, huh?"

"I'd say I don't quite have the word I need to describe how I'm feeling. Maybe I'll invent one. And I'm open to suggestions."

"Now that's an interesting challenge. Words to describe…" Cavnee paused to think. "Splendid anticipation," maybe?"

Bly was about to reply, when the far door to the lab opened and Danyin walked in. Instead of replying to Cavnee, Bly strode to meet Danyin.

211

"Morning, Dan! You ready?"

Danyin gazed up at his friend. "In a hurry, are we?" Bly began to apologize for his rushed manner, but Danyin waved away the apology. "I'm as excited as you are, Bly, and I'm ready. I've had a leisurely morning, and I see no reason to hang about chatting. Let's do it. Let's make some more history."

Danyin turned to Teesh and Cavnee. "All right. Are we ready? Recorders rolling?"

Cavnee nodded from his chair. "Smile. We're already on." The recording was both for posterity, and for Braelind, Saras, and Maryl, who would not be present. Braelind had decided the travelers would benefit from an uncluttered environment.

Danyin and Bly walked to the webbing area. This time Bly knew what to expect. He didn't need to be manipulated into place, as he had with Mekkel. He extended his hands, ready to have them grasped by Danyin's. Both stepped in to the other, heads side by side, each chin resting lightly on a supporting shoulder.

"Thank you," whispered Bly.

Cavnee looked at Teesh, whose gaze was fixed on the webbing ring, and the two kisans entwined within. Cavnee spoke in a quiet voice. "Looks like you've got the next move, Teeshisune."

Snapped from his reverie, Teesh first rolled his eyes at Cavnee's jokingly familiar address, then nodded. Looking down at the monitoring board, he began the DT process. Teesh looked up, and both he and Cavnee watched as the bodies of the two travelers disappeared under the encircling webbing, their combined weight pulling the threads, the threads pulling back, until a comfortable stasis was achieved, like sleepers wiggling into the cocoon of a well-blanketed bed.

"Are you both ready?" Teesh asked? He received a unison reply.

"Ready."

"All right. Here we go." Teesh turned his attention back to the monitor, and set the process in motion. As the vibrations began, the two travelers seemed to drift into sleep. Almost immediately specks of light began waltzing across the screen, reflecting on Teesh's face.

Cavnee rose and walked to Teesh's side. Both watched the monitor and the representation of Bly and Danyin's travels. The traveler's bodies, now uninhabited, were of less interest, and left in the care of the web and built-in safeguards.

As was typical on a dual DT, the two sets of blinking dots slid slowly across the screen, a dot here or there straggling or progressing away from the others, but each set maintaining its own path, all of the specks moving forward.

Then a change. Teesh sharply inhaled. "Remember this is not unexpected," said Cavnee. "We guessed we'd see this." The migration of the dots had changed. The two sets seemed to be seeking each other out, like feathery seeds blowing in the wind, controlled by a matchmaking breeze that made them mingle, and continue their travels intertwined. The two sets stalled mid-monitor, intent on coalescing.

"Just another minute." Teesh glanced at the webbing area, then to a small monitor beside the larger one before him. "Dan's looking good." It had been earlier agreed that Bly and Danyin would be allowed to go further than Mekkel and Bly had, as long as neither traveler, especially Danyin, was showing signs of distress. Looking over to the web, Teesh could see there was light perspiration on Danyin's forehead, but his expression was neutral. As a small sigh escaped Danyin's lips, Teesh began to work the monitor controls.

"Ok, that's good. As Braelind told us, caution's the word for this first trip. Let's bring them back now, nice and slow."

Upon return, they'd been separated. Danyin, with Braelind and Saras in one room, and Bly with Teesh and Cavnee in another, both asked to relate their perceptions of the brief dual DT.

Seated across from Bly, Cavnee recognized the look on Bly's face. It was the look Saras had after a pleasurable DT. It was the look he glimpsed in his own mirror at home after an hour of intimacy with his partner Linny. It was bliss.

Bly tried to put the feelings into words.

"The core sensations were similar to my trip with Mekkel. It was something like you feel after three glasses of mendo, only in this case, your head is still clear." He gave a delighted laugh. "You're in control, and your mind feels capable of solving any problem -- but the intoxicating effects are there. A tempered exhilaration."

Teesh, in a chair next to Danyin, nodded. "It almost sounds like there was a chemical reaction."

"Yes," said Bly. "The words I was using made it sound that way. But to be more accurate, I'd say it was only chemical if emotions are chemical. Which, who knows? Maybe they are. It was..." Bly stopped and tightened his lips, searching for the right words, like a lover who wants to share his secrets, and doesn't want to make a blunder.

214

"It was as if I became immersed in Dan's emotions. And I say emotions, not thoughts, because each brush brought a rush of feeling, as if I stood in a room filled with hundreds of suspended multi-colored scarves, random ones touching me gently, and each one, each color, each texture, setting off another feeling. And many of those were feelings of ecstasy."

Teesh nodded again, encouraging Bly to continue.

"By ecstatic, I don't mean sexually ecstatic. It was like having new and brilliant thoughts appear you hadn't imagined before. Like the moment you understand something, an idea say, which will now displace a long-cherished, but damaging belief. To use banal terms, I'd say I felt waves of confidence, security. Also, calm, joy."

Teesh thought, but did not say, "*As if you're unconsciously extracting what you most need?*"

Now Cavnee spoke. "Did you feel you could control what was going on? Move around, to use your analogy, in the room of scarves, and, hold longer onto some pieces than others?"

Bly shook his head. "No. There was no control. Except now. Now, I feel the control to examine what touched me. I feel like I'd like to walk and think for hours." Bly suddenly straightened in his chair. "What am I thinking? I can't believe I didn't ask this already. How's Dan?"

Braelind could see the moisture on Danyin's forehead. He knew Danyin had checked out fine physically. But subtle damage, psychic damage, was never immediately apparent. Still, Danyin's oft-seen hint of smile was there.

The kisans who'd examined Danyin for signs of physical harm had been excused, Danyin assuring them he felt fine,

215

nothing to worry about, for Baata sake, let him get on with important things. Only Braelind, Saras, and the eye of a recording RT remained in the room.

"I understand why my trip with Bly was short. You needed to be sure things were going smoothly, that I wasn't in pain, and so on. But I'll tell you. I would gladly do another DT with Bly right now, and stay all day. I would dive in deeper, and swim through those thoughts, and let them wash over me."

"So your experience was nothing like Mekkel Sord's?" asked Braelind.

"I don't know. I can't be sure. Bly told us he was tense and frightened at the start of the DT with Mekkel, despite Mekkel's attempts at calming him. And Bly seems to have recently gone through what seem to be enormous changes at a very basic emotional level. So. Was I better equipped given my skills a Listener? Or was the experience inherently gentler?"

Saras spoke. "You mentioned Bly's thoughts. How did you perceive them? Was it like an animal Transference experience?"

"No. And yes." Danyin spoke slowly, wanting his words to accurately describe an experience only he and Mekkel had encountered.

"With animals, as we all know quite well, we feel linked during a Transference, to various degrees, depending on the situation, and the animal. We perceive, and imagine we interpret correctly, feelings like anxiety, joy, boredom. We see images, which we interpret as memories of the animal, or shared memories of the species. This trip had all those elements and more. It was a tumult, but a subdued tumult, to use what may seem an illogical phrase. But I think an accurate one."

"And, of course," said Saras, "Transference, kisan to kisan, were impossible in the past. The tumult, in that case, wasn't subdued. It was deadly." Her sigh was dramatic. "Dear Danyin, this may open doors that were bolted tight to us before."

Braelind broke in with his measured baritone. "Now's not the time to look beyond the moment. We know we'll need future tests to see if Bly is an oddity, or if there are others, probably other Group Kisans, like him. The temptation is great to discuss ramifications, but right now is the time to capture Danyin's immediate impressions."

"Yes. Understood," said Saras. She straightened and continued. "Danyin?"

"Yes. In practical terms, I felt this DT with Bly brought me to places I've only been able to perceive second-hand through my clients. The sadness and confusion others relate to me affects me deeply. One of my main goals, when listening, is achieving empathy and, with careful listening and questions, I think I do achieve empathy -- or something close to it -- regularly. This experience with Bly? Instant empathy. Like a mixture called Someone-Else's-Emotions poured over me and bang, I understood. Intimately."

Saras tilted her head, listening, but remained silent, as did Braelind. Danyin continued.

"There were images. And there was language. Conversations that must have taken hours in real time stored on a speck, and understood in a moment. But I heard each word, or imagined I heard and understood, each word. His memory was mine."

"Do you think they were real memories?" asked Saras.

"Good question," said Braelind, with a laugh. "Real memories, or those conversations we constantly have in our minds?"

"I don't know. The conversations seemed real. And that underlying current of sadness. That was real. It was either proof Bly has a long way to go in turning his life around, or proof that some pain will always be there for him, whether buried, or a scratch away from the surface. Maybe some of both. "

Saras collected her thoughts, then asked, "You said you instantly, "intimately, understood" Bly. Can you tell us what you understood?" Brae nodded approval at Saras' line of questioning.

"That may have been an overstatement. Yes, I did feel that I wore Bly's innermost being like a mantle, snug around me, and an exciting feeling it was. But I would need more time to truly piece together cause and effect. And even then, I'd just be speculating."

"Which of us completely knows our own mind, let alone the mind of others? But, being connected, as we were, took the guesswork away, as far as mood and reaction. How often do we smile when we're sad, and hide the melancholy of a moment from those around us? Only a lover, or dear friend, might see through the ruse. With Bly I was privy to the face behind the face."

Braelind leaned in. "And it was pleasant to you? Not a hint of what Mekkel Sord felt? Of course, even if all seems well, we should wait a few days to see if there's an aftershock."

Danyin sighed, seemed about to speak, then squeezed his eyes shut, appearing suddenly weary.

"All right," said Braelind. "That should do it for now. Do a solo free association RT as soon as you feel up to it. We'll leave, and you can do it here. Then stay slow and low for a few days, to note anything you remember."

"Sounds fine. I'll get going on the RT now. I don't need a break yet."

Braelind, now at the door, turned to face Danyin. "And Mesterdide."

"Yes?"

"Take time off. I know you'll say you don't need it, but assume I insist. Which I do. Enjoy yourself. Spend time with Maryl. She can have some time, too. We're going to be busy for a long stretch, I think, so you both might as well take some time now."

CHAPTER 37

Danyin had tried to relax, to contemplate, consider, the space his mind had inhabited with Bly's. He'd shared lengthy unedited thoughts on the VRC's RT, and more at home. Finally, now, his head felt emptied, and his body restless. Maryl had suggested the visit to the Athletics Arena.

"Brae told me to remind you that he doesn't want you back at the VRC right away, and that he wants you to have a real break before you return. So why not some exercise? I could use it, too. I feel like I haven't done a real workout in a month."

"That's because you haven't, my sune. Not that it shows, of course. But that's a wonderful idea."

At the arena they considered the choices that hour on the schedule. "Game of batden going on," said Maryl. "Want to get in on that?"

"Maybe." Danyin thought of the slippery skins he'd need to don from calf to thigh, and fingers to elbow. They'd enable him to shimmy along the floor to move the slick oval away from other player pairs, and ultimately into one of the four wall slots. "I do enjoy a bit of batden, but it seems strenuous after lazing around for so long. I might need to work up to that."

"I feel the same way. Maybe something more self-paced?"

They'd settled on the leaping space, easier for Maryl with her half tisani heritage, than Danyin with his less agile kyan genes. But they'd had fun, Danyin taking running jumps, and sliding on the lower curves and hollows of the space; Maryl making her lover laugh at her pseudo-daring bounds of height and length, accompanied by comical faces of abject fear before each.

Cleaned up after their exertions, Danyin's arm draped over Maryl's shoulder, they'd walked into the fragrant twilight to a dinner out.

"More mendo?" Danyin asked.

Maryl put her hand over her glass. "No thanks, I'm still working on what I've got. Anyway it's probably a good idea to begin digesting now before the DT. But the meal was delicious."

Danyin nodded and sipped at the small amount of liquid still in his glass. "It was good to have the space and time of a few days to consider what happened with Bly. But I'm ready to leave the cocoon now."

"Are you?"

"I am. So, tell me. Anything new I should be expecting at VRC? I know you got the nudge from Brae not to clutter my mind with anything extraneous the last few days."

"True, I did. Well, there is something. I've already talked to Sumee about this, since it's a topic close to her heart."

"Romance?"

Maryl almost dropped the drink she was sipping with her laughter. "Dan, you're amazing."

"Well, I know that Sumee enjoys talking love and relationships with you, her Marylsune. So what's going on? Something between Bly and her no doubt? You said this was related to the VRC?"

"Yes and no, not related to Sumee and Bly. It's our favorite humans."

"Oh. Our surrogate babies? Rob and Lena? What are those overgrown kislings up to now?" Maryl and Danyin both felt disappointment at not finding partners soon enough to share parenting. But they had each other, their mynies, and their distant Earth "kislings." "You know they fight, and it's usually nothing."

Maryl looked genuinely sad for a moment. "Well, this time it's something. Not that it will affect our research since we can still visit both of them as we always have. But, you know how it is. I'd thought of them as always being together."

"Sure, me too. So what's made you think they're really in trouble this time?"

"It's what Lena told a friend in her living room. And my host was wide awake for at least part of it, because the friend kept playing with her while Lena spoke. She said Rob was "history.""

"Oh yes." Danyin sighed. "We've learned what that word means. She give any reasons?"

"She talked about incompatibility on an inner level."

"Oh, Baata above. Kisling talk. Of course, I was there myself many years ago. She say anything else?"

"Yes, one of the things she said is now on the Listen List, so we can work on what it means. It's the word "suburban." She said twice that Rob's tastes were too "suburban.""

"What in the world could that mean, do you suppose?"

"We don't have a clue."

"I wonder," said Danyin. "Do you think it could be a relationship breaker for us if my tastes were suburban? I guess depending on what it means, it could."

222

Maryl gave Danyin a mock frown. "Well, the reality is, I'd be hard pressed to come up with anything you'd be remotely likely to do, or be, that would be a relationship breaker for us."

They leaned into each other, lips brushing, fingers entwining. Danyin whispered. "I feel the same way." Leaning back, Danyin asked, "Still up for that quick DT tonight? Or does heading home make more sense?"

Maryl disengaged one hand from Danyin's and reached to the side of his head, fingers brushing through his hair. "Let's still go to the lab. It will give me even more energy for later."

"Well, then. I vote for whatever gives you the most energy."

Arriving at the lab they found Mal, briskly adjusting instruments and scrutinizing monitors, though the lab was empty, save Jobe, eyes slit, mouth agape, seated beside him.

"Why, if it isn't Jumpy and Snoozy," said Maryl.

"Hey Maryl, Danyin. You know I was hoping you two would be showing up one of the nights I was on."

"Why?" asked Danyin. "The charming way our mouths fall open when we're in the web?"

Jobe flinched fully awake. "Hey. What's goin' on."

"Hold on." Mal walked to a nearby cabinet and reached in to an uncovered opening in its side. Peering in the cubby, he sought something with his hand. The cabinet was part of Teesh's territory. Maryl knew that if Mal was fishing around in there, Teesh had earlier given him the go-ahead to do so. "Ah, got it."

He pulled out a small object, no larger than the two hands he cupped it in. It was wrapped in fluffy brown paper. "A

223

present." Mal walked to Danyin and Maryl, extending his hands.

"For both of you. A gift. From Mr. Vindin and his partner. Mr. Vindin tells me his partner made it. And it's beautiful. Mr. Vindin gave me a peek."

"From Teesh? What is it?" asked Maryl. "And what is it for?" She turned to Danyin. "Are you celebrating something?" She turned back to Mal as Danyin shook his head. "What?"

"Your fiftieth co-DT."

Maryl shook her head, pleasure lifting her smile. "You're telling us Teesh was keeping track of how many DT's we've taken together?"

"Well," said Mal. "The fact that you've done quite a few together is obvious to anyone. And Mr. Vindin, in case you don't know it, is actually a pretty sentimental guy."

Maryl and Danyin laughed. "I guess I didn't know it," said Danyin. "I'm surprised. And touched. Shall we see what our gift is, my sune?"

Maryl, who'd taken the softly wrapped package from Mal, now clutched it to her breast. "I say no. I say, let's wait until after the DT. Let's open this together at home."

"I guess Teesh isn't the only sentimental one. All right, let's wait."

The DT turned out as Maryl had hoped it would be: uneventful. They both opted to choose two previously unvisited hosts in separate locations. Webbing together didn't necessarily mean going to hosts in the same place. They'd both had the urge to bring back tales to the other, instead of directly sharing the adventure.

The two trips were routine, and both opted to do only brief hovi entries, noting the trips occurred, instead of descriptive RT's. By the time they reached home, both were rested, and ready to continue where they'd left off earlier at the restaurant.

"You know, there were just not enough pets on that visit," said Maryl.

"I think I can help fix that," said Danyin and proceeded to more than compensate for Maryl's touching and stroking deprivation.

Danyin, relaxing sleepily in bed, was startled to wakefulness when Maryl suddenly said "Oh yes," and left the bed and the bedroom. Danyin looked at the time. Still not terribly late, but he was ready for sleep.

Maryl returned and sat on the bed, the soft brown package in her hands. "Shall we open this now?"

Danyin, lying on his side, propped himself on his elbow. "Sure. Allow me to watch, while you do the hard work."

Maryl smiled as she unpeeled the cushioning layers of the present. "I'm guessing this is going to be a carving. That's what Teesh's partner specializes in. Did you know he's pretty well known for his work?"

"No. Didn't know."

Maryl continued lifting alternate sides of the multi-layered packaging. "So the question is, what will this be a carving of? Oh my." Maryl breathed the last words, as the gift appeared in the nest of wrapping. She lowered the opened bundle so Danyin could better see what she held.

"Two mynies," said Maryl.

Danyin sat up in the bed and lifted the carving from its cushion. He moved the piece from one palm to the other, gently using a finger to follow and feel the smooth variegated black, gray and white wood. The figures slept nestled into each other, forming an almost perfect circle, broken only by a few errant toes, and the triangle-shaped ear of a back-leaning head.

Danyin handed the carving back to Maryl who examined it, her feeling of pleasure, so much an element of that day, once again clear on her face.

"Well," said Danyin, "I think Teesh must have described it perfectly to his partner."

"Described what?"

"The sight of us. When we're in webbing together."

"Dan. I don't know where you get your beautiful ideas, but I love them. They fill my heart." As she leaned to kiss him and move into the bed next to him, Danyin made room for Maryl and the object of love she placed between them. He embraced Maryl and felt her gentle vibration.

CHAPTER 38

"Down boy, down Merle. Jesus." Matt pulled the dog back by its collar and leaned down to encircle his arms around his pet. Rob was still standing outside the just-opened front door, regaining his balance after Merle's loving greeting.

"Holy Christ, Rob. I swear this dog loves you more than just about anybody, and acts like a damn fool with you because he knows you don't much like dogs. He wants to impress you, and thinks jumping on you is the way to do it." He shook his head as he ran his hand lovingly down the dog's long back.

Rob walked into Matt's tiny living room, wiping imagined dog fur off his jacket front with the hand not clutching his fiddle case.

"Go on in. I'll put Prince Charming here out back for the duration."

Rob nodded in appreciation. "Thanks, Matt. No offense, big guy," he said to the dog who looked lovingly at Rob, tongue lolling. The dog gave a quick plaintive yelp.

Rob spoke as he turned and walked down the hall to Matt's bedroom, which doubled as a rehearsal space. "Sorry fella', it's no use. Kind of like being gay, straight, or bi. You either like cats, dogs, or both. I'm afraid cats are my thing."

Matt leaned down to receive a wet kiss from the dog, as he spoke soothingly to him. "Just no accounting for taste, Merle. But I love ya'."

A few minutes later Matt joined Rob, a beer in each hand. "I think you're safe now," he said, offering Rob a chilled bottle.

Rob laid down the fiddle he'd been tuning, and accepted the beer. He untwisted the cap and took a sip as Matt did the same with his beer.

227

"Take a load off," said Matt, gesturing toward the long narrow couch that filled a wall in the small room.

"Yeah, thanks. Sounds good. But I'm ready to play anytime."

"Me, too. Just thought I'd like to unwind a few minutes."

"You still have a lot going on at school?"

Matt snorted his ascent. "Shitload of work. I mean a lot of work. Dang. I'm trying to remember that people bringing in their sick little kitties and pups to me might not welcome swearing once I'm a vet. I think all the cursing I hold back at school, I let out at home these days. Sometimes it's worse than it ever was. Gotta' figure out a way to let the words seep out of my ears like smoke, and not make themselves heard." He sighed. "I'm working on it. Least I knew I said that last one."

"Well, I'll try not to make you curse. I'll try to play in tune and be a good boy." He put on a foolish grin.

Matt laughed. "Look at that. Lena like to kiss that crazy face of yours?"

Rob's smile disappeared as he put down his beer on a side table, and leaned to pick up his fiddle. He resumed tuning.

"Hey, just a joke, friend. What? Something up with Lena?"

Rob felt the knot rise in his throat as he worked to focus on tuning. He took a quick breath in and out, feeling the knot loosen, the danger of showing too much of what he was feeling now gone.

"Yeah. I guess she's out of the picture." He looked at Matt. "For good."

Matt clamped his mouth shut, and stood up to reach for his banjo where it leaned just beyond Rob against the couch. He picked it up and started tuning. After a minute he stopped. "Was that your idea or hers?" he asked.

Rob kept plucking at the fiddle as he spoke. "Oh. It doesn't matter, does it? I guess I don't want to talk about it right now. Maybe some other time. All right?"

"Sure, no problem, bud." Matt turned away and bent over his banjo as he tuned. "Goddamn bitch," he murmured.

CHAPTER 39

Danyin walked into the lab and saw Teesh. A few weeks earlier, Teesh had been dismissive of Danyin's thanks for the carved gift.

"Oh, well, that was his idea," Teesh said, pointing to Hiri across the room, staring at a console.

"Wha..?" Hiri had turned his gaze from the screen. "What was my idea?"

"Baata, you kislings have good hearing, don't you?" said Teesh.

"Kisling? I'm not exactly a kisling, Mr. Vindin. I mean I work here with you, backing you up..."

"All right, sorry. You're just younger than me, that's all. Seems an easier task to accomplish all the time, I'm afraid."

Hiri left the lab and Teesh busied himself with objects on a nearby lab table, turning his back to Danyin. "Maybe it wasn't his idea. Maybe Jobe. I don't remember. Anyway, Bon did a great job, as usual. I'll let him know you like the piece."

Danyin had walked to Teesh's side and put an arm around his shoulder as the scientist leaned over his work. "Teesh, my friend. What are you embarrassed about? Both Maryl and I were touched and grateful. We actually slept with the little wooden buggers the first night, and you can tell Bon that. Thanks."

Danyin loved the piece. He felt Bon's carving was a perfect depiction of the emotional connection he felt with Maryl -- entwined, sensual, and comfortable.

With no embarrassing thank you's to deal with on this day, Teesh looked up with a nod as Danyin entered, followed a moment later by Cavnee.

Cavnee headed to Hiri's usual spot near the monitoring board and Danyin called to him. "Cav! Great to see you. But what are you doing in the co-pilots seat?"

"Oh, I still do this now and again to give the usual kislings a break. I don't mind. It's kind of relaxing."

"Well, it's fine to see you. I feel we'll have especially personalized care today. Where's my merry co-traveler? Is it possible he's already bored with our trips after…what is it now? Getting in the range of a dozen DT's?"

Teesh answered. "Bly's coming. He called to say he was going to be a little late because, uh, he got held up at Sumee's place. But he's on his way."

"Ah. That's a great reason to be late. And now I can expect exceptionally cheerful thoughts on this trip. Good. It's worth the wait."

Moments later Bly arrived, striding to Danyin. "Dan. Sorry to be late. I was…"

"I heard. Enjoying the company of our Sumeesune. No problem at all. Shall we?"

The webbing process took only moments, both travelers accustomed to positioning themselves quickly and comfortably; those monitoring them familiar with the appropriate settings and preparations.

Calls of "Ready" rang from Cavnee, Bly, and Danyin. Teesh began the process.

"This is almost getting boring, you two. So at least squirm a little in the web, would you?"

Danyin laughed. "No promises. All right. Let's go."

Teesh began the DT. Cavnee settled into a side chair, hovi in hands, and the bodies of the two kisans sagged into the enveloping, grasping fibers of light.

Maryl would later wonder how one's life could change from one breath to the next, as hers had that day. From the moment she'd received the RT, said "Yes?" and received her response.

CHAPTER 40

If they'd been speaking, their voices would have had an edge of echo, the acoustics such that sounds were slightly amplified. As it was, only an occasional breath could be heard. That, and the sporadic sound of water displaced from water.

The liquid they were immersed in, blue as Bly Goodin's eyes, lapped just below the two chins, of the two cheeks pressed together, Bly's and Sumee's. Bly barely returned his Sumee's underwater embrace, his nude body unmoving beneath the surface, his face impassive above. The two had shared this oblong space many times, fingers smoothing skin and sleek wet fur; probing underwater depths in each other's bodies; and, ultimately, deriving calm from the smooth concave comfort of the vessel, the warmth, each other. But Bly's lethargic demeanor was not one of calm. He could read snatches of Sumee's worried thoughts, and feel the concern rippling from her.

Bly spoke to the air, his voice barely above a whisper. "There were times I was closer to Dan then I am to you now. His being and mine."

Sumee remained silent, both the therapist and lover within her acting as guides.

"As if my heart had been reborn. And my body. My legs. My arms. My mind. I wanted to touch the hair on my head, knowing it would be a new thing. A thing you hear of in songs. A thing you whisper, when you fall in love."

Sumee's voice was quiet. "My sune." She pressed her face closer against his, and placed a hand on Bly's opposite cheek. What she heard was no longer new. The word combinations changed, but the meaning stayed the same. Bly's guilt drove him to confess the intensity of his experience and, through retelling, punish himself over and over.

"You were in a place the rest of us can only imagine. And," she caressed Bly's cheek, "I think, in some ways, you're still there. I hope you'll come back to me, Blysune. Not to forget what's happened, no. But to let go a little. Let more of yourself come back to me. It's lonely without you."

Bly turned to Sumee, meeting her eyes for a moment before once again looking ahead. "I want to. I do. Believe it or not, I'm struggling to. I just still can't believe Dan won't be coming back."

It was true. Though weeks had passed, Sumee wouldn't soon lose the memory of the call from Cavnee, his voice urging her to hurry to the VRC. Then arriving to hear, before she even entered the room, Bly's croaking yells, diminished in volume only, eventually, through repetition. Then seeing the body, and Maryl on the floor beside it, quietly petting the hair, stroking the chest, her pale face glistening with the tears which, like Bly's screams, seemed to go on and on.

RT || Cavnee Rith

"All of us who were there yesterday, at the DT where we lost Danyin, Danyin Mesterdide, are doing an RT. Of course, we've all been interviewed. Extensively. I understand this is for ongoing study. So. From the beginning."

Cavnee usual wry smile was absent; all energy instead transferred to pacing strides. The occasional buzz reminded him he'd broken the invisible filming sight lines, and he needed to reign in his travels.

"The trip started off as usual. More than usual. So boring and typical that we joked about it."

Cavnee cleared his throat, urging the welling emotions to remain silent and crouched for a little longer. It had been only a day. He'd have time alone soon, where he could once again let the creature sadness out.

Would the tragedy have been easier to take if he hadn't been there? Hadn't seen it all? He inwardly marveled that he'd even been there. He rarely assisted with DT monitoring anymore. It had almost been a lark, since he'd had some reading to catch up on anyway.

"Most of the trip went as usual. At least, as usual for those monitoring from the sidelines, like I was. Until we went to bring them home. That's when we saw something was wrong."

The recollection was vivid. The dots on the screen, moving together like batden players and their discs, usually close but with separating slips and slides along the way. Teesh initiated the return, only absent-mindedly checking the screen, his thoughts already on what he and Bon would be making for dinner that evening. Cavnee, in the seat reserved for the back-up, was startled from his reading by Teesh's yell.

Cavnee, needing only to stand and lean over to see what Teesh was seeing, quickly understood why Teesh was simultaneously scrabbling with instruments, pressing the alarm, and giving Cavnee instructions. "Go to them."

The monitor revealed a problem. One series of dots on the screen slid quickly to the right, as they were supposed to, their movement a visual representation of the return of "self" to the body of one of the kisans. The other dots moved just as swiftly to the left, like two sides of a soap bubble expanding away from each other. Until it burst.

Teesh jabbered as he slammed his hand on the monitor then continued slapping the unresponsive controls. "I don't know what's happening to Danyin. It seemed like he left Bly and was heading for a host, and then just slipped out. But to where? Why can't I get him back?"

And he couldn't get him back. Neither could Cavnee or the succession of technicians that came at the sound of the alarm that was rarely activated, rarely heard. They came from all areas of the VRC, from days off at home cut short, from doing business miles away. And Maryl came.

In his RT, Cavnee related all he could remember of what became a blur of faces and activities, alternately working on the monitor, or prodding the motionless forms of the two in the Web, one breathing on his own and appearing fine, one connected to a machine that simulated breathing. He remembered the sounds of the machine indicating that it, too, was failing. That it was unable to correct the defect it would never experience. The death of flesh.

"It was tough. When they finally unwebbed them, Bly had to be quickly moved back, while Danyin was laid down. But Bly already knew. He knew he'd been mentally "unattached" from Dan at the end of the DT. He knew that the body next to his had to be pried away. He started yelling."

"Maryl arrived soon after. She's tough. She just walked up, lowered herself to Dan and…well, this part isn't useful. So I'll end here. I will say I was relieved there was no…burning smell…like Gwinde had. Whatever happened must have been different than what happened to her."

At this thought, Cavnee could no longer hold back the tears.

CHAPTER 41

Maryl had thought she'd take in Mally and Dally, the mynie twins she loved as much as her own brood, but ultimately she couldn't. They seemed out of place with anyone but Dan, his imagined ghost the third presence that seemed always to be with the two. They ended up with Cavnee.

Part of her felt like she'd forsaken Dan's actual offspring. Another part felt she needed to do whatever was necessary to sustain herself through each of the hours that threatened to crush her with the grief that could, for minutes at a stretch, make drawing a breath seem the most laborious of tasks. In those minutes, any number of a thousand past scenes with Dan replayed in her mind.

Maryl's mynies knew. She'd returned from the VRC, unaware of the ache in her knees from their time bent on the hard floor by Dan's body. She'd walked a few feet into her home and stopped. Crying and remembering, time had stilled and her body had halted. Emotions called for full reign, and the body acquiesced. After what might have been an hour, or might have been minutes, Maryl felt something soft caress her elbow once, then again, then again. She turned to see Willo, her chubby furred body wobbling, balanced on the edge of a living room seat, arm stretched out, paw in mid-air, reaching out to her.

"Willo." She scooped up the mynie in her arms, and realized that both Claudi and Valin were at her feet, their usual distaste for each other forgotten in the importance of comforting Maryl. Both heads craned up, both pairs of eyes watched her. She felt Willo begin a tenuous purr, more subdued than her usual uproar, as if asking "Is purring all right?"

"It's all right," she said. She sat down, Willo still in her arms, both Claudi and Valin jumping to either side of her on the roomy seat, Maryl finally acknowledging the ache in her knees, and the ache in her being. The mynies leaned into Maryl, knowing this was what they needed to do for now. And there they stayed, tender purrs and soft crying the only sounds.

The clutter of Maryl's home which had been patiently kept at bay by Danyin, returned. The mynies reveled in the newly created sleeping spots. The détente between Valin and his former nemeses had broken permanently, and evolved into both full-fledged friendships, and the occasional full-throated rivalries.

"If Dan could see this, he wouldn't believe it," Maryl told her pets, the three curled together in a heap of dirty clothes. She reached down and gave each of the three heads a light pet in turn. "And I don't mean the dirty clothes. Although, that would surprise him too, since I had gotten a lot neater when he was around." She sighed. "All right. I should make an effort to get this place back into shape. Tomorrow. Today VRC."

"You know you can take as long as you need," Braelind reminded her when she'd called the day before. She knew, she'd said. It was enough. And she'd gotten permission to do a DT the next day.

Cavnee greeted her as she entered the lab. He'd been to see Maryl during her mourning, and had brought her out for meals with his partner Linny. But he still greeted her with a hug. It wouldn't be status quo for some time. Maryl asked after Mally and Dally, and was assured they were fine, but probably wouldn't mind a visit from Maryl. Especially if she brought along a few bumpees.

238

Teesh, too, had seen Maryl while she was away from the VRC, he and Bon stopping by for reminiscing. He walked over to Maryl and laid his hand on her back.

"Glad to see you, Maryl." He brought his hand back to a pocket on his jacket, his capacity for reassuring physical contact depleted. "What say we get started right away?" he said as he walked to the monitor and Cavnee followed.

Maryl noticed they were set up in a different part of the lab than usual. Of course. They wouldn't use the space Danyin had died in. She couldn't believe she hadn't even considered that she was re-entering the place where she'd knelt by Danyin's body, the body so familiar to her for years, so unfamiliar then in its unresponsiveness to her touch. She shook her head as if to shake the memory out. No. She still felt good about this place. She and Danyin loved it. All that past wasn't going to be wiped out. But she'd use the new webbing area. That was all right.

"So, Braelind told us you had a particular DT in mind?" asked Cavnee. He knew what Maryl had requested, but he didn't say it. Let her have the option of changing her mind, and no harm done.

"Yes. Aim me for Einstein. I know I might land in Mooshie, but if you can try for Einstein, I'd appreciate it."

Teesh nodded as he bent over the monitoring screen, making adjustments and making no comment.

"You sure, Mar?" asked Cavnee. "Not too, I don't know, nostalgic? So soon?"

"Maybe. But, that's where I'd like to go."

"You got it, gorgeous."

Maryl smiled. Teesh rolled his eyes. Life was moving on.

CHAPTER 42

She was filled with the warmth of the Earth's sun.

Einstein chose the moment of Maryl's arrival to rise from the kitchen tiles, stretch, yawn, and push through the cat door to the backyard. He walked to a sumptuously flower-adorned bush Maryl knew was called "lilac." The color reminded Maryl of the Kisa clouds. The fragrance, almost a taste to the cat, a sweet taste, sent a shiver of pleasure through her host's body and, by extension, her own. She could, at this moment, imagine those who were light years away, and only meters from her body. Cavnee grinning the grin that so annoyed Saras and Teesh, glancing up and saying something like "Things are looking good. She's smiling."

Maryl thought of Danyin, of the many times her partner had visited Einstein, and been where she was now. Seeing through the eyes she was seeing through now. She felt he was with her. She tried to move her thoughts from such musings, not wanting her body in the web to be frowning, or crying, or anything else that would cause Teesh to pull her back.

Einstein settled under the aromatic bush, kneading the grass to create an even more comfortable bed. Within moments he drifted into sleep. And Maryl heard a voice.

"Is that Maryl?"

Maryl's body in the web jerked in shock. In the lab Teesh jumped.

"I'm bringing her back," he said simultaneously working controls to pull Maryl from the DT, and turning on the alarm to bring help.

Cavnee nodded as he hurried to the webbing, kneeling down, arms pushing into the webbing to hold Maryl. "Ok."

"Is that Marylsune?"

The endearment faded as Maryl was jolted back to her body, gasping for air, eyes flying open. Her arms strained against the webbing to return Cavnee's touch.

"Cavnee. Baata. Someone spoke to me. While I was there. In Einstein. That's never happened. Not even in a co-DT." She blinked, realizing she'd been staring wide-eyed, all her energy pointed toward the memory of the voice she'd heard. "I think it was Dan."

Cavnee leaned further in as the webbing retracted from Maryl. "All right, you're all right. Take a deep breath." The webbing slipped away from Maryl, leaving her in Cavnee's embrace.

Maryl tried to steady her breathing, to catch the breath that had lately seemed in such short supply, and was now so suddenly abundant.

Danyin sighed. Or had the sensation of sighing. There was no one, so far as he knew, now there to hear the sound. If it was a sound. He felt a warm breeze ruffle Einstein's fur. His fur. Einstein settled in to the spot in the flower bed where the earth was cool was under his belly, and the sun was hot on his back. Danyin, too, settled in.

Braelind, followed by a cadre of kisans responding to the alarm, had joined them, though Maryl had barely acknowledged him as she paced the webbing area. Braelind motioned to the responders to wait before doing anything.

"I should go back. I know you all did the right thing to pull me back, but I'm all right now. I need to know, VRC needs to know, what's going on. Is it a vestige of Danyin from his early visits? Or is he there? And if he's there, then what? Oh, Baata." Maryl grasped her forehead in her hands, rubbing her temples, as if willing the answers to her questions to work their way in through her massaging fingers.

The others stood in a semi-circle around Maryl as she walked and spoke.

"Maryl. What do you mean you "heard" words? Are you sure you didn't just hear something through the cat's ears? A person leaning down and whispering could have surprised you."

"Brae!" She stopped and looked impatiently at the VRC chief, knowing her voice was loud and not caring. "It wasn't that. I would recognize that. No, I wouldn't say I heard words. They were…images. Images with the force of words. Like reading a story that said "Danyin said "hello," so I knew Danyin was speaking. But it felt akin to hearing. As if, in that realm, what Danyin was doing passed for speaking."

Braelind nodded. "All right. Let me tell you what we know. Let's sit down."

Maryl's mouth opened, her breathing once again cut short by surprise and confusion. "Brae…?"

Braelind sat in one of two chairs in the area they'd been standing; Cavnee bringing two more. Braelind indicated to the emergency responders they could leave, and Teesh shooed away others working in the lab before also joining the circle.

"We were planning to tell you soon, so this moment works fine." He paused. Braelind Carsinsen, no matter how momentous his message, would not be hurried.

242

"It's been remarkable. Later, I'll play you the RT's we've been gathering, and I'm sure you'll agree with that assessment. All right. To begin with the known past. As you know, travelers frequently experience dreams of cats during Earth DT's. These dreams sometimes reveal sounds and images of the cats' experiences from that day, or scenes we believe are from their past. The dreams also may depict experiences of days and pasts of others in their species, some from the present, and some from distant times. Some dreams seem to appear only once. Others appear often, and throughout the species. Strong memories of joy, pain, and surprise, relived and remembered."

Maryl felt a panic of impatience threatening to break through in the form of words that would reflect her growing anger as she listened to Braelind recount these long-known facts. What had been withheld from her?

"So why am I telling you what you know? And where does Danyin come in? I'll tell you. He comes into the story about a week after his," Braelind paused, looked at Maryl, and continued, "death." Maryl responded with the smallest of nods, her expression grim and her mouth resolutely shut. "It was Burk, who you know. He rushed to do an RT transcript the moment he returned, to be sure he remembered everything he'd seen and heard. Then he sent it to me."

Maryl squeezed her eyes shut for a moment, guessing where Braelind was going, a small part of her almost not wanting to hear. But a larger part did.

"Burk said he'd started off the DT in an unknown cat, one we had no record of any traveler having visited before. Not unusual so far. The cat was awake for a while, sat and watched its owner, took a bite of food. Then the cat went into the bedroom, jumped up on its owner's bed, and went to sleep. The first dream images were so prosaic that Burk had been on the verge of pulling out. Then the unexpected images appeared, and Burk realized the cat wasn't dreaming some mundane dream featuring a mouse or a squirrel." Braelind's gaze had never left Maryl's, and he didn't move it now. "The cat dreamed about you."

"Me?" The word squeaked out after Maryl's sharp inhalation of breath.

Braelind nodded. "The cat dreamed from the perspective of someone who knew you well. The vision showed you in a language class, an English class, from years ago. And then some scenes from the Athletics Arena, maybe not all that long ago, was Burk's guess."

Maryl's words came out as half-whispers. "Dreams from Dan's perspective. His dreams."

"That's what we guessed. The question was, did Danyin leave his dreams from the times he visited hosts and slept as his hosts slept? Were they images left when he died? Or...?"

"Or," said Maryl, "is he there? Is he somehow still dreaming, thinking, living. In a sense."

"Yeah," said Cavnee, "in a sense we know zero about."

"But we're working on figuring it out," said Teesh.

Maryl spoke breathlessly. "All of you knew? Except me? Why didn't you tell me?"

Teesh and Cavnee remained silent, Maryl's gaze still on Braelind. Braelind had the answers, and Maryl wanted them.

"Maryl, of course it was my call. I felt we needed to know more before we told you. If you're angry, be angry with me."

Maryl stood up. "Yes, I'm angry. I'm angry with you. Brae. What if Dan is...there. Out there? What if it's only temporary? What if I've lost the chance to connect because you were trying to protect me?" Maryl balled her hands and closed her eyes, trying to keep her anger from exploding into a screech. Drawing in and releasing a long breath she spoke again. "We've worked together how long?"

The three kisans were silent.

"Send me back. Send me back now. Nothing can happen to me. Nothing was wrong when you pulled me back. Now. Now."

Brae looked at Teesh who shrugged his agreement. "I pulled Maryl back because of her shocked reaction, and because, well, I'm jumpier than usual. And with good cause, I might add. But, in truth there was no real reason to pull her back. There was no indication of physical danger."

Brae nodded.

CHAPTER 43

Through Einstein's half-slitted eyes, Maryl could see Lena. Looking up from a cool shaded flagstone of Lena's backyard, Einstein saw the young woman reclined nearby on a chair made of what looked like bands of cloth. The slim cloth bands of the chair weren't much slimmer than the two strips of clothing Lena wore, one across her chest, and one below her belly button. Einstein made a small half meow as he stretched on the flagstone.

Lena, skin glistening, eyes covered with darkened glasses, glanced over at Einstein. "What's going on, Einny? You getting a tan, too? And you don't even have a swimsuit on, you nasty boy." Lena stretched her arm out toward Einstein, the cat's head just beyond her reach.

Her hand hovered in the air for a moment as Einstein lifted his head to sniff the tips of Lena's fingers. The image was a recent one. Lena running in the front door and heading straight for the bedroom, unaware of Einstein padding along behind her. She tugged a dress over her head revealing a nude body, one pale stripe across her chest, and another across her hips, the rest of her skin contrasting the light areas with a creamy light brown. She stood, hands on hips for a moment, scanning the room. "Ah," she said as she lifted first the top and then the bottom strip of cloth from where they'd been dropped by the side of her bed. The image faded.

Lena adjusted her body to a more comfortable position on the chaise. She was in heaven. If Rob had been here, he'd now be reciting to her a laundry list of health hazards she was exposing herself to by roasting in the sun with nothing on but baby oil, sounding much like her parents. So what? Die young, stay pretty. True, if she lived a long life she'd probably look like a saddlebag, sooner rather than later. And chemo would be no fun if she got cancer. Lena sighed. Crap. Crapcrap. Rob had gotten to her even when he wasn't there, and was out of her life for good. She got up.

"Right back, Einny. Got to get some damn suncrap on." She muttered as she opened the screen door. "Maybe I can still get some color with 15…"

Maryl listened. Or what passed for listening.

Nothing. Einstein, settled comfortably, and on the edge of wakefulness, heard only the commotion of nature around him. The same things Maryl heard. Bugs barreling through the grass. A bird, somewhere down the block, making a shrieking racket that sounded like a psychotic tirade, but was probably no more than high spirits and a full belly. Even the breeze made its presence known with a low whooshing sound.

Go to sleep, thought Maryl. Maybe Dan could only communicate if the cat was asleep. Or maybe Dan was in another cat. Or maybe Dan was nowhere. Maryl fought a wave of helplessness. She couldn't do anything to make what she wanted to happen, happen.

Great, she thought. Just when I was coming to terms, even a little, with Dan being gone. And now this.

"Better than nothing, though, don't you think, Mar?"

It was Dan's unmistakable brogue.

Maryl knew her body, her real body, so far away, must have jerked in the web. She willed Brae, Teesh, and Cavnee to leave her alone. They must know she was all right. A moment passed and nothing happened. She wasn't pulled breathlessly from Einstein. She was still there.

She didn't know how she did it, but she did it. She replied.

"Dan? You're here? Danyin, do you know where you are?"

"I'm here. With Einstein. And, well, I think I've figured out that I don't have a two-legged body to go back to, right? Wait. No need to answer. I know. I see it now. I'm sorry, Mar."

Could Danyin see the image in her mind that would forever burn brightly? The memory of kneeling beside his still body?

"Dan, I'd say this is one time you don't need to be sorry."

"I guess this situation confers eternal forgiveness on me, eh?"

In the lab, Teesh and Cavnee heard Maryl sigh, and noted the quickening of her pulse. "Still ok," said Cavnee.

"So, you know. You saw it…in my mind?"

"Kind of. You gave me dozens of images in reply to my question."

"Before this, you didn't know what happened to your body? You didn't have pain?"

"Ah, the whole thing was short. Over really quickly."

"What whole thing? Tell me. I know, I can tell, sense, you want, what, to spare me? Don't. I've been "spared" enough lately, believe me. I want to know, Dan. I have to know." Would Danyin perceive her bitterness at having been previously so maddeningly sheltered?

"All right. But I know you. Don't dwell on it after I tell you. It's over now, all right?"

"All right." Maryl imagined Danyin, in the flesh, telling her his story. He'd be taking off a warm layer of clothing, rolling up his sleeves, maybe asking for a beverage to better lubricate his story tongue.

"All right. Are you ready? I'm going to show you."

It was like a hovi show. Reminiscent of the dreams she saw through her hosts during Transference, but brighter. Maryl saw scenes of Kisa. She saw Sumee laughing, drawing her face near to snuggle, kiss. They were Bly's thoughts, she realized. Dan was showing her what he'd seen on his DT with Bly. The thoughts started dissolving, and she knew that Dan had understood that the dual DT with Bly was ending, that he was being pulled back. But he wasn't pulled back. With a heart thudding jerk, he found himself in a host. A terrified host. He heard tiny high-pitched mewls, and knew they were coming from the creature he inhabited, a kitten.

The kitten galloped through leaves and branches, heart pounding, hardly able to see through eyes that had little practice with sight. Not a newborn kitten, but not many weeks since its birth. The kitten didn't understand what had happened to two of its littermates, but felt the shock of their pain wafting to her, telling her to run.

Danyin knew what happened next, though the kitten never did. It had been a boot, worn on a heavy foot, which had come down on her, stomping her once, twice, the pain and fear escalating for a long moment which was just as suddenly gone.

And then Danyin was elsewhere. Not in his body. But somewhere else, where he felt dazed, but pain free.

Maryl tried to reel in the net of emotions she felt after witnessing the kitten's murder. Anger, sadness, disbelief at the cruelty of the act. But she remembered that she needed to try to control negative reactions that would be seen by Teesh and Cavnee, both ready to cut short her visit with Danyin, if they felt they should.

"You found you were in Einstein."

"Yes. I didn't know it right away, but it became obvious soon enough. I don't know how I got here. Did I travel half way around Earth? Or a hundred meters? I don't know. When I eventually did realize where I was, I tried to get out. All the usual ways. Nothing worked."

"After a few days, I decided to channel my fear into what I knew best. The kind of observing VRC taught us. Observation duties. At that point, I thought I would still make it home again."

Maryl was silent. There seemed no use in describing the despair she'd experienced since his body had died. He'd seen it. Maybe even felt what she'd felt.

"It's when I finally stopped trying to "leave" that I realized my relationship with Einstein had started to change."

"Change? How?"

"I've tapped into a deeper, I guess I'd call it, communication, with this cat. Deeper than anything I ever felt during a DT. I can more intimately perceive his thoughts and anticipate his reactions. I more thoroughly experience his sensations. As far as I know, the cat doesn't perceive me. I've tried talking to him, creating images of things I'd like him to do, like jump on a chair, let's say. But he doesn't seem to "hear.""

Maryl could sense Danyin's excitement. She knew the feeling. It was the feeling of a mind ablaze with new revelations.

"I'll tell you Maryl, this body… Einstein controls it but it feels like mine. My tongue, with bristles brushing against sharp teeth. The delectable aroma of the food Lena gives us. The haze of complete joy that envelopes me as I fall into sleep in a safe environment."

"My perception of his memories are the greatest change. They feel unblocked, tumbling in all the time when we – he's – asleep. Both personal memories, and species memories."

"So everything you're experiencing is beyond what we – I – experience as a visitor?"

"Well beyond. And Mar. I've discovered something. Something exciting I'd be willing to bet my life on. Well, let's say I'd be willing to bet Einstein's life on it."

"Danyin."

"Mar. One of my poor attempts at humor. I guess it's easy to lose a body, but hard to get rid of a rotten sense of humor."

On another world Maryl sighed, and a tear trickled down her cheek, and Teesh gave a small nod, acknowledging both the sound and the show of emotion, and confirming both were all right.

"Amazingly enough I "heard" that. A sigh. Ah, Mar, my sune, my love. Believe it or not, things could be much worse. Of course, I flashback to the life I lived with you, to Mally and Dally, to my work, my patients. It's hard when I think of all that. But. I think what I've discovered eclipses the importance of my one little life."

"Danyin, nothing eclipses the importance of a life."

"Mar. If you really thought those words through, I know you'd take them back. But I love that you said them. Let me rephrase. I've discovered something that will alter the history of our species. And maybe our future. Let me show you."

"Show me? Like you showed me your...the kitten's death?"

"Yes. But this is different. You'll want to see this."

There was a pause.

"Dan? Danyin? "

"I'm here. But I'm tired. Dead tired. I won't be able to show you now. I'll tell you, the flame in Einstein burns brightly, but not for long. Come back again later. Maybe tomorrow. "

And then there was silence. Silence as perceived in this small new universe. Einstein's world.

CHAPTER 44

Though he sensed the underlying agitation, the body he inhabited was physically comfortable. He caught a glimpse of Rob's face through Matilda's eyes as she glanced upward. That's one depressed man, he thought. Matilda lay pressed against Rob on the bed, folded into the curve of his thighs and stomach, while Rob listened to music. Half-listened, the visitor guessed.

The visitor was most surprised by the feeling he was getting from Matilda. It felt like empathy. As if the cat knew how unhappy her person was, and wanted to comfort him, seeming to even intentionally looked up at him now and again, gauging his mood and feeling a swell of – what? sorrow? – when she saw how little his expression had changed, how sad he still looked.

Matilda knew that her person had been coming and going as usual. But in between times he was different. Ever since that other one had stopped coming over. This seemed fine to Matilda. But she understood it wasn't fine for her person. She burrowed in to Rob while Jon, her visitor, shared and noted her emotions.

CHAPTER 45

Maryl had left the exhausted Danyin. The essence of Danyin. She returned to find him the next day, an emotional RT recording and a sleepless night the boundary between her visits. On the first return visit, Maryl couldn't make contact with Danyin. Or on the next. After five more trips, marking five more failures over the next few days, Maryl agreed someone else should try while she took the time to rest. Sleep had been elusive since her initial contact with Dan.

"Maybe my exhaustion is part of the problem," she admitted, finally echoing the opinion those around her had been gently voicing.

As Cavnee positioned himself to be wrapped, he nodded to Maryl, his friend overtired, but still seated in a lab chair, not quite able to leave. "Mar, go. If I make contact, you'll know every second of what happened when I return. And I've got your messages for Dan. Don't worry."

"I won't worry. But look," she gestured to her seated body, "I'm resting now. So let me just see you off, Cav." She smiled a half smile, as if her fatigue reached even to the muscles of her face.

"All right. But as soon as I slump in here," he gestured with his head to the strands that now held him, "you leave. Yes?"

Cavnee's vision faded on the image of Maryl half-smiling, not answering.

As soon as Cavnee saw the clutter of discarded sheets of white paper around him, and spotted the familiar sight of Lena's computer, he knew, from earlier trips to Mooshie and Einstein, that something felt different. He felt different. Or maybe Einstein did.

254

"Mesterdide? Are you there? Dan?"

"Cavvv. Nice to, uh, see you, my friend."

Maryl saw the lurch of Cavnee's body in the Web. "He's made contact. Teesh. Can you bring him back and send me?" As soon as the question left her mouth, Maryl retracted it. "No, I'm sorry, forget it. I know we need to take advantage of any contact." She sighed. "We don't dare break the connection. All right. I'll relax, just sit here." Teesh nodded, knowing it would be wasted breath to encourage Maryl to leave.

"Wow. Maryl said that "talking" to you was a weird sensation and she was right. I feel like some pop-up section of my brain that's been glued shut my whole life just sprang open, and it's finally being used for what it was meant to be used for."

"Interesting. Well, it's great to have you pop in."

"Mesterdide. So it's true that your ridiculous stabs at humor live on."

"Cavnee, this minor loss, just one little body, isn't going to ruin my love of wordplay. In fact, I'd say words are rather important at this point."

"I guess so." Cavnee tried to suppress the response that flitted through his mind. "I know. And I'm sorry." He mentally pushed the condolences aside and continued. "Listen Dan. We've been trying to get you for days, and weren't able to. Do you know why?"

"I don't know why. As far as I know, I've been here all along. In this cat, in Einstein. And it hasn't seemed long since... did you say it's been days? That seems wrong. But I guess it's not, if you say so."

Cavnee hoped his next thought couldn't be perceived by Danyin, the idea that his friend might be slowly losing the ability to communicate with other kisans. Was his "essence" dissipating? Or integrating into his host? Who knew? It was all conjecture for now. Maybe Danyin would go missing for short periods, but keep reappearing. At least for as long as Einstein was around.

There was no reaction from Danyin to the spate of mental conjecture, and Cavnee felt relieved that there seemed to still be a "talking state" and a "thinking state" at his disposal.

"So Maryl couldn't get through to me? I know my sune. She must be frustrated beyond belief."

"She is. But she did the smart thing. She's beyond exhausted and agreed that sending someone better rested, wouldn't be a bad idea."

"That's my Maryl. I love that she does the right thing, even though it must have made her want to spit to send someone else to me."

"You got it. Exactly." Unexpectedly, Cavnee imagined the lump that must be forming in the throat so distant from where his mind resided. The contact was exciting, but how could he not also be sad, he thought? Dan and Maryl were his friends. But he needed to focus.

"All right then, Cav. You'll be the messenger of what I now know. Prepare to make history. But make sure the corasans mention my Maryl in their songs, won't you?"

"Ok, Dan. I will. Tell me."

"I'll show you."

The images, just as Maryl had described them, were like a hovi show. But they were suffused with an almost dazzling light, like midday on their two-sunned planet. Cavnee knew, that back in the lab's web, he must have gasped.

256

The figures were dark, so dark their features were difficult to distinguish, though the space they were in was brightly-lit. The contours of their bodies were as smooth as the surface of a pond undisturbed by a breeze. Was it possible they were unclothed? No – there must be something covering them, though if there was, it appeared to cover them from the top of their heads to the bottoms of their feet.

The bodies of the dark figures, two of them, weren't dissimilar to a kisan's body. Or a human's. The appendages were familiar, and the height no more or less than the average. It was the darkness that proclaimed the alien nature of the figures; a sense of light being absorbed instead of reflected.

From a position below one of the figures, Cavnee watched a piece of the scene unfold, realizing he watched from the perspective of a cat on one of the elevated soft surfaces, so often seen in dreams, and sung in songs of the Baata.

Cavnee's dream host was awake, but unable to move. As the figure leaned over the cat, Cavnee understood that it felt neither uncomfortable nor afraid, despite feelings of wanting to stand, followed by the inability to do so.

There was one thing the cat could move. His eyes. Nestled in the soft surface, the cats' eyes moved from one side to the other. On a nearby surface, a match to the one the cat laid on, the cat perceived another creature like himself. Another cat. Beyond were the other raised, soft surfaces which were something like beds, and something like tall work tables, holding much larger figures. Kyans. No. They were humans. The cat knew they were humans.

Cavnee knew a smile must be appearing on his face as he realized the lilt of Danyin's accent still seemed intact, though his friends' voice, or what now passed for vocalization, should no longer be influenced by ancestry or region. Maybe I'm imaging the accent, thought Cavnee. Danyin's words narrated the scene.

"When I see this vision, it's different from what you or any of the other VRC'ers, or even our sweetly singing corasans, have seen before. I have Einstein as my antenna and everything is in a new focus. I know you can't see this, Cav, but I've seen this space from a few vantage points now. Six viewpoints, as a matter of fact. Half the number of cats actually in this room, each with its own soft bed. And you're right. A matching number of humans are there, too. Here's what I've seen."

"The dark ones have thin flat black squares made of a hard material. Small. Some kind of medical tool, I'm certain. They use them to gently scrape the skin of each person's arm, moving the square up and down over a patch of skin dozens of times. They later do the same thing to a shaved spot on the side of each cat."

"Though the squares seem to be only moving over the skin, the feeling, you know, as I experienced it through Einstein…"

Cavnee added the next thought. "…who is experiencing it through the thoughts of the original cat in this vision. The cat that sent out this experience for other cats to share in their dreams."

"Yes, that's right. The feeling was that the square was plunging deeper, pulling minute matter from the skin. The spot tingles afterward."

"So – it's some specialized tool they're using? A collecting tool?"

"Exactly what I think. I've watched it over and over now. Felt it. And I believe I understand. Take a bit of cat DNA here, and a bit of human DNA there, and you have it. Put them

258

together and the kisans are born. No, the kisans are created. Like our melem story. The kisan myth about the creation of a new species from a combination of four different species. But this time, it's not a myth."

In the distant web, Cavnee released an exhale, and Teesh checked his monitor. "He's still ok," he said. "He can stay for now."

Cavnee worked to focus, and absorb what Danyin told him. "And this time they used two species?"

"I don't think so. I think three."

"What do you...oh you mean the dark ones included themselves in this... recipe? Baata. That is hard to get my mind around as anything but a story some crazy corasan might come up with for fun."

"I know. And if it's true, which I believe it is - we are, in fact, an engineered race."

"Oh ..." Cavnee's thoughts blurred as his mind tried to wrap itself around Danyin's conclusion. "So, we're... a false race."

"I know this is a jolt, Cavnee. But I've had some time to think about it. My first thought was the same as yours. Eventually though, I asked myself: Can any thinking, living, soul-filled creature be termed anything but real and true? And my answer is no. No matter our origin."

"Well. I don't know. I suddenly feel like a science experiment."

In the web, Maryl and Teesh saw that Cavnee's face was a map of concentration, his forehead a series of lines, his mouth tight.

"Appears that the joking is over," said Teesh. "Something's going on." He glanced down at the monitoring screen. "But he's still all right."

Danyin continued his theorizing. "If it's any comfort, I think there was a reason as old as time for what happened. I think it was all about survival. Most of the dark ones in the lab were dying. And I'm guessing others, not in the lab, were dying. So, I believe they were trying to keep a bit of their species "alive," if the worse were to happen; if the whole species were to die out completely."

"How do you know they were dying? You heard them speak? And could understand them? Or…are you implying the cats could understand them? Dan, I know you were…are…a mynie lover, cat lover, whatever. But how would you guess all this from this vision?"

"Because, with my link to Einstein, I knew that at least some of the dark ones were ill. Gravely ill. A cat can do that, and a mynie can do that. They can sense illness and the imminent approach of death. In addition to everything else I tell you, remember this: be sure experiments are set in motion to test what I've just told you about mynies and cats, and their ability to sense the ending of a life. You'll find it's the truth."

"All right, got it."

"And I felt something else from the dark ones." There was a pause from Danyin. "It's hard to describe. My first impulse would be to call it kindness. But maybe it's better described as "lack of malice," since a selfish intent was certainly part of their actions. After all, they took what they wanted. I don't believe they asked permission."

Cavnee made a conscious effort to mentally reinforce all Danyin had told him, so he could pass on as much as possible.

Though he was beginning to feel overloaded, he didn't want to break the connection. Who knew if the communication could be regained?

"I've seen one other vision that supports the theory of the creation of kisans. It involves an image of the cats emerging into the sunlight of two suns. Around them they see cats, humans, and kislings but no dark ones. They're in an area filled only with the natural world, no structures, no pathways, and no signs of civilization."

Cavnee understood. "As if they'd been in a vessel that brought them there. One that had traveled for years. Two of the three original species, and one new species. Kisans. But the kisans were still young."

"Yes. And the image is unexceptional, unless it's connected with the room of beds and the dark ones. Corasans who've seen the second vision in their dreams, see what they interpret as just a band of young kisans, older kyan-type kisans, and mynies. We've never connected this harmless dream to the Baata."

"Baata. Right. What about Baata? Everyone hoping for an address in the afterlife is not going to be crazy about this news."

"Ah. I've thought about this as well, my friend. And you know what? It doesn't mean there isn't the equivalent of a Baata somewhere. Maybe even one with beings that would put their stamp of approval on all this scraping, and mixing, and matching! Can't say I believe it, but there's no denying there's still a lot to think about. And I'll leave it to you to help those lazy VRC'ers kick their brains into action."

"All right. Will do, Dan."

Neither spoke for a moment, and then Cavnee continued.

261

"Dan, there's another obvious question. How could anything, any kind of vessel, make it through the virrius and not be destroyed? If these dark ones sent out some sort of ship, what was it made of?"

"I don't see the exterior of any kind of vessel in the visions, so I can't tell you. If the dark ones are still around, they can probably tell you. Though maybe finding their planet, and whatever virrius-resistant substances they have there, would be enough. And then figuring out how to get there, of course. That could be the tricky part."

"Yeah. Tricky."

Cavnee detected a change in his perception of Danyin's voice. It hinted of Maryl's exhausted drawl after her nights without rest. Danyin confirmed Cavnee's thoughts.

"Right now, you should go. The same fatigue that hit me when Maryl was here is hitting me again."

"All right. Just some quick things from Maryl."

"Yes, tell me please."

"She says her apartment is a mess, but she's working on it. She says Mally and Dally are doing great. And she thanks you for calling her cootie, though I'm not sure I know what she meant by that, since I don't know what cootie means."

Cavnee heard, or imagined he heard, the echo of a laugh. "That's right, you don't study English. Cutie. That's the word. Cutie. You tell Maryl I'm still her stud. Thanks, Cav. Talk to you again."

CHAPTER 46

RT's had poured into the VRC, their core pleas funneled to Braelind. *My partner/ kisling/ beloved friend is dying. Can we do a DT to give him a longer life?*

Word about Danyin, about his disembodied existence, had gotten out. Gotten out in the way things get out, even when pledges of silence have been solemnly made. News of a miracle is hard to suppress, and the survival of Danyin Mesterdide's essence, beyond the death of his body, was a miracle.

The imagination of a species had been captured by a universal desire. If we can't live forever, that ultimate of fantastical goals, can we at least extend our time? Even if it's only a spirit-like version of ourselves that lives on?

Word of the new wonder spread like the warmth of hope after the chilling revelation that old wonders were gone. The same haphazard information leak that told of Danyin, told also of what Danyin had revealed about the kisans. About the reality of the connection between mynies, kisans, and a third, unknown, species. About an origin that rent their mythologies and left them scrambling for new prisms to peer through to understand a newly scattered history that must be pieced together again.

As Maryl walked down the dimmed VRC hall, she saw a shaft of light from an open doorway cutting through the dusky lighting. Stopping short of the opening she spoke softly, hoping not to startle her friend within. "Brae?" She moved her head forward to peek into Braelind's room in time to see the look of irritation wrinkling his forehead relax, as he turned to face her.

"Maryl." Braelind was seated at a small table, and took his hands from the hovi he'd been clutching and studying.

"Suns have long set, Brae. Isn't home beckoning?"

"You know how it is. Sometimes a work question doesn't quiet itself in a decent stretch of time. Then you and your brain have to stay put for a while."

"Anything I can help with?"

Braelind leaned back in his chair with a heavy exhalation. "As a matter of fact, yes. I'd planned to talk to you first thing tomorrow, but if you're willing to push into your sleep time, I'd be grateful."

Maryl entered the room and settled herself into a lounger across from the research chief that allowed her to stretch her legs. "I'm yours. And I'm guessing from your preamble, that you've got some difficult things on your mind. Probably involving Dan. All I can say is, please, just tell me what's going on. I may be able to help."

"Maryl, it's rare that your judgment has not been wise."

"Thank you."

Maryl waited as Braelind took advantage of the intimate space and after-hours vacuum to be as deliberate as he wished.

"Since it appears VRC'ers are not the circumspect group I imagined, you may already know what's on my mind."

Maryl cast her eyes down. "If I were the blushing type, I'd do it on behalf of our beloved VRC, Brae. I'm guessing you're talking about everything to do with Dan. The fact of his being able to communicate with us. And what he told us about Baata – or the lack thereof – and the further fact that there's probably not a kisan or kisling in the whole world who hasn't heard about it all."

Braelind's smooth forehead fell back into creases as he nodded his head.

Maryl's voice was gentle. "You know what, Brae? All these leaks are big, huge. But I think it's all right."

"Do you, now?" He leaned back in his chair. "Please, my friend, share your insights."

Maryl paused, absorbing the unique nature of the moment. Braelind looked weary. Wearier than he'd been in years. He was letting down his guard and asking her, for just a few moments, to take the reins he normally held with ease.

"Well, first Dan's situation. We have no real idea how it happened. And that's the answer to those who want to be where Dan is. We don't know where that is. Maybe someday we will. But there's no way we're going to slaughter volunteers on our way to the answer."

"But who knows how many crazies will try it on their own?"

Maryl dismissed the thought with a flick of her hand. "Crazies will always find a way to die before their time. They've got their eyes two strides ahead, and miss that important next step."

"Nice observation. Think I'll use it for a future fatherly lecture. All right. How about the fact that we've single-handedly shredded a world belief system?"

Again, Maryl waved a dismissive hand. "We haven't. First of all, plenty of kisans won't believe what they've heard. The Baata, in all its mystery, will be the Baata. And those who accept what we've discovered? So what? The mystery of life is the joy of life, and whoever created us didn't leave out a capacity for wild and marvelous imaginings. We'll never be without religion and myth."

"You know you're simplifying the situation, Maryl. The path to new beliefs may or may not be a gentle one."

"I know, Brae. But here's one truth. The truth is, it's late. The truth is, the questions on our minds have thousands of possible answers. The truth is, you look like you've gone to Baata but haven't lain down yet! Listen, you and me, we're going to be involved, neck deep, for a long, long time, in difficult, ongoing research in our work life, and a seismic cultural shift in our personal lives. So, for tonight, let's take it easy." She cupped her hand to ear. "I hear no bellowing from outside. When I looked at the hovi earlier, they were still showing the batden game finals. So, for the moment, peace reigns." She tapped her hand on her chest. "Still breathing." She smiled. "You have any of that nasty mendo on hand? Not delicious but it helps me sleep."

Braelind returned Maryl's smile, turned his chair around, and reached into a wall cubby, withdrawing a bottle filled with shimmering green liquid.

"Helps me too."

Maryl's mind wandered to the early days of the VRC. The Virrius Research Center. Charged with investigating anything and everything related to the lovely lavender tendrils that made their skies breathtaking, and their wanderlust frustrated. Could they ever build a transport that would pierce the toxin without harm? Could it be put to useful purpose? Was there a cure for Grett's, the lethal disease sarpac riders contracted after brushing the virrius?

266

Questions remained unanswered. But they had achieved one of their goals. They'd broken through the virrius. Not in the way expected, and probably not the only way possible. But they'd done it, and Braelind Carsinsen had guided them in the pursuit. VRC investigations had led to the development of local Transference, then distance Transference. They were learning about cultures heretofore unimagined. And they'd triggered the explosion – or at least dissection - of lovingly held beliefs.

Maryl watched Braelind gather glasses for their drinks. No. It wasn't simple. Braelind, second-in-command of the agency that had effected world-altering changes, appearing off-stride for even an evening, was sobering. But as she watched Braelind, hand steady, pour their drinks, she relaxed.

CHAPTER 47

Valin flicked his tail, and accented the movement with a sharp meow. Willo skittered away from the bowl she knew perfectly well belonged to the complaining mynie; she just didn't always care, since she could move quickly when necessary. And Valin was always wasting food by leaving it sitting there.

"Valin, I guess the real "you" is finally showing," said Maryl. "Who knew you'd migrate to top of the pack, my sweetiesune? Well, best of luck to you, since you've got some tough girls to deal with. Don't be surprised if Willo and Claudi attempt a coup now and again." Valin lovingly circled the lounger Maryl reclined in, but flicked his tail as if to say "don't I know it."

Maryl shifted her attention back to the mini-hovi she'd been studying, but the tinkling of the RT's song pulled her away once again. The song was a default choice for the device, fast and stupid, and not her taste. But it was anonymous, unrelated to memories, and just what Maryl had needed after the long months of coming to terms with the idea of never making contact with Danyin again. Over time the anguish had decreased, and the acceptance had grown. She knew, compared to others who'd lost those they'd loved to sudden death, that she'd been lucky. She'd had a chance to say goodbye.

Maryl thought about selecting a new song each time an RT came in, forgetting by the end of each transmission. She glanced, as always, at the identifier, and glanced again. It was blank. She half-smiled at the thought of a lifelong piece of luck disappearing. The identifier wasn't working, and that was something that had never happened to one of her RT units. She tapped the identifier window but the screen remained unchanged, blank, as if no RT caller was there, as if a ghost were calling.

Saying "oh well," Maryl activated the RT. The kisan, a pure kyan, by the look of him, appeared in a standing position before her. He wore blue slacks and a shirt crowded with the pattern of large-petal flowers, both fashions reflecting an Earth-style lately adopted by kisans. The kisans couldn't quite mimic the blue jeans they admired, but they got close. The ones her caller wore seemed like a good imitation. The flowers on his shirt were a vivid orange. Sumee would not approve.

The caller spoke. "Maaaryl. Ah. It is so marvelous to finally have a chance to speak with you."

"Mah – velous" is what the caller said. It was an Earth affectation. Everything "Earth" was all the rage these days.

"Hello. Did someone recommend you call? Are you with the VRC?"

The caller gave a clipped laugh, reminding Maryl of a more genuine rendition of Mekkel's "Ha."

"No, no one you know recommended that I call you. Though I know of you, and your fame."

"Fame?"

The caller smiled. "Wrong word for you and yours. My apologies. I should say I know you're respected for your work. My name is Jon."

"Jon." Maryl recalled there was a time when Jon was only an Earth name. But now names that had never been heard on Kisa – names like Tyler, Rich, Sadie, and Peg - had caught on worldwide. Kislings were now growing up with these new names, and even grown kisans had adopted them. Maryl repeated her question. "Are you a VRC researcher?"

269

"Ah. I can only regret that I'm beyond the recruiting arm of the VRC. But, yes, I'm a researcher. Like you. Much like you, actually."

He switched languages, now speaking the Earth language of English.

"I wonder if you'd be willing to practice some English? I believe that's a fairly strong language for you, what with your many *visits*," he emphasized the word, "to English-speaking places."

Maryl's eyes narrowed. The request was as odd as the call. But she'd play along. "Why are you on my RT? It's unusual to get an RT from someone I don't know. This is a protected connection."

"Oh, yes, this is unusual." And then Jon did something on the RT that made Maryl stand in astonishment. He pulled into view a small table with a cup on it.

Maryl gaped. "There's a table in your RT. And a cup. A complete cup. That's not possible." She reached out and swatted her arm through the image of Jon, the table, and the cup. It passed through the images, as it would pass through air, as it would pass through any RT. "Do you have them both heated? But how? I don't see the source of any heat." She slowly moved her hand toward the cup, reaching to grasp it. Again, her hand clutched at nothing but itself. Maryl took a step back.

Jon shook his head. "No, dear Maryl. Neither object is heated. Well, a bit of heated liquid in the cup. But not enough to make it so clearly visible."

Maryl laughed in delight. "That's wonderful. Having two complete objects in an RT. Where are you? Is this something Brae set up? To tell me about this? This is monumental."
270

"It is nice, isn't it? But, no. No one you know set this up. In fact, what we set up was a space around me as empty as possible, so as not to startle you. You'll note the image is angled so you can't see the floor, which, by the way, you would be able to see if the angle were tilted downward. This cup is your clue that I'm someone who has things to say that are worth listening to."

Without thinking, Maryl took a step back from the RT image before her. "Who are you? And whoever you are, I say why don't we meet in person?"

Jon shook his head. "That, I'm afraid, is something that cannot be arranged at this time. Though wouldn't it be lovely to share a cup of tea."

"Tea?"

"Yes, tea. That's what's in my cup. Real Earth tea." Jon lifted his mug and took a sip. "PG Tips, actually. Delicious. Mmm." He replaced the cup on the table. "Ah, I can see from your expression that you understand precisely what I'm saying, and don't believe me. How could I be from Earth?" He shrugged. "But I am."

Maryl gasped at the sight of another object in the RT, as the image shifted and showed a chair, which Jon walked to, carrying his tea cup, and sank into with a relieved sigh.

"Ah. It's been a long day." He took a sip from his cup. "I know," said Jon, waving his free hand in the air. "All of it takes getting used to. But that's what we do, isn't it, you and me? Make miracles of the stuff of everyday lives." Jon squinted. "Oh yes." He fumbled on the chair seat beside him. "Good I didn't sit on these," he said, as he put on a pair of eyeglasses shaped like flattened ovals. "Just another little something we didn't want to spring on you, you understand. Ah. Interesting to see you through human eyes instead of mynie eyes."

Maryl only glanced over her shoulder as she backed up to a lounger behind her, not wanting the image before her to disappear. "I think sitting down is very good idea," she said. She perched on the cushioned edge and inhaled deliberately to slow her hammering heart.

Jon continued. "Since you explained yourself so wonderfully when you sent your first RT's to us, let me do the same for you. And it will be even simpler for me, since you know so much about us. When we received your RT, we knew nothing about you." He shook his head as he watched the disbelieving expression on Maryl's face. "Really there's just one point that's essential for you to understand and believe, and then we can enjoy our conversation: I'm from Earth. I'm on Earth right now. You might say that we are now having the mother of all long distance conversations." Jon reached for his mug and sipped his tea, looking expectantly at Maryl, as he cradled the cup in two hands.

Maryl shook her head. "Let's assume I believe you. How could your technology be so advanced, and we know nothing of it? Did you create the RT based on the data we sent you?"

"Ah, our technology. The answer to whether we used what you sent us is no and yes. We'd already had a version of what you call the RT when we received your transmission. However, your blueprints did give us some ideas on tweaking what we had. Thank you." He smiled. "I'm fairly certain you have no idea of most of the technology we've been dabbling in. In fact, almost no one on Earth has any idea, so don't feel like you're not in the club. No, technological savvy isn't our problem on our little planet. But, after years of visiting, wouldn't you say we have plenty of other problems?"

Maryl thought of the comparisons she and others had made between the Kisan and Earth societies, over the years.

She answered carefully, still unbelieving of the scenario Jon presented, but willing to go along. Why would someone from Earth, at first contact, be emphasizing the problems of his planet? "I'd say that Earth isn't alone when it comes to problems. Here on Kisa we have our share."

"Mmmm, yes. One question, Maryl, before I talk more about myself. Tell me. What do you think is the worst behavior you've observed on my planet?"

Maryl surprised herself with her ready answer. "The killing of cats."

Jon laughed his light laugh again. "I guess it does show how barbaric I am, that I think of that particular behavior – along with the killing of any number of other animals - as negligible, in the vast litany of our cruelties." He nodded. "But...I suppose if I were you, killing cats would be pretty close to the top of the list."

"What do you mean by that? If you were me?" She leaned toward the RT image, her hand slicing through a phantom table as she gestured.

Jon glanced at the table. "Watch the table, please. That was a great jumble sale find."

"What?"

"Sorry, sorry. Just trying to keep things nice and friendly. Kidding. I've got no scripts. To answer your question, I think killing cats would seem even more horrific to you because of your chimerical make-up. You know, you and most kisans being a combination of three entities, including cats."

Maryl was silenced by the words. Her lips parted, her mind considering the surety of Jon's statement, speaking as if he knew what he said was fact, instead of speculation.

"That's the theory."

Jon put down his mug and slapped his hand on his knee. He knew he had more information than Maryl, having seen the vision of the dark beings from visual angles the kisans had not. He had seen the storage containers filled with the remains of species proven incompatible with early experiment attempts. But still. The evidence should have been clear.

"Maryl. You know. You all know. You've had so much evidence dumped on you that you need waders to get through it. The mynie dreams, the cat dreams, your conversations with Danyin…"

"You know about *Danyin?*"

"Maryl, isn't it obvious? Just as you've been visiting us, we've been visiting you. In fact, our paths were similar. We tried human to human Transference. It was a tragic failure for us, just as kisan to kisan attempts were for you. But moving to animals was possible. Even animals that were very, very far away."

"Here? On Kisa? Through mynies?"

"Through mynies mostly, though some other animals as well."

"And you've been able to pick up so many details through animal Transference?"

"That should come as no surprise to you. Think of your own visits. And we've been doing it much longer."

"Longer?"

"Yes. Much longer."

Maryl felt a wash of frustration. How could the VRC have been so in the dark about this? "Who are you? Are you acting on your own? Representing a particular country?"

"Well, certainly I live in a country. But, no, I'm not attached to any government, and neither is anyone in my circle, shall we say. The people in my group? Mmm. Many countries are represented. Though..." He paused, lips pursed. "Some of us come from places that don't really have any government to speak of."

Maryl spoke slowly. "So, you and your circle...you'd all like to be the government?"

The laugh from Jon sounded heartfelt. "No, no. The government types may be buggers sometimes, but eventually we'll let them handle the boring follow-up. They're so good at that. Good at jumping on coattails, if you know what I mean. We're handling the delicate beginnings. Certainly, when we found you all those years ago there was talk, talk, talk about bringing the news right to the officials. But then we said, wait now. Why don't we get our ducks in a row, find out more? Eventually we'll hand it over. And if I have a say in it, that'll be when I'm old and gray. Or possibly gone. And," he took a sip from his cup, "I do have a say in it."

"So your group is private. Are they," she paused, realizing she was believing what Jon was telling her, "are they humans who wanted to make contact beyond their planet?"

"Actually, this little invention, the RT, as you call it, was just one of the many our group came up with. Probably the best, I'll give you. We're tinkerers, you might say. Great minds and decent ethics, matched with lots of lovely money. Brilliant. Good things happen when those things collide."

"But why do you say you'll be old and gray before you reveal what you know? You're not terribly old now." Maryl judged Jon to be about her age; not young but someone with years of life still ahead of him. "Why will it be that long?"

"Because," said Jon. "We think we have more to learn. First of all, most of us, hereabout, have trouble accepting beings across oceans, let alone galaxies. And then, of course, our immature and opportunistic tendencies, shall we say, could be problematic. If we released the RT to the public? There'd soon be 3-D images of beer commercials crowding the sidewalks, and pornography pieced together by teenagers, appearing in nursery schools..."

Maryl interrupted Jon. "It wasn't perfect overnight for us when RT's were introduced. And it's not perfect now. Why do you think we have identifier panels on our RT's? We needed to create guidelines, protections as the technology evolved, and use increased. But I wouldn't say it was a mistake to share RT's with our world. Definitely not."

"Ah. But VRC has its secrets, yes? And, if I am who I say I am, everyone on your world may not learn of me for some time. Otherwise, it could be too shocking. Cause a panic?"

Maryl didn't reply. Her caller knowing of unrevealed VRC work surprised her for an instant, until she thought of the RT conversations she'd had from home with Claudi, Valin, and Willo relaxing nearby. Who knew how many other researchers shared such conversations with their beloved pet companions present, in what they thought were private situations? Jon's conjecture about concealing, for the time being, the news of human to kisan contact with Earth, would probably emerge as truth.

"Maryl, you're right, of course, about your planet having its share of problems. But, you've also had successes we can only hope will be in our future. That's part of the reason I'm contacting you – we're contacting you. We want to learn from you. Having RT conversations is going to be one way to do it. And we'd also like to be able to experience more directly what kisans experience day to day."

Maryl understood. "Through our mynies."

"That's right."

Maryl felt the gentle plop of a mynie landing in her lap as she stared at the RT image. Maryl turned her eyes to her beloved Willo, the loving golden eyes staring into her own.

She turned back to the image in front of her, finishing a sip of what he said was tea, and replacing it on the table. She met Jon's eyes. "Is someone here now?"

Jon smiled. "You never know, do you?"

CHAPTER 48

A lovelier day for the ceremony would have been difficult to conjure, should magic have been an option. The event's location, adjacent to Bly's childhood home, was choked with alternating trees sporting purple flowers and white flowers, the thousands of small petals still and bright in the lavender-veiled sunshine. Kisans spanning generations chatted in standing groups, or gathered sitting on ground coverings, relaxing as they awaited the start of the joining.

Bly looked even more handsome than usual, Maryl thought. And why shouldn't he, thought Maryl? Pleasure could do that to even the homeliest kisan; shine through and convince onlookers they were seeing pure beauty. And Bly had natural advantages.

She knew Bly's outside was not a perfect mirror to his inside. She'd witnessed the ache that pulsed to the surface at unexpected times. But his long journey from silence and despair had progressed far, and she thought the happiness she saw was genuine.

Sumee still hadn't arrived since Wilina, and others back at the house, were fussing with her clothing and hair. Maryl thought she would talk later to Jon, or one of the others, about this behind-the-scenes detail of the ceremony. How did it compare to what humans did?

The timing for the ceremony, two days after Sumee, Bly, and their entourage arrived, had been good. It gave Sumee time to recover from the half bottle of mendo necessary to get her through the long journey, and made her admit that her initial suggestion that they do the joining in front of a friend or two, right outside her home, all in sarpacs, would not really have been as satisfying.

Maryl had been standing apart from others, head tilted upward to enjoy what for her was the too-rarely-indulged-in feel of sunshine. Garin, finishing a conversation with a nearby group, walked up to her. "You're Maryl, yes? I haven't even had a chance to say hello, what with all the preparations the last few days. I'm Garin."

"Garin, of course." They greeted, cheek to cheek. "Bly's told me what a support you were to him when he visited."

"And Danyin told me a lot about you."

Maryl was silent for a moment. She knew Danyin had met Garin and Wilina, and some of the others, on his trip to Bly's home. No one had yet mentioned it, but she'd been thinking of it. She thought of Dan when she'd seen the thallies in the courtyard near her room. Dan had told her of his encounter with them after he returned from the trip to Bly's family, and the memory sent a pleasing thrill through her even now. Which was good. Her first thoughts associated with Dan these days were past memories of pleasure, instead of more recent ones of loss. Maybe the room she was staying in was the same one Dan had stayed in, the room she now shared with the figurine of two intertwined mynies, packed at the last moment, and now tucked by her pillow.

"I enjoyed talking to your Danyin. I was able to visit with him, one-on-one, for a short time, late one night, after Wilina and Bly went to sleep. He was ... hilarious, wasn't he?"

Maryl laughed. "He was. I laughed a lot with Dan."

"And caring," said Garin. "I'll tell you, he extended himself for my little brother."

"Yes. He loved Bly."

The two paused. Garin broke the reverie of memory. "So, what have you got there?" he asked. He gestured to the portable enclosure at Maryl's feet. "I heard that you'd brought a mynie with you. That's unusual, isn't it? Or is this yet another Earth hobby we've picked up?" Garin crouched down and looked through the clear opening of the holder, crisscrossed by air slots, at the brown-and-white, long-haired beauty. "What a lovely mynie."

Claudi, awakened by the talk, peered from the carrier at her admirer. "Meow."

"That's my girl Claudi. She just seems to have a traveling bug, so I'm indulging her."

"Meow," said Claudi mournfully. Maryl imagined the mynie was saying "No. I'm traveling because you're making me. I hate it."

"Well, what an unusual mynie," Garin said, as he leaned down to look in at Claudi.

"Also, Sumee loves Claudi, and knows she's like a kisling to me. So Claudi was officially invited."

"That's great. It's fun to see her here. Adds to the festivities, I'd say. Hey there, beautiful," Garin said as he placed a fingertip into one of the open slots of the carrier.

Maryl knew she couldn't -- wouldn't -- give Garin the real reason of Claudi's presence, at least for now. Only Braelind, Teesh, Cavnee, and Saras knew of the agreement to bring mynies to as many public gatherings as possible, or knew anything of Jon and his band of researchers. Brae's boss, though rarely seen, was also wholly informed. For now, Braelind wanted this communication to be one of those rare secrets that would continue living up to its name. Maryl had argued to include a few others in the confidence, to expand
280

their skill set, but had been refused. Brae had responded that more time was needed, but it wouldn't be time without end.

The small VRC group continued their contact with the Earth researchers, jointly making decisions about what steps to take for the time being. With help from their Earth connections, they integrated improvements in the kisan's RT's, Braelind, for now, taking credit for the innovations. Hiri voiced the common surprise. "Who knew he still had a working researcher in him? Thought he just knew how to make speeches."

Braelind had been modest, knowing the real truth would come out someday. He had enough real accomplishments to keep him warm at night, and didn't need to be credited with inventions not his. The improved RT's meant that those who couldn't attend Bly and Sumee's ceremony were able to watch remotely, all the decorations and landscape viewed in three-dimensional splendor.

Garin straightened from his visit with Claudi, as the sound of joyful cries broke through the gathering. It was Sumee, held aloft on a pedestal as if floating in an old RT image. Four of the older kislings in Bly's Group held the pedestal and Sumee aloft, some hands steadying the base, others the ravishing corasan.

Sumee was clothed in a solid white cape, draped around her like a cocoon from neck to knee, dangling glittering strings waving from the edges of the enveloping wrap.

The guests parted to create a path to the site of the joining, where Sumee and Bly's corasan friends would sing a song celebrating the anticipated joy the couple would share as joined beings.

Bly, already at the place of ceremony, awaited his cocooned love. As she was gently lowered to the ground, and her bearers moved back, Bly stepped forward. Slowly he began to unwrap the generous package that was his Sumee, not even he knowing the surprise she had for those who knew her well. As Bly pulled the material, and Sumee turned to accommodate the pull, a gasp escaped Bly and Sumee's closest friends. She stood revealed, smiling wickedly, and laughing at the look on Bly's face. She was gorgeous. And she wore orange.

Maryl smiled, strangely elated at the sight. As she watched Sumee and Bly come together, and the rituals of the ceremony unfold – the Corasan songs, declarations from family members, petals dropped from sarpacs – she thought of Danyin. She and Danyin would not be joined. They were only joined as imagined by Teesh's partner, in a carved figurine, a piece of the essence of each of them forever curled together. But only a piece. Now Dan was even more intertwined with his host, their link inextricable until death. And then? Most likely that was the end. But who knew?

Maryl glanced at Garin, still by her side. Her heart stirred at seeing his eyes moist with emotion, and joy in his smile. This tisani had a beautiful heart. At that moment, she knew she'd be seeking Garin's company after the ceremony.

When the formal vows concluded, Sumee pulled back from Bly, squeezed his hand, and leaned over to speak to him as the crowd yelled their approval. Bly nodded as Sumee turned and walked to Maryl, reaching for both of Maryl's hands with hers. Maryl spoke first. "Sumee, I'm so happy for you today. And you're as gorgeous as ever. But Sumee, my sun. You're wearing orange?"

Sumee grinned. "I know. My nemesis color. What can I say? I knew, for me, this day would be different than any other day. And I had to travel to make it to this day! And it was horrible! But, I'm here and it was worth it. How better to thank the Universe, and remind the people I love most to resist the expected, than to do the unexpected?"

Maryl embraced her friend. "As the saying goes on Earth, "will wonders never cease?"

Claudi, a few meters away, added her melancholy comment. "Meow."

Jon, much farther away, suspended in the twisted wire cocoon in the basement launch area, thought his response to Maryl's question. "I don't think so. No, I really don't think wonders will cease. And, hopefully, you'll forgive us our little fibs, when the time is right to tell you more."

David, suspended near Jon in an adjacent metal web, was wrapped in his own thoughts, considering, yet again, how they could solve this lingering problem of visual clarity. Seeing through the eyes of humans and kisans was still, inexplicably, somewhat cloudier than seeing through the eyes of cats and mynies. Though he didn't know it, he sighed, briefly expanding the silver web that cradled him, as he watched Sumee through Maryl's eyes, the kisan appearing hazy and bright, like morning sunbeams piercing the horizon.

Sumee disentangled herself from Maryl's arms. "All right. Enough with the grand sentiments. Get me out of this awful color! Bly!"

End

ABOUT THE AUTHOR

Ellen Metter grew up in beautiful northern New Jersey, but now calls Colorado home. Passions include walking about in cities or nature, live music, and conversation. With artist Loretta Gomez, Metter authored the first humor book on the topic of choosing to be childfree, Cheerfully Childless.

Metter is a sane cat lady, and asks "Why not consider adopting a cat? Or another cat?"

EllenMetter.com

40176967R00172

Made in the USA
Middletown, DE
05 February 2017